SOUL'S BLOOD

SOUL'S BLOOD

by

Stephen Graham King

A Division of Bold Strokes Books

2016

SOUL'S BLOOD
© 2016 By Stephen Graham King. All Rights Reserved.

ISBN 13: 978-1-62639-508-4

This Trade Paperback Original Is Published By
Bold Strokes Books, Inc.
P.O. Box 249
Valley Falls, NY 12185

First Edition: January 2016

Credits
Editor: Jerry L. Wheeler
Production Design: Stacia Seaman
Cover Design by Gabrielle Pendergrast

Acknowledgments

First off, I need to thank everyone at Bold Strokes Books for giving this book a home and welcoming me into the fold, allowing me to share it with you. Special shout-outs to: Cindy Cresap for keeping me and the process on track, Jerry L. Wheeler for his stellar editing (You made me better, my friend!), and Gabrielle Pendergrast for the perfect cover design.

No one creates in a vacuum, and over the years there have been several people who have read various versions of this story and offered their invaluable input: Kim Gaspar, Gordon Portman, Suzanne North, and Colleen Manestar. Apologies to anyone I have missed. I forget things.

Thanks to Paul Regehr for his long-ago assistance with fight choreography.

Thanks to Tango Palace in Toronto and City Perks in Saskatoon for keeping me caffeinated and sugared up during the revision process.

And finally, thank you. Whether you've read my work before and come back for more, or you've picked this up just because it intrigues you, I am ever grateful you've come along for the ride.

For the Sistren:
Susan, Linda, and Jennifer
At my side, wherever I go

CHAPTER ONE

Galactum Year 148

Keene found him in a bar deep within the Grift, hunched over a quisling table in the back. He fugued, and the image Zyd had provided appeared before his eyes, the smoky, cramped room blurring behind it. Though the light from the game grid cast dramatic shadows on the man, the face matched. Definitely Nord, Keene thought, watching him down a shot then give a nervous wave of the empty glass to call for another.

Keene 'pushed a drink order to the bar's system, found a booth with a good view of Nord's table, and took in the sad sameness of the bar while he waited. He'd seen a thousand others like it, in a thousand other Grifts, around a thousand other spaceports across the Galactum. Deevee panes floated in air clotted with the spicy-sweet haze of fizzstick smoke, streaming wagers and odds on everything from races to sporting events to the games happening at the tables themselves. Underneath it all, Keene could hear the barely audible whisper of cards and the click of Slapjack tiles on the hard tabletops.

Got him in my sights, Blue, positive ID. Zyd's intel is solid. He looked in Nord's direction, opened his node and 'pushed the image to her as a server dropped off his drink.

Good. Her satisfaction caressed his node. *I'm on my way. Mark him and wait for me.*

Will do. Watching Nord, he took a sip of his cider, and it fizzed on his tongue. Not bad for a place like this, he thought. Too bad he wasn't planning on drinking it.

He reached into his pocket for the tracer tablet, dropped it into his glass, and watched it dissolve into a pillar of whitish bubbles and disappear. He clutched the glass, took a breath to steady himself and focus, then eyed the mass of people between him and Nord. Seeing an opening, he 'pushed to reserve his table and stood.

He wormed his way through the crowd, keeping the glass above his head to protect the contents. With the same honed skill he used to gauge weight distributions and lading of cargo, he calculated the distance he had to cross, the mark he needed to hit, how he needed to stumble, and just the right tone of embarrassed apology in his voice.

There.

A gap opened in the crowd just where he needed to be. He moved left into the sudden void and was directly in front of Nord's table. He shifted his body weight and stumbled into a short, doughy-looking man concentrating on a screen. Keene's glass fell from his hands and hit the floor near Nord's feet, the marked cider fanning out in a sheet under the table.

Nord started to rise, but Keene put a hand on his skinny shoulder, applying just enough pressure to keep the smaller man seated without him realizing he was pinned. Keene grabbed a napkin from the table and wiped at the frayed hem of Nord's coat for cider stains that weren't actually there.

"Shit, I'm sorry. I can't believe I did that. Someone knocked my arm. What a waste of good tope, eh?"

Nord gave an irritated shake of his head. "Never mind. No damage done. Forget about it."

"Thanks, man, really." Keene shifted and saw Nord's shoes planted firmly in the puddle of cider, drops spattered across the toes. He smiled down at Nord. "You enjoy the games, my friend."

He turned and walked back to his booth, a half smile on his face. He settled back into the seat again, and ordered another cider.

Marked and ready. I'll wait for you here.

He felt Lexa-Blue enter the bar shortly after that, the sensation in his mind like a shift in atmospheric pressure. He kept his eyes on Nord as he felt her make her way through the crowd to him. He knew she was in the booth with him an instant before he felt the seat shift under her weight.

"Hey, trader, wanna get squishy?"

He turned to her just as she picked up his glass and took a sip. She grimaced and put the glass back in front of him.

"How can you drink that stuff? Tastes like piss. Fizzy carbonated piss." She lost focus as she ordered a drink for herself.

"I didn't order it for you," he shot back at her. "And for the record, I'd love to get squishy, just not with you."

"Yeah, yeah, like it's my fault you're a bum chum, and I don't have a dick." She cuffed him in the arm. "I could have one grown, but they're more fun when they belong to someone else."

Keene chuckled, knowing that even a dick was not a prerequisite for getting her attention.

"Where is he?" she asked, looking around in a slow circuit of the room.

Keene pointed to the table where Nord was still sitting, yet another drink in his hand, three empties on the table in front of him. "Vrick was right. He spends all his money either here or at the casino, so we were bound to find him at one or the other. He looks just like the image Zyd gave us."

"Vrick was right? Don't tell him that, or we'll never hear the end of it."

I heard that, Vrick said through both of their nodes.

Quiet, you. You are replaceable, you know.

Replaceable? Without me, you'd be mucking out a garbage scow.

"Leave em alone, Blue," Keene said. "You know how bored ey gets planetside."

Bored? Vrick's snort of disbelief reverberated through their nodes. *I'll have you know I'm watching seven different ballet, opera, and theatre performances and scanning the local library for books I haven't read. 'Push me when you need me.*

Without turning to Keene, Lexa-Blue asked, "You sure he's tagged?"

"See for yourself," he answered, pointing at the floor beneath Nord's table.

She followed his gaze, shifting the wavelength of her vision. She felt a slight tingle in the scar that bisected the eye socket from brow to cheekbone as her view changed. The floor below the table glowed brilliant green, the bilious tracer covering Nord's shoes like splatters of paint. Satisfied, she shifted her vision back to normal just as the server delivered her drink.

Keene felt the wisp of mischief from her as she arched an eyebrow and looked up to catch and hold the server's gaze. The server's eyes went wide when he noticed her scar and the smooth darkness of black sensor gem set where her right eye used to be. Keene didn't need to be nodelinked to him to sense his profound unease at such an obvious and perfectly correctible deformity. Through their link, he felt her spark of satisfaction at the reaction, and she turned away, dismissing him with body language that all but left a rime of frost on his serving tray.

"You enjoy doing that, don't you?"

She shrugged, but her pleasure at the casual provocation was a spiky simmer through her node. He had worked by her side enough to know this agitative side of her, her urge to provoke those around her. It had taken years of partnership before she had told him where the scar came from and why she refused to have it corrected, why the sensor looked like a chip of polished agate rather than a human eye. Still, he often felt for the victims of her compulsion, who ended up having her atavism shoved in their faces. It had bothered him when they met. He had avoided her eyes, but that had just provoked her further. Finally, getting used to it was his only defense. Without any reaction from him, she soon lost interest in provoking him and the door opened for friendship.

He felt her hand on his arm. "I think he's on the move."

Nord stood from his constellation of empty glasses and headed for the door, his small frame disappearing in the mass of people just as a roar of approval rose at a change in the score of the zoomstick game.

Lexa-Blue rose from her seat to follow, but Keene held her back. "Let him go. We'll know wherever he goes, so there's no harm in letting him have a head start." *Track him, please, Vrick.* "Finish your drink, Blue. Vrick will keep an eye on him for us."

When their glasses were empty, they stepped out of the noise of the bar into the late autumn evening, the warmest since they had arrived on Highland. Above them, three tiny moons cast an intricate lattice of shadows across the street, cords of light and dark twisting and crisscrossing each other into the distance. A lazy drift of mottled clouds, fat with the threat of rain, stretched into stripes as they were taken by currents of air.

To follow Nord, they had to sidestep a bewigged, corseted woman flanked by two men in nothing but fig leaves and gold body paint. Once past the revellers, Keene saw Lexa-Blue scan for their quarry's footsteps on the pavement. Through their link, he had a flickering, visual echo of how they glowed, ferny bright, to her sensor eye. Looking back at him, she pointed in the direction of Factory Town, and Vrick showed them his position relative to theirs. *He isn't moving all that fast. You should be able to catch up to him if you hustle.*

They quickened their pace, following the footprints through the garish lights lining the streets, past the bars, clubs, and restaurants that made up the Grift. Their path led them away from the bustle of activity toward the quieter, industrial section of the city. At one point, they came up short at the end of a slidewalk, Lexa-Blue losing the trail.

Don't panic, Meat. I have him on the grid. He took the Half-Moon exit. The trail picks up again there.

Keene felt a bubble of humour from Lexa-Blue at the hush in Vrick's tone. Ey spoke through her node, making eavesdropping impossible, but still es words were a whisper-touch, stealthy and intimate.

Sure enough the pattern of footprints continued again exactly where Vrick had said they would. They followed him through the streets, deeper into the industrial section of Port City, into the warren of square, unadorned factories. Night shift was well under way, and the streets were deserted, with nothing to interfere with the rhythmic sounds of machines and the wave power that drove them. Off in the distance, ships lifted and landed at the port proper. Nord doubled back several times, cutting through laneways and shortcuts, obviously trying to lose anyone tailing him, unaware every footstep led them closer to him.

How close is he? Lexa-Blue asked Vrick.

He's slowing down. I think he's almost made it to wherever he's headed. Again, the positional data came through their nodes, showing a shrinking distance between them and Nord. They slowed their pace, keeping out of his line of sight.

He stopped on the next street over, just down the alley. If you stay just this side of the wall, he shouldn't see you.

They took a few steps back and waited, Keene sensing Lexa-Blue focusing her thoughts. Gadgets and tech were his area, but the rough stuff was her specialty, and he was happy to let her take charge. No point in messing with a formula that worked. He moved closer to the wall, meditating in a different way. Where her mind coiled, filling her with a kinetic energy that might burst into action at a moment's notice, Keene grew quiet and still, his essence becoming smooth as a mirror pool, ready to follow her lead.

Lexa-Blue fugued, and her dark, pocketed shipsuit tightened close against her steelskin so nothing would catch, no fold of cloth would hinder her movement, and Keene followed suit. This was her domain, and she knew the night well, could feel its touch on her skin. It was a remnant of the time when she had hidden her face from daylight and inquisitive glances, for the hours after sunset had always been more forgiving. The reticence to be seen was long gone, but her love of the dark remained. She stepped from the shadows into the growing dusk and felt Keene follow. As she hugged close and silent to the wall, she seemed less substantial than the rising shadows. At the mouth of an alley, she stopped and scanned the ground again. At her feet, the trail of glowing tracer footprints crossed her path and led to her right.

Taking a careful look in the direction of the trail, she saw him about twenty-five metres further along, by himself in the glow of a light post. Lexa-Blue smiled, her gaze hard and predatory, and her energy coiled tighter as she 'pushed the image of their quarry to Keene's node.

They saw Nord in the chill, bluish glow of the streetlight, fidgeting with his sleeves, his belt, his cuffs. She took in his ratty, stained coat, and a flash of distaste coursed through her. As she watched him, his hands shook as he pulled out a fizz-stick and lit it, the tip flickering blue-white, and the shaking eased as he inhaled. She watched as the initial hit of smoke seemed to calm him a bit, easing his jitters. He inhaled again, sucking more greedily this time.

They watched him and waited. Zyd's information seemed accurate. When they had delivered the cargo of exotic foodstuffs from Mandragora, Zyd had hired them in their less publicized, but more lucrative sideline, something Keene called "Creative Problem Solving." Nord had stolen a valuable bit chip of information that Zyd proclaimed essential to his business. Not wanting to sully his reputation by getting his hands dirty or trust his local precinct of GalSec, he had hired them to quietly recover the chip.

Someone's coming, Vrick said. *Opposite direction, you're okay. He won't see you.*

Lexa-Blue kept her hand near the gun strapped along her thigh. Through her node, she felt the power cell cycle and confirm its charge, the diagnostics signalling perfect working order.

She zoomed in on Nord's contact as he came into view, the images flowing like water between her and Keene. The new arrival was taller than Nord, but fleshy and mean, the set of his eyes like granite. He wore padded, beaten zoomstick leathers, scarred and split at the joints, showing years of use. Her instincts told her the bulge at his waist was a gun, and Nord had a good chance of ending up dead once the deal was struck. For a moment, she considered letting the deal play out. Once the new arrival had the bit chip and killed Nord, one shot would take him out. The polymers of the chip could withstand a couple of bounces off the pavement. No muss, no fuss.

She felt the smear of Keene's disapproval. *Fine,* she 'pushed. *We can do it the hard way.*

They watched the pair converse in whispers for a moment, Nord's nervous eyes darting around, on the lookout for intruders. They both reached into their respective pockets, Nord pulling out the bit chip, the other pulling out a credit chit.

Bingo, Keene thought to her. *A little subtle intimidation and we should be able to…*

Before he finished his thought, she drew her gun, stepped from the shadows, and fired. The stun charge caught Nord's contact full in the chest, lifting him off his feet and sending him hard to the pavement. Before the energy flare had faded, she trained the gun on Nord.

"Or you could just shoot him," Keene said aloud as she advanced on Nord, her gun not wavering a millimetre. He followed her into the open, raising his own gun to cover her.

"Give me the chip." Her voice was flat and cold.

Nord's lip twitched, and his eyes widened at the implacable tone in her voice. She saw him look frantically from side to side, gauging his chances of getting away from her, his hand clenched around the chip. She took a slow step toward him, the gun aimed right between his eyes.

"We all know he was going to kill you once you gave it to him. I, on the other hand, am willing to let you live. Mostly." When he didn't move, she activated the tracer beam, and a pinpoint of red heat appeared on the skin between his brows. "I'm not playing games, Nord. Now."

Stay chill, Blue, Keene 'pushed. *Last thing we need to explain to GalSec is another body.*

Nord looked at Keene, then back to Lexa-Blue, and she saw a muscle in his jaw go into frantic spasm. She heard a sharp click and a stiletto shot from the cuff of his filthy coat. He slashed desperately up and across her torso, his panic and adrenaline making the cut frantic and deadly as the blade sliced through her shipsuit and sparked across her steelskin. Faster than she could think, faster even than Keene could fire on him, she twisted out of the way and struck back, her fist catching him hard in the jaw. With an echoing crunch of bone impacting bone, he jerked backward, his head hitting the light post with a resonant gong-like peal. He crumpled into a heap as the light above him began to flicker.

She bent down at his side, pressing the gun against his temple in case he had any more tricks planned. When he didn't move, she pried the bit chip from his fingers. "You lose." A smirk formed on her face as she looked up at Keene. "Better than being dead, though."

Keene looked down at Nord. "Is he going to be all right?"

She touched her fingers to Nord's neck and nodded. "He might have a concussion, but it's no less than he deserves. Vrick can call Med-Aid once we're on our way." She stood and crossed to the stunned form of Nord's contact. She knelt and picked up the chit that had fallen at his side. Examining it, she smiled again and held it out for Keene to examine. "An unexpected bonus."

Keene saw it was a bearer chit, no payee or payer registered. All one had to do was present it for deposit.

He raised an eyebrow at her. "You know this isn't ours to keep, don't you?"

She shrugged. "Finders, keepers." She stood and, through her node, instructed the shipsuit to loosen, changing it from a skin tight layer to a comfortable coverall. She slid the chit and bit chip into a pocket and sealed it.

Nice work for someone who's sixty-five percent water, Vrick said. *The car is on its way. Should be there in a couple of minutes.*

Thanks, Vrick, Keene 'pushed, crossing his arms across his chest. He whistled tunelessly and off key while waiting for their rented groundcar to make its way to them. He took in a deep breath, smelling the salt tang of the evening mist from the ocean. Somewhere in the distance, a disgruntled murmur of thunder promised a storm before morning. Beside him, Lexa-Blue examined the slash in the front of her coverall, a stripe of burnished silver showing through the gap. Finally, she detached the top half entirely, leaving only the dark cargo pants, and then made as if to throw the torn fabric away.

"Hey," Keene said. "I can fix that. Hang on to it."

She shrugged and tied the sleeves around her waist, then stretched and shadowboxed in place, attempting to work off the thrum of adrenaline from the confrontation.

Keene watched her and shook his head, knowing this was a battle he couldn't win. He watched the trained play of her muscles as she moved, the fringe of her short dark hair dancing over the fair skin of her face. She was a beauty, he thought. The kind of beauty that eats its young. He knew how ferociously protective she was of him and of Vrick. He had seen her break bones without a second thought or a whisper of regret when provoked. Beside her, he felt large and clumsy, and not just because he stood half a head taller than her and was broader, more solid. She moved gracefully, with a control he had never had and knew he never would. His milk chocolate skin and coarse, cropped hair made him feel like her negative, her shadow, sometimes. He was just a farm boy with a talent for tech when he had fallen into her orbit. And now he bounced from planet to planet and danced along the edge of the blade with an astonishing regularity.

They heard the hum of the car's anti-gravs at the same moment, between grumbles of thunder. When he saw the car rounding the corner, Keene stepped away from the light. "Come on, Blue. Zyd's waiting."

Vrick, better call Med-Aid now.

Already done. You'll be long gone by the time they get here, Vrick told them both.

Lexa-Blue executed a smooth bow to her imaginary sparring partner, did a neck roll, and followed Keene to meet the car as it slowed to a hover between them. The doors moved laterally back along the car's chassis to admit them.

"I'll drive," Keene said, taking the driver's seat and releasing the auto-drive. Beside him, Lexa-Blue slid into the passenger seat, webbing herself in. Hand on the throttle, Keene geared up the grav cushion, moving the car into the dark street, away from the industrial district deeper into the heart of the city proper. They drove in the companionable silence of long-time friends, Lexa-Blue looking out the window while Keene concentrated on driving.

"Is it just me?" he said, after they had left the industrial section and headed into the city. "Or are the Grifts all starting to look the same?"

She snorted, but he knew it wasn't directed at him. "How long we been working together, junior?"

He suspected she could provide the exact date if she wanted, but he humoured her. He knew he would never forget that afternoon he had walked across the hard, flat surface of that landing pad on Goldslick, to take his place with her and Vrick. He would always remember the swagger in her step as she greeted him, defying him to say anything about her scar and her eye, and he thought about how long it had taken to win her acceptance and her trust. "Just over five years now."

She smiled, a tickle of friendly condescension and something else in it, he thought. Weariness? No, that wasn't it. It was an acceptance that some things were just what they were, and nothing could change them.

"I took my first steps on the concourse of a space port," she said. "Knocked over a rack of sim-chips when Da wasn't looking and scuppered a deal he was trying to set up. I've been on every port on every planet in the Galactum a dozen times over, and after a while, they're just a blur. Everybody has something they need to get rid of and something else they need more of. The trade and the ships are the only way to spread it around. Ships need crews, and crews need downtime. They need to relax after a trip or set up the next one. They need to find passengers for the next run or to jettison the ones they just had. And they need places to do it. Bars, clubs, theatres, jiggle-joints, squish-houses—they need it all and they need it close by. It's where they do business, and where they play when business is done. Anyone local with more than three neurons firing who wants to make money off them gets as close to the Port as possible. And no matter where you are, it's pretty much all the same juju."

He nodded, agreeing with her assessment and looking again at Highland with a new, more jaded eye. Holo-signs, lurid and sweat shiny, beckoned and bludgeoned his attention, all subtlety gone in their quest for the attention of any trader, pilot, or crew happening by. In the Grift, the only chaos was bright and noisy. Light from signs, storefronts, streetlamps, and floating holos drowned out the few stars not already hidden by the glow of the moons.

The flow of traffic around them increased steadily, hemming them in and forcing Keene to reduce speed. He steered the car away from the clogged main artery only to find himself caught in a press of bodies that had spilled out of a bar to clog the street, waving emerald and silver banners.

"Looks like Comet 10 took the Zoomstick Cup. Pay up, Blue."

"Yeah, yeah, put it on my tab," she said, with a dismissive wave of her hand.

"One of these days, I'm collecting, missy. Don't think I'm not." He spotted a gap in the wedge of bodies and edged the car onto a side street, where he was able to speed up. He turned left at the second intersection, then right three streets later, pulling into the long, curving drive at their destination.

Amid the gaudy lights around it, the façade of Wave was understated and elegant, a whisper amid the screams. Set back from the street by a manicured lawn and gardens, the main body of the club was a wide, four story dome of burnished bronze surrounded by four turrets, each ten stories tall.

Keene stopped the car at the main entrance, and they both stepped out, a young parking valet in vibrant sea blue walking toward them. Keene fugued a moment, transferring control of the vehicle to him, then felt Lexa-Blue fall into step beside him as they climbed the steps leading to the entrance.

At the top of the landing, Wave's sigil appeared in the corner of their vision. When they opened to it, the sigil bloomed, announcing their presence to the club's AI, which instructed them to wait for their escort to Zyd. Though he managed entry to his domain with state of the art systems, Zyd preferred his staff to be flesh and blood, rather than the AIs and holos many of his competitors used. The club's systems were state of the art, but he never let his guests go without the human touch.

Inside the lobby, Wave's AI instructed them through their nodes to wait for escort. They waited in the crowded lobby only a moment when they recognized Licia, one of Zyd's attendants, emerging from the hallways into the club's interior. Delicate as a china doll in a sheath of the same swirling blue that the valet had worn, she came to a stop beside them and inclined her head in greeting.

"Welcome back to Wave," she said, the lilt of her voice cutting through the background noise. The flicker of a smile on her face hinted of mysteries and secret seductions. "Your weapons, please?"

She presented them with a lock box, and they surrendered their guns. Keene sensed the momentary hesitation from Lexa-Blue as she released her grip on hers.

"Licia," Keene said. "Good to see you again. You look lovely."

Her smile widened at the compliment. "The Master is waiting in the Atlantis room. If you would follow me?"

She led them back the way she had come, down the curving smokeglass hallways to a door that unfolded before them like the petals of a copper flower. They followed her through and were transported to the bottom of the sea.

At the heart of the centre dome, the Atlantis room was the main dining area of Wave. The holo field above the tables recreated every sight and sound of the sea bed to the finest detail. As Keene and Lexa-Blue followed Licia between tables, ripples of far off light refracted through crystal clear water dappled shadows on their faces. A school of glossfins flitted over their heads, then broke like surf against the hide of a kraken passing over them ponderous and slow. A haunting echo of whale-song followed them across the dining room to Zyd's "captain's table" where their employer was holding court.

A man given to excess in everything, Wave's owner weighed almost a hundred and fifty kilos. An impeccable dresser, his dark suit was pressed and expertly tailored. He had gene spliced his skin a pale sea green to accent his wide-set sapphire eyes, which were prone to sparking with mischief or wrath when provoked. Now, they sparkled only with delight as he saw them approach, a beaming grin splitting his face.

"Come, children, sit, sit. We must eat." Zyd indicated the seats to his right with an expansive wave of his arm. Licia stood just behind him on the left, her hand resting lightly on his shoulder.

"Oh, Zyd, we couldn't possibly," Lexa-Blue said, already sitting and opening the menu.

"You'll have to forgive her, Zyd. She was raised by wild dogs," Keene said as he sat as well. "I'm hoping to teach her how to use utensils real soon."

Lexa-Blue cuffed him on the shoulder, not even looking up from the menu.

Zyd rolled his eyes. "Now, children, do behave. Mischief at the table sours my stomach."

Lexa-Blue smirked at Keene sidelong, but he managed to keep a straight face. "We promise to behave. Is Owen-Ra still your chef?"

Zyd looked affronted. "He is the best in three sectors. Would I allow anyone else to grace my kitchen?" He snapped his fingers, and a waiter came forward and filled their glasses with wine. They glanced at each other, trying not to smile. Zyd's grand, theatrical gestures were legend.

He showed admirable and uncharacteristic restraint by waiting for them to taste the wine and order dinner before coming to business. "You have it?" he asked.

Setting her wine glass down, Lexa-Blue smiled and pulled out the bit chip, sliding it across the table. When he saw the chip, Zyd's whole body relaxed, and a glint of hunger came into his eyes. Pulling out a portable reader, he slotted the chip into it and checked its ID signature. He smiled when he saw the results of the scan. With a swift movement of his hand, the block disappeared into his pocket. "I trust you sustained no injuries on my behalf?"

Lexa-Blue chuckled. "No. Caused a few though."

Zyd's smile flickered, then slipped back into place. "Now, children, you know how I despise violence."

I'm sure there's a stash of bodies somewhere that could tell us.

We don't know that for a fact, Blue. "I'm sure no one would be so unwise as to provoke your anger, Master Zyd," Keene said aloud. "Besides, that's what you have us for," Lexa-Blue assured him. "To keep things from coming to that. Don't worry. Other than a nasty headache in the morning, he'll be fine."

He has a broken jaw. Vrick sounded vaguely disgusted.

Mind your own business.

Zyd clucked his tongue at her and shook his head. "Such a naughty thing you are." Zyd's eyes glazed over, then he focused on them again. "Your payment is on its way. Thank you, my friends. You have done well as always. Now, more importantly, dinner."

Before their meals had even arrived, a porter appeared and presented them with a credit chit for twice the agreed upon fee. Zyd knew full well of Lexa-Blue's superstition about transferring credit through Know-It-All. She liked a chit in her hand, something tangible rather than, as she put it, the idea of payment.

When they protested the extra money, Zyd cut them off with a sharp wave of his hand, ending all discussion on the subject. "A small bonus for a job well done."

Lexa-Blue handed the chit to Keene, who pocketed it, then smiled at Zyd. "You're the kind of client I like doing business with."

Zyd waved away the sentiment, lifting his wine glass. "Now then, we can enjoy our dinner in peace."

He signalled the waiter again, who refilled their glasses as if on cue just as their meals appeared, then fugued for a moment before refocusing his eyes on them. "There. Suites have been prepared for you, and I expect you to enjoy yourselves. The pleasures of Wave are yours for the night."

A good day all around, Keene thought, reaching for his wine glass.

❖

High above the port, a massive spacecraft made orbit, gleaming in the light of the stars. In the main screen on the bridge, the storm over the Port swirled dark and angry. Standing in the midst of the ship's bridge, one man watched lighting spark through the mass of clouds. He shook his head.

"From one storm to another." He sighed, knowing better than to interrupt the crew as they brought the vessel into the planet's gravity well. They had performed admirably in keeping the ship in one piece during the gamma storm they encountered on their journey in-system, but he could tell their nerves were worn. They had not known the reason for their trip here to Highland, but what they had left behind was preying on everyone's mind even though honour and duty had driven them all to exceed their usual limits. He wished he could offer them furloughs to the planet's surface, but the urgency of their mission would not allow it. If all went well, they would be on their way home before the end of the next day. The most he could offer them was a good night's sleep with the relief crew manning the helm.

He turned at the sound of the commo officer's voice.

"Consul? I have received a transmission from the surface, receipt coded to you, text only."

"Transfer it to the Captain's chair, please." Being nominally in command of this mission, the Consul took his place in the main chair of the bridge. He placed his hand on the lighted panel and pressed a short sequence, keying an eyes-only, privacy holo. Words formed in the display. *They have been detained. Nothing more I can do. You have until tomorrow. Once I have made the introduction, our business is finished. We will not speak again.*

Choosing to ignore the hostility of the message, he killed the holo and turned back to the commo officer. "Open a tightline channel to the Technarch, full privacy."

The air shimmered around the Consul's chair, running like water for a moment before solidifying into amber light. He waited until the channel engaged, the holo image of his leader coalescing inside the privacy field. Hazel eyes fixed a penetrating gaze on him, with a power he felt even these light years from home.

"Well?" The Technarch's voice was terse with concern.

"They were detained as you requested. I was able to convince Master Zyd Quarto to keep them occupied until we arrived, and he succeeded. They will be at his establishment until tomorrow. We are in orbit now and will make contact then. Damage teams have the repairs under control, and we should be ready to return as soon as contact has been made and our…guest is aboard."

The Technarch nodded in satisfaction and brushed a tendril of hair back from his face. "Good. There have been no incidents since you left, and I am hoping it stays that way until you return. Inform me when you are under way again. You have my gratitude, Amory. You have done well."

The Consul bowed his gratitude for the praise, but by the time he had straightened, the channel had been broken.

CHAPTER TWO

Keene woke the next morning, his face awash with sunlight, feeling the tickle of a breeze across his chest. The storm had hit as he and Lexa-Blue were finishing dinner, winding up to rattle the windows with thunder as he staggered, half-drunk and sated, back to his room. It had blown itself out as he slept, leaving the sky a clear, hard blue. Lying with the warm light on his skin, he stretched, allowing himself fifteen more minutes between sheets as soft as a lover's skin. Usually an early riser, the glut of tactile sensation was decadent luxury.

Finally he knew he could put it off no longer. With a sigh, he threw back the covers and rose. Positioning himself near the windows to take full advantage of the sun and breeze, he began a routine of stretches that led into the workout Lexa-Blue had taught him. Of course, I look like I have three broken feet when I do them next to her, he thought, but who wouldn't?

Twenty minutes of martial arts and shadowboxing later, when his dark skin ran with sweat, he called it quits. Indulging in one last luxury, he ordered a full breakfast: pastries, fresh fruit, thinly sliced meats, eggs done just right, and a pot of Zyd's special coffee blend. After an invigorating shower under pulsating jets of water, Keene wrapped himself in the downy bathrobe Zyd had provided, coming back out of the bathroom just as his breakfast tray arrived, delivered by the most beautiful young man he had ever seen.

Time to rouse my missing partner and get ready to make tracks, he thought.

Blue? he 'pushed, drizzling amber-sweet honey on a slab of bread.

The mental grunt of response made Keene smile.

Come on, Sleeping Beauty, time to get up.

The only response Keene sensed was a ripple of pleasure, an erotic warmth leaking through the node, followed by a distinct image of a light, arching tongue tracing the curve of a small firm breast. He blushed, even though he should have grown used to it by now. She loved to show him more than he was interested in seeing if he happened to contact her at an inopportune time. It was one of the downsides of having bleeding edge comware splicing your brains together.

Hey, keep that to yourself, missy. I don't need to see it.

No, you need to do it for a change. That guy from Ulysses, what was his name? He was all over you. He'd have gotten squishy with you, and as far as I could tell, he actually did have a dick. What stopped you?

Not all of us think with our gonads, you know.

Too bad for you.

He sighed, knowing this old discussion all too well. He changed the subject. *How much did we eat last night?*

I lost count after the fourth course. But I think I worked it all off on the dance floor afterward.

Keene remembered the sight of her, sinuous and unrestrained as she danced, and he wondered if her current companion was the ambassador's daughter with the hair like a fall of autumn leaves. No, he decided. More likely it was the shaven headed men's zero-ball champion she had been dancing with when he wandered off to bed. Not my type at all, he thought, but obviously come up to her pathetically low standards.

I heard that.

I'm sure you did, Blue. It's time to send Prince Charming on his way. We have work to do.

He heard a string of good-natured, creative profanity from her but sensed she was getting up. With an affectionate grin, he sent the link back into idle and tucked into the meal with relish. He hated to leave this hedonism behind, but business was waiting. He was determined to enjoy his last few moments in this particular heaven.

Eventually sated, he stood and began to dress. As he was buckling his boot, he felt a whisper through his node, Wave's system letting him know he had an incoming call. He accepted the call with a thought, and a small holo formed in the air before him. He recognized their host.

"Good morning, Zyd," he said. "I was just about to call you. Everything was perfect as always. Thank you."

Zyd waved Keene's thanks away with a sweep of his manicured hand. "Pish and tosh. Only the best for my darlings. Though, I would ask a wee small favour in return. There's someone I'd like you to meet if you can sacrifice a moment or two of your time."

"Of course," Keene said, his curiosity piqued. Anyone Zyd recommended was bound to be…interesting. "We'll be right there."

"Thank you, handsome boy." The holo compressed and was gone.

Wakey shakey, Blue. Zyd has someone he wants to introduce you to. You have exactly the amount of time it takes for me to walk to your room.

He opened the door to the common room and crossed.

Naked or not, I'm coming in.

As he raised his hand to the door sensor, it slid aside, revealing Lexa-Blue, dressed and ready.

"Sorry, you'll have to get your cheap thrills somewhere else. All the lovers have gone home," she said, blowing him a kiss. "Better luck next time."

"Come on," he said, chuckling. "Zyd's waiting."

She did have very good taste in lovers, this he had to admit.

Zyd's office sat atop the north tower, sleek and clean, with no clutter and nothing out of place. While showy and operatic for the public, Zyd was all business in this room. When they entered, they found him behind his slab of a desk, dark and glossy as chocolate. He was not alone.

By one of the windows stood a man flanked by two uniformed guards, resplendent in red and gold. He was short and middle aged, with a prim, officious look about him. His dark suit bore the same ornate crest as the guards, and his hair was greying at the temples. The aura about him suggested he was used to wielding power, but at the same time that the power was not his.

He seemed to focus his attention on Keene, and, without waiting for an introduction from Zyd, he came toward them with a purposeful stride. Keene and Lexa-Blue noted the flash of affronted fury across Zyd's face.

"You are Sei Keene Ota Chiaro?" At Keene's nod, he bowed low and went on, ignoring Lexa-Blue completely. Keene didn't need his node to feel her bristle at the insult. He laid a light hand on her arm. Good one, stranger, Keene thought. That's two people in the room you've pissed off. Why do I think I'm next?

"I am Amory Jaekir, Consul to Daevin Adisi, Technarch of the

Brighter Light. The Technarch requests the honour of your presence. He must speak with you on a matter of the utmost…"

Jaekir's voice trailed off when he saw the shock on Keene's face, but he recovered his poise and continued. "…importance. His Highness has heard of your talent at…solving problems and requires your assistance. He asked me to bring you to him at once."

Keene shook his head, stunned by the mention of the name and the request that came with it. "I'm sorry, but that's not my problem. My responsibilities here don't give me the luxury of coming just because Daevin calls. He'll have to work this out on his own."

An indulgent, gentle smile formed on Jaekir's face, as if dealing with a truculent child who is unaware of his place. "I'm sorry, but that just won't do. I'm sure your business ventures seem important at the moment, but we are dealing with a matter of planetary importance, and every moment is precious. We must hurry. Now, if you will come with me." He reached out and took Keene's elbow.

Keene narrowed his eyes, and he looked down at the hand on his arm, feeling Lexa-Blue tense at his side, ready to step in. *Easy, Blue. I've got this one.* He very deliberately pulled his arm out of Jaekir's. When he spoke, his voice came out low and measured. "Perhaps you didn't hear me, so let me make this perfectly clear for you. I'm not coming."

Jaekir sighed, the sound heavy with impatience, and he reached again for Keene's elbow. "I'm afraid the Technarch was most insistent. I'm not to take no for an…"

Keene reacted instinctively to the unwelcome touch, shifting his weight and delivering a stinging blow to the Consul's forearm. Through his node, Keene felt Lexa-Blue readying to draw her gun. He wasn't certain she wouldn't shoot up Zyd's office.

To his credit, Jaekir maintained his composure. Only a quick hand movement prevented the bodyguards from retaliating.

"Consul Jaekir." Zyd's voice was a low, controlled drawl, hinting at limitless menace. "Correct me if I'm wrong, but Brighter Light is indeed part of the Pan Galactum, is it not? And as such, it is subject to all laws enshrined in the Constitution." His sapphire eyes narrowed to slits. "Am I correct?"

"You are," Jaekir answered stiffly.

"And our friend here has committed no crime on your world. There are no warrants for his arrest or extradition." Zyd steepled his fingers and leaned back in his seat. "Is this also correct?"

Jaekir's body was rigid. "Yes."

"Then, it would appear our business here is concluded." Zyd indicated the door, the motion precise and unmistakable. "Don't you agree?"

Jaekir said nothing. He stepped back, bowed low again, and exited, signalling the guards to follow.

"You, sei, are my hero," Lexa-Blue said.

"Don't thank me yet," Zyd said, his brow furrowed in concentration. "I have a feeling you haven't heard the last from that one."

He offered them coffee, and they accepted, avoiding all mention of the shadow the Consul had left in the room. Finally, with one last round of thanks, Keene and Lexa-Blue left him, fetched their car, and drove away.

"You going to tell me what that was about?" Lexa-Blue said from the driver's seat. "Who's this Daevin character?"

He felt her waiting in the sudden, prickly silence for him to explain, but he said nothing. He was a million miles away and ten years in the past.

The memory enfolded him in such clarity its edges were sharp as cut glass, and he was back in Molly's Books on Auxford, the day he and Daevin had met. The details flooded over him, immersing him in sight, sound, and smell. He saw the stacks of books, always on the verge of toppling, the rows of shelves lined with bit chips and vids, the milling crowd of students and faculty. He heard the creak of the rolling ladders, the hiss of steam and the clink of cups from the mezzanine cafe, the constant murmur of conversations, Molly's laughter. He smelled the mingling aromas of coffee and baking and incense. The whirl of sense-memories made him ache with longing, filled him with the desire to reach out, to touch it all again.

And amidst it all, the locus on which all of the memories turned, was Daevin. Daevin as he had been then, just crossing over the line from handsome to pretty, his hair falling to his shoulders in loose auburn waves. Daevin uncomfortable in his ring of bodyguards, everything about him uneasy with his own power. Daevin looking at him with eyes a deep, penetrating hazel-blue. Eyes that locked him, warmed him, melted him. And that first, diffident smile that went through him like a beam of light.

"The Technarch, as he calls himself now, was someone I knew from school. From a thousand years ago, it feels like.

"It was the first day of Wintermas break, and my marks had been better than I expected. I went into town to the bookstore to buy myself a present and there he was," Keene said. "When I saw him standing there, all I wanted to do was take him to bed. I never expected anything more. We did the dance, all that meaningless small talk so throbbing with subtext that the air crackles with it. We talked about books, and I realized he was more than a pretty face. He was passionate and funny and full of this energy that just drew me in. We went upstairs and talked for hours over coffee. I remember stretching my leg at one point and it touching his, not on purpose, but not quite by accident either. It was the first time we touched."

"Pretty scorching stuff. Practically pornographic. You could have been arrested," Lexa-Blue mocked. She was rewarded with an affectionate scowl in return.

He was silent a moment before speaking again. "It's a funny thing when it happens. Like some soggy romance holo or something. Makes you stupid."

"It was mutual, then?"

Keene blew out a sharp breath. "That's putting it mildly. It just about killed me to say good-bye, but he was going home for the holiday. With my parents gone, I didn't have any family to visit, so I just stayed in Auxford. It was one of the longest months of my life. When school started again, so did we. We took it slow at first, but it didn't take long for things to speed up. Sort of like a snowball rumbling down a mountain."

"It wasn't good?"

Keene shrugged. "Is a first love ever good? We laughed a lot. We fought a lot because we were so different. I mean, there I was an orphan who was only in school because my parents' will stipulated I use my inheritance for my education, in love with the heir to one of the most powerful leaders in the Galactum. We broke up. I was devastated. We stayed friends. We got back together because someone played a sappy song. It was explosive, passionate, maybe even a little obsessive."

Keene stared out at the passing streets, his words raw and earnest. "But I loved him. I've never loved anyone else like that."

"What happened?"

"We were together for about two years. We slept together when we could, which wasn't often. He was always surrounded by spyeyes and bodyguards, and they reported his every movement to his father, who kept him on a pretty tight rein. Old Dad had some pretty strict ideas about his heir maintaining a high scholastic profile and saw me as a threat to Daevin fulfilling his potential. I guess if you've invested that much in someone and taken them into your family, you want to make sure they make good on it."

"Hold on a second," Lexa-Blue interrupted, confusion on her face. "Daevin's adopted?"

Keene sighed and rubbed his eyes. "Brighter Light is a corp colony. They altered their family units centuries ago to align with that structure. You have your birth family and what they call your real family. You stay with your birth family until you're eighteen. All that time you go through extensive tests to determine your aptitudes. Depending on what you are good at and what the Families need, you are adopted by one of them once you finish your basic schooling. Old Dad decided Daevin had what it takes to be his heir, so he adopted him and sent him to Auxford for some higher education. You can see why he didn't want anything to interfere with Daevin's schooling. The funny thing was, we got each other through some of the other's worst courses. He would have flunked xenopsych without my help, and he got me through quantum math. It was pretty hard to get any privacy, but we managed to keep it together."

"And then?" Lexa-Blue prompted.

"Daevin was called back to Brighter Light when his father fell ill, and he told me he probably wouldn't be back. He asked me to go with him, but the idea of being a…royal consort was more than I could handle. Besides, I wanted to finish school and travel. I asked him to let someone else take over, which I can see now was a pretty ridiculous demand, and being a selfish pronk, I was furious when he refused. It wasn't a very graceful ending."

Keene's face turned wistful and he sighed.

"The irony of it all is that after he left, I lost it. My grades went to hell. I ended up dropping out. I was too proud to tell him I was wrong or let him see how badly I had screwed up. I wanted a new start, so I joined the Merchant Fleet." His face clouded over once again. "I found out later that his father had died, and I sent him a letter. We corresponded for a while, but it just sort of faded away. I haven't heard from him in years."

"Until today. What do you plan to do about it?"

Keene snorted. "Nothing. That's one pot I don't intend stirring up again after all these years. If he had wanted to know me, he could have made the effort then, not now. And definitely not with a stupid gesture like this. Any bond between us died a long time ago. Would you cross the sector because the first boy you kissed when you were thirteen asked you to? I doubt it."

She smirked. "I was ten. And he was cute. If he still was, I'd consider it."

This made Keene laugh. "Just drive."

They spent the rest of the morning and into the afternoon running errands in Port City proper: connecting with potential clients, completing other transactions, ensuring the stocks aboard their ship were replenished. They arranged for a new cargo of medical supplies for a hospital on Splinter to be dispatched to the landing pad that afternoon for loading. After a relaxed lunch, they split up for some personal time. It was late afternoon when they reconnected and returned to the landing pad where the Maverick Heart waited.

"Okay, I'm going to clear up some export datawork so we can get out of here once our new cargo arrives," Keene said as they got out of the car. He fugued onto the traffic grid, and the car hummed away in the direction of the rental office.

Lexa-Blue nodded. "Vrick and I will check out the repairs and make sure we're in shape for space. Unless anything went wrong, we should be ready by the time you're done."

With a nod, Keene left her in the Maverick Heart's shadow and went into the ship. Settling into a comfortable chair in the lounge, he closed his eyes. An animated sigil formed in the lower right corner of the dark becoming the character alpha, then melting into omega then repeating. Focusing on it, he opened a link to Know-It-All and queried for the link-code to the Dockmaster's office. When the code came up, the digits and characters were a soft powder blue, Keene noticed, with an icy mint aftertaste and spoken in a cool professional voice. A thought triggered the link-code, and he sensed the yellow buzz as the call signalled at the other end.

When the export clerk opened the channel, Keene noticed the tell-tale blurring at the edges of her image that told him she was jacked rather than nodelinked. He felt a flash of tech-rat pride at being one interface jump ahead of her. Get with the times, he thought to himself. Jacking is so passé.

How may I help you today, citizen? She was too perky to be believed. No one should enjoy their work that much, Keene thought.

As usual, he had mixed feelings about always being the one to deal with the Dockmaster's office, but while dealing with the bureaucracy taxed his patience, he knew that if Lexa-Blue had to deal with a clerk as chirpy as this, mayhem would result.

He sent an I.D. spurt through the link, then the manifest and its documentation from the ship's records. The clerk beamed as she received the data and sent back a confirmation for Keene to file with their records.

Thank you. See you next trip.

And thank you for visiting Highland. Safe Journey.

Keene winked at her and closed the link. Before logging off Know-It-All, he checked in with the Met Station. A new image pane opened, and the long range forecast came up, floating over a gorgeous aerial view of Highland's ocean. As weather stats and detailed forecasts scrolled through the pane, a subsidiary window opened at the upper edge of the weather readout. Keene groaned as he recognized the familiar synthetic face with the sickening, unctuous grin.

Greetings, citizens, this is Noah Tall, with another Info-clip brought to you by Galactel. Do you find that quantum resonances interfere with your...

Keene tried to kill the ad stream with his home-coded mute program, but the artificial huckster didn't respond. Time to upgrade that piece of code again, he thought. Having absorbed enough information from the met report, Keene logged off and opened his eyes.

Through the lounge's main port, the bright afternoon light blazed off the hard concrete. Highland's two suns were well past their zenith, but already he could sense the shift in the quality of their light that signalled the change in the seasons. He and Lexa-Blue had spent enough time here to recognize the signs of the approaching off season. As well as the change in sunlight, the increased traffic in and out of the port indicated many were concluding business before the harsh Highland winter took hold.

A winter that will see me half the way across the Galactum, he thought. The met report had confirmed the first of the ice storms would all but shut Highland down in less than a month.

And after the time we had coming in-system, he thought, I can do without storms for a long time. Things should be nice and quiet for the next while.

❖

Slipping off her leather glove, Lexa-Blue ran her hand along the underside of the ship's hull. Having shed the heat of their descent days ago, the metal-ceramic composite was cool to the touch. Though the Maverick Heart had begun life as a private yacht, the ship had been retrofitted decades earlier for deep space cargo hauling, with the addition of a racking system that cargo pods could be added to. The ship was squat and squarish, but even with the additions to its hull, the lines were clean and tight.

She remembered the day she had first seen the vessel on another landing pad far across the Galactum, waiting for her interview.

Fewer than two hundred sentient ships had survived the Consciousness War. Many of those had turned their backs on humans altogether, disappearing into the black of space. Of those remaining, some travelled space alone. The invitations for human companions were rare, and without even knowing she was being considered, she had made the short list compiled by the Maverick Heart.

She had been without a berth for months, reduced to begging for temp slogs on crummy, third-rate barges that ran the same five port run week in and week out when the summons had come.

In the interview, when she had seen how clean and spacious the ship was, her desire to hide the intense need for the position had made her tart and mouthy. She'd been sure she'd blown it to bits and put her crew through hell until the miraculous acceptance had come through.

Penny for them, the Maverick Heart said.

What in the seven hells is a penny?

You humans and your sad little meat brains. Learn some of your own history, Meat. Vrick's voice rang with affection.

I'm nothing but a meatsack, but that's why you love me. What's our onload status?

The new cargo hasn't arrived yet.

Lexa-Blue frowned. *When was it due?*

About an hour ago. I just figured that it was delayed somehow. Meats are pretty unreliable. I haven't been able to get through to Pryn's people. I wanted to check with you before I did any snooping.

She rubbed her chin and sighed. *Give them another fifteen, then dig away if you can't get through.*

Will do.

Uneasy at the change of plan, she closed the link and stepped out of the ship's shadow into the sunlight. Pryn ran a tight operation. It

wasn't like her to miss a deadline or keep people waiting. It was one
of the things Lexa-Blue liked about dealing with her. Still, she knew
unforeseen complications were always possible, and their relationship
with Pryn went back a long time. Until she had confirmation something
had gone balls up, she was prepared to wait.

She turned her face to the suns, letting them warm her face and
wash away the worry for now. Life is good, she thought. Steady work,
good partners, plenty of nice planets to dirtside on and a not too wild
trip in-system. True, the gamma storm had shaken them up a bit as they
came out of interspace, but they had made it through with only minor
damage. I'd hate to think what it must have done to anyone who had
been closer. Still, a gamma storm beats a pirate cruiser with a weapon
lock on your ass. She stood there daydreaming for a few minutes, just
enjoying the sun on her skin, until Vrick spoke again.

*No word from Pryn yet, but repairs are complete. All systems
up and running. The hull ruptures are sealed and test well within
tolerances. All my diagnostics are clear. Do you want to have a
look? What am I saying? Of course you do.*

The put upon tone in es voice made her laugh as she walked along
the ship's port side to the engine cowling. Where there had once been
scorched gouges in the metal, the hull was now unblemished. She
micro-inspected the repairs as Vrick fed es diagnostic data through her
node. Satisfied the ship was one hundred percent space-worthy, she
stepped away. *You look beautiful as ever, Vrick. No reason to wait
any more. Go digging and see what you can find out about our
cargo. Do whatever you have to. Just don't get caught.*

Later, when Keene joined them on the flat, hard landing pad, he
saw storm warnings in the flat line of her mouth and the furrow of her
brow.

Vrick, tell him what you told me, she 'pushed to them both.

The ship's words were measured and careful. *When Pryn's
people didn't get back to me, I did some digging. I was able to break
in on a call and reroute it from their commo. They were expecting
the Trade Liaison on the end of the line and ended up talking to me.
I'm no expert in human behaviour...*

Keene knew that wasn't true. Vrick usually understood human
reactions better than the humans having them.

*...but I think they were hiding something. All I could get out
of them was that they no longer required our services as the cargo
was cancelled. The interesting thing is that I sliced their commo

records, and the cargo that was meant for us was loaded and on its way to us when they called it back. Then they paid another crew a short notice bonus and rerouted it to their ship. They cut us out on purpose. Their system re-encrypted before I could find out why.*

It was Keene's turn to frown. "We've been working with Pryn almost as long as you and I have been together. Why would she freeze us out like that? It doesn't make any sense."

Lexa-Blue didn't say anything, but he felt her seethe.

"Come on, Blue. Nothing we can do about it now. Let's hit the Trade Nexus and see if we can line something up. Once that's done, we can get hold of Pryn and see what her problem is."

He knew she could be volatile, but her moods came and went quickly, so he waited, then felt the gnarl of tension in her ease a bit. She turned for the ship's hatch.

"Who needs that rucking prunt anyway," she said. "Bigger and better things." Once they had entered the ship, Vrick spoke up.

"There's a message coming through for you, Keene."

"See?" Lexa-Blue said. "Probably our next cargo coming through already!"

"Let's hear it, Vrick."

"Aud, vid, or full holo?"

"Summarize."

"An Amory Jaekir cordially requests the honour of your presence at a meeting to discuss his offer further."

They looked at each other, incredulous at the offer.

Keene shook his head. "He just doesn't give up. Tell him I haven't changed my mind and I have no intention to. If that's not good enough for him, he can shove it up his ass."

"Shall I quote you on that?"

"Use some of that Class Nine intelligence, Vrick. Just deal with it."

"Not to worry, Keene," Vrick's voice was gentle. "I'll take care of it for you."

"That Jaekir's one pushy little fucker. He's not going to give up, you know." Lexa-Blue stood and tossed Keene's coat to him. "What's say we take off for a while? We can wait until tomorrow to sort out another cargo. Let's just kick back and have some fun. Come on, you need some serious night life."

"Squish, stims, and humping senso-vibe, huh?" Keene smiled for the first time since Jaekir had come into their lives.

"Give the boy a prize," she said, leering.

"Blue, that's the best offer I've had all day."

❖

The next morning, they sat in their galley, planning how to replace Pryn's cargo. Taking a bite of a sweet, nutty pastry and a sip of coffee, Lexa-Blue fugued to add a name to the list she was compiling. Then she 'pushed it to Keene. "Anyone else you can think of to add?"

He closed his eyes, and the list opened in his mind. He scanned it, agreeing with all her choices. "Don't forget the Sceptre. There're always deals being made over the Slapjack tables." He added the name, divided the list in half, and 'pushed one half of it back to her.

She nodded, but he felt a squirm of frustration from her. He pushed a plate with the last piece of her favourite cheese in her direction. "Don't stress, Blue. We'll find something."

She stared at him over the rim of her cup, her eyes narrow. "One thing I've learned in this life is that you should never assume things will work out. The money from Zyd will get us off planet and keep us going, but only for a while. I want to get this resolved. One thing's for sure, we're not letting this Jaekir guy decide our next move."

Keene raised his pastry in a toast. "Hear, hear."

Four hours later, his conviction was flagging. He returned from the Sceptre after painstakingly checking every contact on his half of the list. As he approached the table by the galley, he saw her sitting composed and straight in her chair, tapping the empty glass in her hand on the table in a slow, angry rhythm.

"Looks like you had as much luck as I did," he said.

Tock. Tock. Tock. The glass continued its hollow sound on the table. She looked back at him, her natural eye as dark and cold as the sensor gem.

"Sei Aris is 'unavailable'. Sei Tomek wouldn't see me. Sei Yilena has all her cargo booked. She's lying."

"You don't know that."

She looked at him. "Keene, she's a worse liar than you."

He sighed. "Sounds exactly like the stories I got. Face it, Blue. They've got us."

She cracked the glass on the table with such force, he was afraid it would break. "Fine. Slag this dirtball. We dust off tomorrow and hit

Red Ring or Forest, or head out to the Brink. How far can this guy reach, anyway?"

He looked sceptical. "Brighter Light provides most of the technology that keeps the Galactum running. Even when Daevin was just a student, I was surprised by how much power he could bring to bear when he really wanted to. Now that he's Technarch? I wouldn't be surprised if he could hound us to the Brink and back if he put his mind to it. But he wouldn't do that unless he really needed help."

"Why are you defending him?" Her voice rose, and Keene held up his hands to ward off her temper.

"Hey, easy. I'm not defending him. It's a dirty trick to play on us, I know. You're right, let's just go. There's bound to be something out in the Brink systems."

He wasn't convinced they could hide from Daevin's reach, but he knew her pride wouldn't allow her to cave in to Jaekir's pressure. Leaving the planet was at least something. Staying here wouldn't get them anywhere. "Come on, Blue. Gravity can't hold us. What say we burn some sky and leave this all behind?"

He saw some of the tension ease from her posture. "You're right. Let's ditch this dirtball and see where the stars take us."

Lexa-Blue stood from the table and went straight to her pilot station and began checking the ship's readiness.

"Eager to get going, Blue?" Keene said, taking his own station. "No happier than me to see this ass end of this place, I'll bet."

She winked at him as her board showed green. "We ready to go, Vrick?"

Ey answered after a fractional hesitation. "The Port system has been stalling me. All it says is that you need to contact the tower directly."

She turned to face Keene, and they exchanged a look, then she fugued onto the commo grid and recited the standard departure spiel, her clipped tone a signal to Keene of brewing anger. "Highland tower, this is Maverick Heart, I.D. code T-3372A, requesting take-off clearance from Pad J-23."

The commo channel was silent for a moment, then they heard the bored voice of a controller. "Negative, Maverick Heart; clearance denied. Please stand by."

Lexa-Blue frowned. For anything short of criminal investigation, refusing departure clearance was a serious breach of Port protocol.

"Highland tower, state reason for refusal," she demanded.

"Negative, Maverick Heart. Please stand by."

Lexa-Blue cut the connection and frowned.

"Vrick, can you do a tap and see if you can find out what's behind all this?"

"Your wish is my command. Initiating tap," ey answered.

A few seconds went by.

"No security coding on the directive," Vrick said. "If it was any more blatant, it would be arrested for indecent exposure. The tower received a polite, informal, but very insistent request from the Brighter Light's envoy to keep us here. Local government is putting pressure on the tower to comply. Turns out they're in negotiations on a deal for a new power grid upgrade. I'll give you three guesses who with."

"Jaekir," Keene said. "We'll never make it past the perimeter defenses without clearance."

"So what the fuck do we do?"

"We don't do anything. I do. Vrick, please contact the tower and request a channel to Amory Jaekir."

CHAPTER THREE

I've got your back, Keene. Stay snappy.

He sensed her off to his left behind the colonnade, as aware of her location as he would be of an arm or a leg. He'd told her not to come, but he knew she would ignore him. Knowing she was there, and that Vrick was jacked into every possible surveillance system, made him feel as secure as he could be until this mess was resolved.

Realizing his hands were balled tightly into fists, he made an effort to shake them out and relax, looking into the fountain. The fat, bright suns overhead made the water shimmer over the stones.

He had set the meeting in the most public place he could think of, by the Flame Fountain in Old Earth Plaza. If Jaekir's intention was to force Keene to accompany him, broad daylight and multiple witnesses might deter him. But even if it didn't, would GalSec even bother to investigate if he "disappeared" at the hands of Brighter Light's Consul? Could Daevin have changed that much?

He's coming.

Keene turned to see Jaekir crossing the square toward him, the smile on his face too warm, too inviting. It was a smile meant to lull you while the knife slid in. Keene knew the ruthlessness that hid behind that smile. Jaekir stopped about a metre away, his hands spread, trying to appear non-threatening.

"I have come, as you wished, alone."

He's lying, Lexa-Blue told Keene. *I've made four armed guards, all within striking distance.*

Keene's mind filled with the positions of the strategically placed guards in relation to himself and Jaekir, the park, and the fountain. He's not the unassuming little mouse he pretends to be, Keene thought. "We have a problem."

"More than you know." All traces of the smile left Jaekir's face, and his tone was grave, all condescension gone. For the first time, Keene could hear real emotion in the older man's voice, and he saw raw worry etched in the older man's face. "His Highness, Daevin Adisi, Ruling Technarch of…"

"Skip the song and dance. Get to the point."

Jaekir looked Keene over with a long, reappraising gaze. "He wants to see you. I am to bring you to him on board his yacht, Sunstriker, which is in orbit. He needs your help. It seems you and your partner have quite the reputation for handling difficult situations, and word of your skills has reached the Technarch's ear. I assure you, the situation is dire."

Keene felt a flash of concern and fought to keep it from showing on his face, but he realized too late that Jaekir had seen it.

"As my partner told you," Keene said, self-reproach giving his voice a harsh edge, "we have a run to complete, and then we'll consider Daevin's request."

Jaekir smiled, and Keene was surprised how genuine the expression seemed.

"Unfortunately that is not an option."

"Don't be too sure of that."

Jaekir shrugged. "Your ship cannot leave this world unless I permit it."

Keene wondered if Jaekir was aware that the Maverick Heart was a sentient, endangered citizen protected by special Pan Galactum statute. The diplomatic hassles of arranging that type of detention were staggering. But he wouldn't put it past the other man to try.

"The ship might stay. That doesn't mean I will."

The older man shook his head, a small smile on his face as he tutted at Keene's statement. "But are you really the sort that would walk away from his partner, his friend, leaving her interdicted on this world?"

Keene's eyes narrowed in sudden suspicion, yet he noted the word choice. Jaekir, and likely Daevin too, were unaware of Vrick's status. Good. Might be able to use that later, he thought.

"One word from me, and your partner will find herself under investigation for smuggling, tariff violations, and anything else I can think of. Her license will be revoked within a day."

Keene felt a sear of rage from Lexa-Blue. *No, Blue! Let me handle this.*

"I know you won't believe me, but it gives me no pleasure to do this. I would much rather be home in front of the fire with family. Traipsing across the sector blackmailing strangers is not something I enjoy in the least."

For a moment, Keene's fury split and doubt seeped through. Jaekir's words seemed sincere, perhaps for the first time since they had met.

"There are other methods, though. Much less extreme." Jaekir reached into an inner pocket.

Keene's hand shot toward his gun. Through the node, he felt Lexa-Blue do the same. Jaekir froze, then resumed his movement much more slowly.

"Nothing so pedestrian, I assure you," he said, his tone even. "Something I was told to give you if all else failed."

Jaekir's hand reappeared holding an envelope. He handed it to Keene, who felt something small and hard shift inside it. He held it a moment, unsure whether to open it. Then, with a decisive motion he tore the end, emptying it into his palm. A folded note and a ring.

The ring.

Keene felt a rush of heat, leaving him unsteady on his feet. He clenched his palm, and the ring dug into his flesh. The ring he had given to Daevin, one of a matched set in simple etched silver. The mate to the ring he had carried for two years after they had ended before pitching it into the sea, walking away from all it had represented. With a flush of shame, he realized he didn't even remember what world he had been on at the time. He stood there, the ring heavy in his palm, his mind reeling. Daevin had kept it. For all these years. With numb fingers, Keene opened the note and read it.

Keene:
Please come. I need your help.
Remember your promise.
Forgive me.
Daevin.

The memory of his promise came back to him in a surge of emotion. He heard his words as he slipped the ring on Daevin's finger. *Any time you need me, just say the word. I'll be there.*

Fates, I was young, he thought. *Do we ever really expect to be held to promises like that? And yet, if Daevin needs me enough to swallow* that much pride after all this time… Still, Keene's hackles rose at the thought of Daevin's ham-fisted manipulations to get his help. The urge to run took him again, the muscles in his thighs tightening to turn and flee. But where to? For a moment, he was afraid to even breathe for fear the slightest motion would tip him over some precipice he could never come back from. The Maverick Heart, his lifeline, was grounded. And worst of all, even if he found some way to secure transport off-planet for himself, Jaekir had Lexa-Blue dead in his sights as his next victim and was more than willing to exercise that power. For a gut-wrenching second, Keene found he didn't care, the desire to escape from this trap was that strong.

No. He couldn't do that to her. In the end, she and Vrick were all he had. His life with them was a prize he had fought for and earned many times over.

"Fine. Count me in. I need to inform my partner I'll be leaving. We can leave tonight after latemeal. Have your rucking yacht ready."

He turned on his heel and walked away. On the path to the park's entrance, he became aware of Lexa-Blue walking beside him, matching his step but saying nothing.

Keene fugued to the traffic grid and hailed a cab, then turned. "I'm going. Tonight. Once I'm gone, you'll both be clear. You and Vrick can find a job and get off this mudball. Once things are taken care of, I'll get hold of you, and you can pick me up. You can take smaller cargoes or hire loading help until I get back. If you stick to the safer sectors, everything should be fine."

The half-truth was bitter in his mouth. She hated spacing alone. Too many things could go wrong, and she wanted someone at her back. She always swore an extra pair of hands made all the difference in a crisis, and no sectors were guaranteed to be safe, short of doing milk runs between Hub and its orbital stations. Some were marginally less dangerous ones, but that was the best that could be said. Even the core systems had been threatened by pirates and worse. A sharp, ugly image jabbed his mind: Vrick, cold and gutted in space, Lexa-Blue's body frozen and adrift in the wreckage. He was saved from the horrific picture by the arrival of the cab.

She didn't even pause to think. "It won't be a problem. Because I'm coming with you."

"Damn it, Blue. He wants me, not you. For once in your life, just step away when you can." He turned to get in the cab, but she gripped his upper arm and spun him back to face her. Despite the strength of her hand, her voice was calm and quiet, not rising to the bait of his anger.

"If you're in this, then I'm in it too. All the way up to my perfectly shaped hoots." She loosened her grip and laid her hand on his heart. "I've got your back."

He looked in her eyes, one sparking jade green, the other solid black, and knew that, just like he had no hope of fighting Jaekir's control, he couldn't fight her on this. The pressure of her hand against his chest anchored him. He knew she would follow him whether he allowed it or not, and relief surged through him. This was what he had wanted, what he had not been able to ask for, what had gotten lost in his desire to protect her from whatever was coming on Daevin's world. He nodded, all that was needed to show her how he felt, and stepped aside to let her enter the cab.

"He wants me to travel on Daevin's yacht, which is in orbit," he told her as the cab pulled from the curb. "I'll let him know you're coming too. Vrick…"

Ruck that, Vrick said. *Where you go, I go. You can travel in that…clunker if you want, but I will be on your tail like a solar flare. Deal with it.*

Keene managed to smile. "I doubt he'll like that much. We could just break off in orbit and head out of the system once we're off planet. Which, come to think of it, isn't such a bad plan."

She shook her head. "I'm willing to bet that this 'yacht' will be armed to the teeth. They could probably disable us with one shot and not even break a sweat, then tow us the rest of the way. And if previous behaviour is any indication, they'd do it too."

I can set up a transponder lock to give them the confidence that they can track our extra-orbital trajectory. Then once we're out of the gravity well, I'll twin the inter-drive with theirs to keep us in contact once we hit interspace. It's standard FTL convoy procedure. If we wander too far from them, both ships could go off course and end up a plasma smear. That should keep them calm.

"If they know anything about us, they know we aren't likely to disintegrate ourselves to get away from them," Lexa-Blue said.

That thought actually made Keene chuckle. "Good point. Of course, who knows what that crew thinks of us."

When they reached the Maverick Heart, Keene and Lexa-Blue

proceeded directly to their control consoles, set along the back of one of the comfortable, right angled couches facing the main port. Taking a chair, Keene scanned across the readouts on the panel. "Are we green, Vrick?"

"The greenest of greens. I can lift off as soon as the Tower gives us permission to leave."

"Think there'll be any problems twinning the inter-drive?" Keene asked.

Vrick made an eminently telling, scornful sound. "I was twinning my drives with my people as a baby. The question is, can that hunk of scrap keep up with me?"

"I have a hunch the Technarch's yacht might be a step up from a hunk of scrap, Vrick." It was all Keene could do not to laugh, but the last time he had laughed out loud at Vrick, the artificial gravity in his quarters had suddenly developed random malfunctions. For a week, he kept waking up on the ceiling.

Lexa-Blue stood and arched her back. "I'm going to the gym to punch something. Let me know when the next crisis hits."

Once she was gone, Keene crossed to the galley, finding and opening a bulb of fruit juice. "Vrick, would you open a channel to Jaekir for me? We need to see if we can convince him of the wisdom of our new plan."

He settled himself on the couch until Vrick told him the channel was open. In the space between him and the view port, a sleet of glowing rain fell, coalescing into an image of Jaekir. Keene outlined the change of plans, bracing himself for argument.

Jaekir listened intently, rubbing his chin between thumb and forefinger. When Keene was finished, Jaekir paused thoughtfully before he said anything. Finally, he locked his eyes on Keene's. "You do know that we'll be watching every move you make. Deviations from our course will not be tolerated."

Keene met the unflinching gaze with one just as hard. "Vrick, send transponder code and begin the prep to twin the inter-drive. All requests from Sunstriker are to be complied with fully. Maverick Heart out."

Jaekir's image broke apart into streams of light, evaporating as they hit the deck. Keene stared through the space the holo had filled, feeling a surge of renewed resentment, then inhaled, willing it down. The waves of emotion began to quiet, a wash of fatigue flowing into its place, and all he wanted to do was to lie down. He fugued to check the time, finding he had several hours until latemeal. He decided to go to his quarters and rest a while. As the door closed behind him, he sagged on the edge of his bed, grateful for the solitude.

He looked around, struck by how bare his room was. Vrick could easily have reshaped the bed to any size he required, but Keene kept it the right size for one. Lexa-Blue's was almost three times as big and often full. Where her walls were covered with an arsenal of exotic weapons, his were bare. He had few knickknacks or mementos, little to indicate anyone lived there at all.

The fatigue turned to a coldness in his heart, he turned to the transparent wall that filled with stars when they were in space. The view of the landing pad and the Port beyond seemed flat, wrong somehow.

What happened to me? My rooms at school were packed with things. My books alone...

I don't even own any real books anymore, he realized. How could I have forgotten that?

When he and Daevin had split up, he had cut away, with surgical precision, huge chunks of the life he had led, desperate to remove the pain. And now, that pain had exploded into his life again.

Did I ever actually heal? Or did I just keep on going until I convinced myself I was all right?

As Keene tried to nap, Lexa-Blue meditated in the Maverick Heart's gymnasium. Her body was still, save for the easy rhythm of her breath, but underneath, her emotions churned. She hated what this was doing to Keene, and further, she hated this Daevin character for causing it all. She realized she was also angry at Keene for dragging her into it, even though the choice to stay and be at his side was hers and hers alone. There was a whisper of relief that he would not leave her by herself. After all, she had been alone when— She cut off the thought. Let that one lie. But the furor in her heart demanded some form of action, some form of release.

She opened her eyes. "Vrick, program me a sparring partner."

"Skill level?"

"One level below mine," she said. "I feel like kicking ass."

"You've got it, Meat."

Stepping out of a storage cabinet, the animate walked toward Lexa-Blue and stopped a short distance away. It bowed low, and she returned the gesture.

As the animate straightened, it launched itself at her. She twisted at the last moment, using its momentum to throw it over her shoulder to the mat.

The animate hit the floor with a thud but kept moving. It slithered around, pivoting on one hand to scissor kick her legs out from under her. She went down in a loose ball, doing a shoulder roll, then came up in a crouch and sprang.

The animate caught her and pulled her close, her back to its front, and squeezed. She jammed an elbow hard into its rib sensors. Programmed to mimic human vulnerabilities, it doubled over and released its grip on her. She pulled away, whirled around, and struck, alternating punches with open-handed chops. The animate staggered backward under her blows, unable to find an opening.

"Hold." The animate stopped. "Vrick, bump up the level a notch or two. This is too easy."

"Done."

She grinned when the animate came at her again.

An hour and a half later, the twisted remains of six animates were strewn around the room. The decapitated head of one had rolled under a bench, its blank eyes staring out at her. "This is not helping."

"Don't blame me. It was your idea to relieve stress by beating six animates to death. Are you done with your tantrum, or do you want to hit something else?"

She did a quick bend and stretch, and flashed em her wolf's grin. "Keene work everything out with Jaekir? Are we on?"

"We're on. Keene and I sorted it out while you were busy committing droidicide. The vectors are already plotted, and we're set to synch the drives when we hit orbit. Other than the impending mayhem and recriminations, we're all set. Cue the excessive and embarrassing displays of gratitude, now."

Lexa-Blue threw back her head and laughed, then headed for the shower.

❖

Keene woke after a restless nap and stayed in bed, watching Highland's sun set. He sat up and tried to rub the graininess from his eyes. When he still felt logy and disconnected, he stripped and headed for the shower, debating whether to use a portion of his precious water ration for a real shower. In the end, he decided it would be bad to use any before they had even left the surface. Instead, he set the sonics almost high enough to rattle bones, emerging awake and refreshed.

He put on his steelskin and caught sight of its metallic glimmer in the mirror. It brought him up short. I'm going to see someone I used to love, and I'm wearing body armour. With a wry smile, he shook his head.

But he didn't take it off.

Over it, he added a soft, loose shirt and dark, close fitting pants. He stopped a moment, picking up the picture of his parents, then the one of him with Lexa-Blue. He smiled, remembering it being taken on Weber's World. As always, he felt he looked awkward and uncomfortable in the image, while she came off as rakish and sexy. Replacing the photo on his bedside table, he set out to find Lexa-Blue and ease the rumbling of his stomach.

He found her in the common room, a glass of wine in her hand. She was reading from an old, leather-bound book he recognized as one he had bought for her years before. He stood there a moment before she noticed him, affection surging in his heart.

Their friendship had been born in this room on those long cargo hauls from planet to planet. Under the curving wall of stars, they had spent hours watching hundreds of holos and classic vids together, had talked and played cutthroat Quisling marathons lasting hours. He had light-painted while she read, occasionally sharing funny or thoughtful passages with him. One of his paintings of her sat half finished, in the frame of his easel by the galley.

A smile formed on his face as he remembered the meals she had prepared for him, synthesizing only the ingredients before cooking them by hand. The thought of those evenings, drenched in wine and laughter, made him realize how hungry he was.

He turned to look at her again, irrationally afraid she might have disappeared while his attention had been elsewhere.

She looked up at him as if reading his mind. "Dinner is just some of the leftover chenyai I made the other day. Hope that's all right."

He nodded and walked over to where the galley opened onto the common room, finding the pot on the warmer. The rich, spicy scent filled his nostrils, and he ladled a bowl for himself along with thick chunks of bread. Balancing the bowl and the bread, he crossed and sat on the couch near her.

"We have orbital coordinates for the Sunstriker and are all set for liftoff. Vrick was just waiting for you," Lexa-Blue told him. "Port Control is suddenly more than willing to grant us launch clearance."

He acknowledged with a small movement of his head, swallowing a spoonful of his stew. "Let's get on with it, then."

They felt the air shift and become more solid as the stabilization field came on, then they heard the engines cycle up with a thrum through the decking. They both stopped and looked out of the window as the lights of the Highland dropped away in the view port.

"Nothing like a little blackmail and imminent peril to end the day, eh?" she said wryly.

"No life like it, my friend." He swallowed another spicy mouthful of chenyai, his eyes watering as he bit into a pungent chunk of the root that gave the stew its name.

Seeing his distress, she stood. "I'm getting a refill. Can I bring you some?"

He nodded, his eyes blurring with tears. She filled her glass and poured one for him, handing it to him as she sat. He gulped the wine down when she returned with it. She took her seat again, chuckling. "So what's say I kick your ass at Quisling after dinner?"

"I just might surprise you, Blue," he said when he regained his power of speech. "Pull up the board, please, Vrick."

A sheet of light appeared in the same space where Jaekir's holo had been, fragmenting into blocks of colour which then ranked into their opening positions. "Your move, Blue. I'm feeling lucky tonight."

She quirked up the corner of her mouth, and a block of red changed position.

He was managing to hold his own when Vrick spoke ten minutes later.

"Just thought I'd let you know we're matching orbits with the Sunstriker. She's coming up on the starboard side."

He and Lexa-Blue watched as the massive yacht hove into view, and they were able to see every breathtaking inch of its hull. The size of a small city, the Sunstriker's lines were proud and strong, showing her to be every inch the flagship of one of the most powerful leaders in the Galactum, yet its graceful curves suggested an artist's touch. The bright white hull of the yacht slid past the viewport, and they saw the plating was marred by signs of repairs. Keene realized the damage had been heavy, and he recognized the tell-tale signs of a gamma storm. The same one we hit, he thought, but they must have caught it a lot harder.

The ship's motion also gave them a clear view of dozens of weapon turrets, from pinbeams to phased plasma generators to inversion torpedoes. She may be pretty, he thought, but she's got teeth.

"We're in synch range, parallel course," Vrick told them. "Synching drives and nav plots for interspace. Complete. We'll be past gravity well threshold in three hours and will transition to interspace then."

"Excellent." Lexa-Blue leaned back in her chair and laced her hands behind her head. "Okay, junior, your move. Not that it makes much difference."

He scowled at her, then looked at the game holo. Seeing his next move, he smiled and made his play. A row of shapes turned green, breaking through her flank. Her smile faded.

"Oh, that's it, mister," she muttered. "This means war."

CHAPTER FOUR

The voyage to Daevin's home world, Orb, would take just under six days. The next morning, Lexa-Blue found Keene in the common room, mug of coffee in hand, surrounded by translucent holo-panes. Some of the panes held blocks of text, others images. She caught a glimpse of a slowly turning, azure blue planet. She poured herself a cup of coffee and joined him in the centre of the swirl of information.

"What's all this?"

He pulled his attention from a pane of scrolling text and looked at her. "Research. I figure forewarned is forearmed. I want to know as much as possible about what we're getting into."

"Good idea. What have you learned so far?"

He sighed and scrubbed his face with his hands, then took a sip of coffee. "Well, I knew everything in Brighter Light revolves around the development of technology, but I had no idea how far it all reached. I tried to find some area of industry they aren't involved in, but there doesn't seem to be one. Food production, medicine, media, transportation, you name it. They either hold key patents, sit on the board, or build key components. If they don't own it, they own shares in it. It's not a monopoly by any means, but they have a lot of pull. As Technarch, Daevin's the head of the family that controls the largest share of resources and technology, and succession is determined like the monarchies of Old Earth. When Daevin's tenure ends, if he has no biological heir, he could bring one into his family by adoption or marriage. It's sensible and yet totally anachronistic at the same time."

He reached into the pane with the image of the globe and it expanded, following the motion of his finger. "But this, I knew nothing about."

The blue-green world, misted with clouds, expanded to fill the display. Brighter Light moved out of sight around the planet's curve and a parcel of land outlined in red came into view. There, on the other side of Orb's major continent, separated by kilometres of undeveloped land, was another colony. Topography overlaid the image, showing the terrain around the colony to be a small, fertile oasis on the edge of a harsh, rocky outback.

"The natives call it Sotari. It's not easy to find any information about it. They're practically hermits. They don't trade with other colonies and Know-It-All hardly mentions them. They have no exports. I'd expect this of a world out on the Brink, not in the core. I couldn't find anything about how they got there or where they came from. I read some crazy rumours that Brighter Light was somehow instrumental in crashing a ship that contained their ancestors, and that's what started the bad blood between them. Considering how desperate humans were to find habitable worlds during the Diaspora, how few can even be terraformed to be suitable, I can see it happening. But it was so long ago, no tangible evidence exists beyond whispers of hints of half heard rumours."

His expression was grave. "I found several carefully worded references to 'disputes' between Brighter Light and Sotari. The Galactum has been forced to mediate on more than one occasion. There are some veiled references to an especially violent incident called Rhokhara's Tears. Look at the date."

"Twelve years ago. Is that significant?"

"Right near the end of Daevin's father's tenure as Technarch. Think there might be a connection?" His arch tone left no misunderstanding about just how connected he thought the events were.

"Sucker bet," she said. "Can I help with the research?"

He gestured to the couch beside him. "Pull up a chair. There's plenty to read."

"I'm going to need more coffee before I can face that." She refilled her mug, sweetened it, and returned to join him. About a half hour later, she looked up from the pane she was reading. "Look at this."

He slid closer to her on the couch, and she gestured at the pane to turn it toward him. "What did you find?"

"It's a sneakfeed I heard about. Sort of an 'unofficial' history of the Galactum. The real story on what's behind current events. It's for traders, smugglers, that sort of thing, to give them a heads up on political situations they may find themselves in."

He looked at her askance and cocked an eyebrow. "You been holding out on me, Blue? How come I never heard about this?"

"A girl's gotta have some secrets." She indicated a passage in the text. "I think I've found out where the citizens of Sotari come from. How good is your history?"

"Secret databases notwithstanding, probably better than yours."

She scowled. "What do you know about the Fauxmosome Revolt?"

Keene's eyes went wide. "That was centuries ago."

The Fauxmosome Revolt was one of the turning points in the history leading to the formation of the Pan Galactum. It had been the origin of the ban on human nanotechnology enhancements and almost all forms of eugenic manipulation. People could change the colour of their hair or eyes, like Zyd had, but they were limited to only the most basic gene tinkering.

The Fauxmosome Corp had spent decades using the then burgeoning science of nanotechnology to enhance the subjects of their experiments. With viable subjects, they had expanded into a breeding program until the subjects rebelled. Thousands of Fauxmosome employees and scientists had been killed, the headquarters and laboratories destroyed. The rebels had fought their way to the nearest port, stolen a ship, and disappeared into the dark.

"Think about it," Lexa-Blue said. "Splice in the right nanotech comware, you have a telepath. Splice in force-field generators, and you have telekinesis. And that's just the beginning. They bonded the nano so tightly to the genes that it bred true."

"Didn't they record a faster mutation rate in the nanobonded genes?"

Lexa-Blue nodded. "Who knows what the descendants of the original subjects could be able to do now?"

"Crikes," Keene said.

"What did you find?" Lexa-Blue asked.

Keene slid a pane through the air for her to get a closer look. "When Daevin's father died, he left Brighter Light in a real mess. Rumour has it that this Rhokhara thing was his fault, but there's not much on exactly what happened. Some serious P.R. muscles must be flexing to keep it hush-hush. Relations between them and Sotari were at an all-time low when Daevin took over, and trust me, that's bad. Daevin's pulled some miracles out of his hat to keep things calm, but the bad feelings run deep. Things must be pretty shaky, because the Galactum's talking expulsion for both sides. Looks like things really are getting ugly."

Keene leaned back in his chair, running a hand over his wiry hair, and let out a low whistle of disbelief. "If the Galactum Council is even considering expulsion, then things must be worse than we thought. With the extent of Brighter Light's involvement in everything, the Galactum must be dead serious. If they cut Orb loose, then the trade ends, and the field is wide open for other corps to take over their market share, and Brighter Light has nowhere to sell anything. Is there anything there about what's going on to make the Galactum ready to expel them?"

She shook her head. "Hints and rumours mostly. Anything that gets reported gets contradicted later. Looks like we just have to wait and find out."

❖

For the next six days, the Maverick Heart travelled through the dark emptiness between star systems, piloting with a control no human could match in the hyper realm of interspace. Twinned to the Sunstriker, ey was in constant communication with the larger ship's drive system and the Limited Intelligences that governed it. The larger ship, with its extensive crew complement, didn't need the same control a ship the size of the Maverick Heart did. The networked LIs, under drive crew control could keep the vessel under control almost as well as ey did.

Almost, ey thought, but not quite.

Vrick spent the voyage feeling like ey was holding back. The mass of the yacht and its contents made the larger ship slower, less responsive as the LIs navigated the twists of interspace.

In this void, beyond the dark, the ship's hull was Vrick's body; its engines es heart; its sensor sheeting, es eyes. The inter-drive field that hurled the ship past Einsteinian barriers also absorbed micro-meteorites and free molecules, converting them to energy that nourished em.

In the time it took a human neuron to fire, Vrick saw an opportunity to take advantage of a bloated red star's gravity well that would slingshot the ships onto a more efficient trajectory, activated the tightline, and communicated the opportunity to the Sunstriker. The LIs on the larger ship pondered es proposal in detail for three tenths of a second, before signalling their agreement. Before a human could have uttered a command to change course, the ships were on their new heading.

As ey flew, Vrick watched Keene and Lexa-Blue in their shipboard routine. Their finite lives, bound by the demands of their flesh fascinated em. Ey reshaped es time sense, continuing to react quickly enough to pilot the ship, but slowed down another input stream to observe them. That first day, ey watched as they spent the rest of the day and the following morning searching more records, hoping to find more information on Orb's situation. Finally, they declared a moratorium on active searching. Keene set up an alert to continue searching without their direct input. Vrick felt the trace as a tiny filament in the web of information flowing into em at any given moment, but ey would know if anything came through.

Once they had filed their research away, Vrick watched them return to a somewhat normal shipboard routine.

Ey watched as Keene finished a lightpainting of Lexa-Blue, fascinated as the motions of Keene's hand moulded pixels created paths of colour that built into a facsimile of Lexa-Blue which was her, and yet not her. Try as ey might, Vrick couldn't quantify the differences in any meaningful way. Ey had debated the concept of art in depth with Keene, studied the subject, and was no closer to understanding why humans created it, what it meant to them, or why Keene could do it and Lexa-Blue couldn't.

Ey observed them as they watched several holos, gauging their reactions, trying to analyze the subtleties of humour and emotion. Ey watched them cook meals and consume them, a parallel to es own consumption and processing of energy. When they sparred in the gym, ey monitored and mapped their bodies, the motions of muscle and sinew, the impacts of meat against meat. Ey ran comparisons on their bio functions and interpreted them against a library of previous readings, sensed their tension at the unknown situation they were flying into.

Ey was rechecking their velocity and vectors when the tightline signalled for es attention, the contact a warm pinpoint of light across es consciousness. It was the Sunstriker, informing em they were coming up on their transition point to normal space.

Ey knew where es human partners were. Always, in fact. Keene was aft, performing routine checks on the water re-filtration system. Lexa-Blue was in the common room, a book open in her lap, gazing out at the warped sluice of colours that replaced normal space outside the ship. Ey knew she was fascinated by the altered visual stimuli the human mind interpreted from interspace.

Ey routed es voice to the vox boxes nearest each of them. "We're coming up on Orb, and we'll be dropping out of inter-drive in five minutes."

Ey saw Keene set the maintenance to automatic and come forward to the lounge to take a seat beside Lexa-Blue, who didn't shift her gaze from the eddies of colour.

"Disengaging inter-drive in thirty seconds."

Lexa-Blue straightened in her seat and leaned forward.

"Retrofire on my mark," Vrick said. "Sub-drive ready. And... mark."

At the sound of her breath catching, Vrick zoomed in on her, seeing that she held her breath for an instant as she registered the dull blue dot, directly ahead. Then the dot exploded as the universe Doppler-shifted into visibility and leapt to surround the ship again. Bringing the sub-drive online, Vrick monitored their bodies, making note of details imperceptible to the human eye. Ey saw the flush that pinked her cheeks, the darkening of Keene's brown skin. Ey felt their hearts accelerate, their temperatures rise. Before Lexa-Blue even realized she had held her breath, Vrick heard the almost silent puff of exhaled air and sensed the minute fluctuation in the CO_2 levels in the room. He saw Keene beside her relax back into his seat.

"They've given me their orbital insertion vector and strict instructions to follow closely. And I quote, 'no deviations from course will be allowed'."

Lexa-Blue smirked over at Keene. "What say we go sightseeing?"

"My mistress's eyes are nothing like the sun," Vrick said. "And she's a crazy bitch too. I'm sticking to the vector, thank you. You may want to get yourself shot down, but I don't."

Lexa-Blue stuck her tongue out, aiming somewhere in the direction of the ceiling to ensure Vrick took her meaning. "Spoilsport."

❖

Their journey insystem was quiet, the Sunstriker breaking away from them in the shadow of a massive space station to take up an orbit while they continued toward the planet's surface.

"Some kind of habitat, do you think?" Keene asked. He 'pushed an instruction and the viewport zoomed in on the silver hull.

Lexa-Blue shook her head. "Too much equipment all over the surface. Those look like telescopes or some kind of external sensing array." She pointed past the station to a smaller satellite in the distance. "Now that, on the other hand, does not look like a scientific instrument."

"There's a network of them." Keene refocused the view. "Definitely space to ground weaponry. I'm just glad it's not pointed at us right now."

As Vrick descended through the upper layers of the atmosphere, their course treated them to a breathtaking view: Orb's watercolour blues and greens vivid through gaps in the mask of cloud. They entered the atmosphere over the northern ocean, then traversed the sere, burnt umber and ochre of the median lands that cut across the continent, the land below gradually becoming verdant with life.

"What do you want to bet that vector brought us down without taking us anywhere near Sotari?" Keene asked, casting a sidelong glance at Lexa-Blue.

"You think? I'm the cynical one, remember? You're the wide-eyed farm boy who looks to me for guidance in the wicked world."

"Guidance *to* the wicked world is more like it." She was about to retort, but he stopped her with a movement of his hand, pointing at the landscape below.

Turning toward the night side, Brighter Light lay below them. Situated along the coastline, the sprawling city-state spread inland, covering thousands of square kilometres. From this distance, all they could see was the patchwork silver, grey, and white of buildings interspersed with the browns and greens of undeveloped areas, cut here and there by the jagged blue of lakes and rivers.

"Looks like we'll arrive late evening, local time," Lexa-Blue said. Ship time was somewhere in the early afternoon. "We'll need to do a sleepshift when we get there."

As the Maverick Heart drew closer, detail became clearer. They could make out the knots of industry blended with rolling tracts of preserved nature. Keene was now able to trace the web of mass transit lines that spread everywhere. The air was full of small aircraft darting here and there, without giving the impression of congestion and crowding.

"It's like Hub, only prettier," Lexa-Blue said.

He couldn't disagree with her. Brighter Light was one of the most beautiful colonies he had ever seen, but the sight left him unmoved.

Frowning, he leaned forward, zooming in as he had done with the orbiting satellites. The view through the port flickered as Vrick replaced it with a holo and zoomed in on the colony below.

"What is it?" Lexa-Blue asked.

"It's as if the planners took the Galactum's requirements for maintaining a balance with nature and applied them precisely but with no imagination. There's no wildness, no spontaneity. Look at the parks, the green areas. They're too reined in, too exact, in perfect proportion to the developed areas. They've tended them within an inch of their lives."

Lexa-Blue pondered his words and looked through at Brighter Light through the prism of his words. "You're right. It's sort of like Kyushu, but without the tranquility of spirit. There's a wildness and a warmth on Kyushu that envelops everything, brings all that precision to life."

"Looks nice to me," Vrick commented. "You meats think funny."

In the distance, Keene was able to discern their destination. A huge, blue-grey monolith of a building vaguely resembling a stack of terraced pyramids with the topmost point cut off, was growing steadily, dead ahead. The structure was situated in an inlet, with ocean on one side and all of Brighter Light on the other, dominating the skyline of the colony. Brighter Light's logo was emblazoned at its apex like the prow of a continent-sized ship.

As they entered their final approach to the building's landing pad, Keene noticed a slight rise in the sound of the engines. It lasted only a fraction of a second and was gone. He recognized it as the ship's passage through a security membrane. Had they not been cleared for landing, nothing would have been left of the ship but shrapnel and vapour. He could see Lexa-Blue noticed it too. Enough years in space, and you knew the sounds your ship made.

"Gotta keep his Holy Techness safe," Lexa-Blue said.

The Maverick Heart came to a perfect landing on the pad shaped from one of the flat roof areas of the pyramid. With a slight dip of the landing gear, the ship came to rest.

Lexa-Blue looked at him and shrugged. "I'm just following you. What now?"

Keene stood and picked up his overnight bag. "Come on, might as well wait out there."

Lexa-Blue slung her own bag over her shoulder, following him to the ship's hatch and then down the ramp. "What? No party?"

Keene chuckled, feeling Know-It-All synch their nodes, the

passive display at the edge of their vision telling them local spring was well under way then offering the variations in length of the local day, month, and year.

A wall of shadow fell across the landing pad as the sun dipped below the massive angles of Daevin's headquarters. They waited outside the Maverick Heart, the ship ringed with landing lights, but no one was there to meet them.

"Not much of a welcome." Lexa-Blue scuffed the pitted surface of the pad with a toe. "I mean, it's not like we weren't expected."

It was Vrick who answered, *Escort is on its way.*

A flood of light spilled out as a door to the landing pad hissed open. They turned as a trio of figures emerged from the light to greet them. Leading the group was a lean blade of a man with a manner like honed steel. As he passed through the door, he looked carefully from side to side, his hand near the heavy sidearm at his waist, and his every move was precise and controlled, wasting no energy at all.

That him? Lexa-Blue 'pushed.

Definitely not. Not unless Daevin's changed a hell of a lot more than I thought.

The man took up a position just off to the side, with a wary eye on Keene and Lexa-Blue. His bearing and the cold, appraising eye he played over them left no doubt he was there to protect the man standing just behind him.

That's him.

Keene felt Lexa-Blue stiffen at his side as she saw him for the first time, felt her take his measure. He had definitely changed from the boy Keene had known and fallen in love with so long ago. He stood taller now and despite being a half head shorter than Keene, his bearing was regal, with a sense of command in how he stood before them, unapologetic. The luxurious designer clothes he had once favoured had been replaced by a conservative suit, with the demi-cape in vogue across the Galactum this year. His hair, shot now with grey, was tied back, baring his face and giving him a new solemnity.

Keene wondered how he looked in Daevin's eyes now. To push away the thought, he looked past Daevin to the woman behind him. He managed to control his shock and a sharp gut-kick of revulsion. Beside him, he felt Lexa-Blue react but control it better.

Standing in front of them was a living nightmare from his childhood. She was slight, her head larger than normal, almost frail in her thinness, and she was ghostly pale. Her skin fairly glowed, bright against the dark of her simply cut gown. Her huge dark eyes seemed to bore into him from above a pair of sharp, angular cheekbones, and he felt that crawling discomfort of someone violating his personal space by standing too close. He had to give himself a mental shake, reminding himself the Wraiths of Vyrta were nothing more than the bogeymen used to frighten children when they misbehaved, as his own parents had done to him when he was young. They weren't real.

Don't stare, junior, it's rude.

And then the apparition smiled. "I am Elai. Welcome." Her voice was rich and melodic, and her smile was so warm and genuine that all of Keene's discomfort faded, and he couldn't help but smile back at her. Through his node, he felt Lexa-Blue do the same. He found himself noticing the fiery gold highlights along the thick braid of her hair.

As if impatient to speak, Daevin stepped past Bach and extended his hand to Keene. "I'm glad you came."

Keene didn't take the hand right away. He let it hang in the air awkwardly between them but finally wasn't able to maintain the slight. He took the offered hand, and Daevin closed his other hand around it. His palm was warm and smooth against Keene's skin, and he felt a crackle of their old chemistry flare up against his will.

"I didn't really have much choice, did I, Daevin?"

For a moment, Daevin's composure wavered at Keene's cold, bitter tone, but his demeanour of command righted itself quickly. Daevin's protector bristled at his side and stepped forward, but Daevin stopped him with an upheld hand. "I suppose I deserved that. I can see I will have to make my case right away. I was hoping we could do this in the morning, but we can certainly do it now." He gestured at the watchful man at his side. "Mordren Bach, my Chief of Security."

Keene shook Bach's hand, noting his dry, calloused palm. The handshake was one sharp rise and fall, with no wasted motion. Everything about the other man was abrupt, hard-edged, hinting at threat and contained violence. His one piece, form-fitting uniform was matte black except for the rank insignia on his left breast, but even the steelskin seemed like it could not contain the lethal energy coiled in his muscles. A recently healed scar wound from his collar under his right ear to terminate in the yellow stubble of his hair. His eyes, the colour of glacial ice, pierced Keene, taking his measure, the gaze untainted by trust. His air of ruthlessness reminded Keene of Lexa-

Blue, but without her warmth or easy humour. Keene felt a territorial ripple pass between his partner and the security chief, like combatants taking each other's measure. *Down, Blue.*

Daevin seemed aware of the potential for confrontation and spoke. "Bach, please inform Sei Parro that I won't be able to meet him for that drink after all and make my apologies. Qoios will be in touch to reschedule."

Bach tensed, but nodded and left them. Daevin turned back to them and indicated the door to the building with a sweep of his arm. "We can talk in my office." He turned and strode from them, not checking to see if they were behind him. Elai looked at them apologetically.

I don't know about you, partner, but I want to find out what this is all about. Lexa-Blue shouldered past Keene and followed. After a moment, Keene did the same.

Know-It-All obligingly provided a map of the building, showing Keene Daevin's personal residence on the upper floors and the Brighter Light corporate offices below. They appeared to be at the lower level of Daevin's quarters, in the section housing his offices and staff. The halls seemed like those of a grand luxury hotel. Muted, relaxing tones covered the walls, and the floors were pale, polished wood. Comfortable looking armchairs nestled in niches set into the walls. The only thing that belied the impression was the nameplates outside the doors. In place of room numbers were legends like "Quantum Interference Laboratory" and "AI Enhancement and Optimization Division." After a ride in a glass elevator up a soaring atrium, they entered Daevin's office.

The room was large, yet simple and functionally laid out, with a huge desk, straight-backed but comfortable looking chairs, and a large standing globe. Behind the desk, a window showed the sea of lights that was Daevin's city. The other walls were blank when they entered but came to life with readouts, reports, and graphics. Streamers of data ran around the room at the top of each wall. The office looked neat and intentionally efficient, but the desk's surface marred that impression. A scatter of flimsies almost fell off the desk's edge, and a book was lying open, spine up. As Elai crossed the room to sit, Keene noticed her gait was stiff and awkward, as if her joints pained her somehow. She made no complaint or sound, but he saw lines of strain around her eyes. She seemed almost unused to walking, as if relearning some skill she had lost. Was it an accident, he thought, or some illness that had caused her appearance and difficulty? He 'pushed the thought to Lexa-Blue and felt her notice it too. He thought he saw a slight smile cross Elai's face. Elai sat in a chair close to Daevin's desk on the right. Keene noticed she didn't wait for Daevin, and he glanced at Lexa-Blue.

Interesting. Whoever she is, she sees herself as Daevin's equal.

And he agrees.

"Please, sit." Daevin's invitation prevented Keene from answering. They sat in the comfortable, straight backed chairs that faced Daevin's desk. "Qoios, store all the data for tomorrow. We'll continue after breakfast."

"Very good, sei."

"Qoios is the AI that runs our the headquarters. If you need anything, ey will be glad to assist you."

Now that they were sitting face to face, a bristle of tension crackled the air between Keene and Daevin.

"So, we're here," Keene said, his voice flat. "What's so important you felt the need to use blackmail to get us here? What crisis warrants sabotaging the business of someone you used to…" He paused and was unable to hold Daevin's gaze. "…know."

Daevin's face darkened. "Is that why you're so angry with me?"

"Not all of us have a world's worth of funds to buy us whatever we want. Some of us have to work for a living."

Daevin let out a sardonic laugh, brittle as a tree branch snapping. "Well, then, if that's the objection, we can clear it up right now." He unfolded his arms and opened a drawer in his desk, pulling out a credit chit and encoder. He tossed them at Keene, who caught them with only a slight fumble. "Name your price. Go ahead. You said it yourself, I can afford it. What is your precious time worth?"

Keene didn't speak, clenching the chit in his hand.

"What? No answer?" Daevin turned to Lexa-Blue. "What's your daily rate? If I were to fill your cargo holds and charter your ship?"

Lexa-Blue met his gaze without looking away, a glint in her eye. "Five thousand, universal. Per day."

Daevin smiled a shrewd smile, the smile of a man who knew he was being offered a premium rate. "Ah, universal credits rather than anything as subjective as local currency. How much of a discount do you usually have to take to receive payment in universal?" He waved her answer away before she could even open her mouth. "Triple your daily rate for the next month and add a twenty-five percent bonus. Will that be sufficient to buy your time?"

Keene looked at Lexa-Blue, who merely shrugged and said, "Business is business, junior."

Still Keene held the encoder, as if uncertain. Finally, he keyed in the amount and handed the chit and encoder back. Daevin didn't even look at it. "Qoios, authorize the payment."

"Done, sei."

Daevin tossed the chit back at Keene, then steepled his fingers and closed his eyes a moment. He seemed to will himself into a state of calm. His face softened for the first time, and he stretched his fingers to loosen the knots of tension in them. "My apologies. The situation has grown...difficult here. I'm afraid it has taken a toll on my nerves."

Against the swell of his anger, Keene felt himself softening when he saw Daevin's face. "What situation, Daevin? What's been going on?" He was surprised that Daevin seemed to have trouble forming his thoughts. It wasn't like him at all. Even when they had first met, Daevin had always had a strong command of the things he meant to say. "Does it have anything to do with Rhokhara's Tears?"

He was using the name to wound Daevin, and he knew it. It had the desired effect. The lines of Daevin's face went hard and cold, and his voice grew thick with anger.

"That debacle cost this planet more than you will ever know. I would gladly throttle all those involved myself if I thought it would do any good." With visible effort, Daevin calmed himself. "You've done your homework, I see."

Keene shrugged, looking to Lexa-Blue and then back to Daevin. "We know the name. We know it was ugly, and we know things have been bad since. Beyond that..." His voice trailed off, and he shrugged again.

Daevin laughed, the sound brittle and humourless. Elai sat, still and solemn, looking like a child in the large chair. "Bad. You have a gift for understatement, old friend."

"Tell them, Daevin. They need to know." Elai's voice was gentle, so full of tenderness for Daevin that Keene felt she had reached over and touched his arm, even though she hadn't moved. Daevin smiled back at her, the expression weary but genuine.

"Rhokhara Canyon is deep in the Median Lands between Brighter Light and Sotari, an area that technically isn't part of either but whose sovereignty is constantly in question. The canyon is the source of a rare form of scarlet crystal particularly resonant to the Sotar genetic make-up. Twelve years ago, a Sotar excavation team was surprised by a Brighter Light strike force. The former Technarch," Daevin's voice went flat at the mention of his father, "had decided the crystal deposits could be exploited in medical equipment and was willing to risk anything to get them."

"Why was it so important to him?" Lexa-Blue asked.

"You have to understand. The control of our technological resources is centred along Family lines. We build our Families to make the most use of the resources available to us. When our people arrived here, the technologies of the ship were our survival tools. They became a form of barter that grew to be the basis of the society that we built. When Rhokhara's Tears happened, the Onestra were trying to mount a hostile takeover of the Technarchy. My father saw those crystals as the only way to maintain his position. It doesn't excuse what he did, but in the context of our culture and the times, I can almost understand it. I don't know that I wouldn't have done the same thing."

Keene wasn't about to get in to a debate over ethics.

"When my father's people arrived, the Sotar leader refused to cede the area. The conflict became violent, and both teams were lost." Keene heard a deep sadness in Daevin's voice. "So much energy was expended in the fight that the scarlet crystal ran molten for three days."

Keene shuddered as he pictured a river of burning red stone.

"Luckily, cooler heads prevailed in Sotari and even my father realized he'd gone too far. He managed to shift blame to the Onestra. It disgraced their family line, but it kept an uneasy peace for almost ten years."

"What happened then?" Keene asked, his voice quiet.

"A meeting was planned to negotiate a lasting agreement to bring the situation to an end once and for all. The meeting hall was firebombed and burned to the ground with everyone trapped inside. Both negotiation teams were wiped out, with no one claiming responsibility. No evidence was found to link the attack to either side, but within days terrorist groups on both sides claimed they were only there in retaliation for what the other side had done. The Sotar group is called Deathmind; the Brighter Light group calls themselves SCI, that's S-C-I. Since then, thousands of people have died in a constant pattern of attacks back and forth, and things are only escalating."

Keene gaped. "And you think we can help you with this?!"

"Maybe." Helplessness rang in Daevin's voice. "I don't know what else to do. You and your partner made short work of those smugglers last year."

Keene was surprised Daevin had even heard of the incident. "Well, yes, Daevin, but we had the whole of GalSec behind us. All we did was put ourselves in the line of fire and hope someone took a shot at us."

"I'm not asking you to work miracles, and I'm not asking you to work alone. Any new insights or ideas can only help." Daevin looked lost, and Keene knew what this admission of need cost him. "I'm desperate." He gestured at Elai, still grim and silent. "We're desperate."

Keene looked at Lexa-Blue, but her expression was inscrutable. "We'll need to talk this over, Daevin."

Daevin nodded. "It's late. I've had a long day, and I'm sure you have too. We can continue this in the morning, once you've had a chance to talk things over. What shiptime is it for you?"

Keene seemed taken aback by the sudden softening of Daevin's demeanour. "It's mid-afternoon for us. It should only take one night of sleepshift to get us on the local diurnal."

Daevin nodded. "Qoios, are the quarters ready?"

"Yes, sei. I can direct our guests there if you like."

"No need, Qoios. I can do it," Elai said, standing stiffly from her chair. "I'm ready to retire for the night, and it's on my way."

Keene and Lexa-Blue rose to follow her, a spark of tension still in the air between them and Daevin. It looked for a moment that Keene was about to say something, but Daevin forestalled any further confrontation, his tone still commanding but suddenly weary. "Rest, old friend. We can talk more in the morning."

Outside the office, Elai's grimness eased, and she smiled at them again.

"Shall I call a porter for your bags?"

Her fathomless dark eyes were kind, and Keene knew she was all too aware of his initial reaction to her appearance. Fortunately, she was both understanding and forgiving. Keene tore his eyes from her gentle scrutiny and shook his head, slinging the bag over his shoulder. "Not necessary, thanks."

"Spacers get used to travelling light when they're onworld," Lexa-Blue added. Elai made a gentle gesture of assent and led off toward their quarters.

"I know it doesn't seem so, but he is glad to see you," Elai said. "I tried to talk him into approaching you in a more open manner, but he is a stubborn man."

"What's your part in all this, Elai? How did Daevin get you mixed up in his affairs of state?"

"I am First Mind of Sotari, their leader. We have a lot in common," she said dryly. "His people are killing mine and mine are killing his. He came to me to try to make things better, to try to make it all stop. And so here I am, deep in the arms of a people who fear me, who think I am the monster who hid under their beds when they were children." She looked at him askance, the corner of her mouth turned up in a gentle smile.

Keene blushed when he realized his feelings when he saw her must have been brazenly on display to her abilities. He felt a sudden desire to apologize but had no idea what to say. He was glad when they finally reached the suite allocated to them for their stay.

Elai stood inside the door as they went into the suite's main room. "Are you hungry, now? Would you care for anything at all?"

Keene shook his head, as did Lexa-Blue. "Just a shower and a good night's sleep." *We're going to need it.*

Elai smiled that odd little smile again and, for a moment, Keene wondered if he had spoken aloud.

"If you change your mind and need anything, just ask Qoios. I'll leave you, then." With a slight tip of her head, she turned and left.

Lexa-Blue tossed her bag on the bed in one of the rooms. "I'm going to get Vrick to sleepshift me and get some rest. We have a big day tomorrow. You want me along when you see him?" His ambivalence must have shown, for she nodded knowingly. "We can talk about it in the morning."

She closed the door, and he went into his own room, which would easily have put Wave to shame. He stripped and crawled into bed, his head buzzing with thoughts.

Time for me to sleep too, Vrick. He lay there, tossing and turning as Vrick used his node to adjust him onto the local day/night cycle. His limbs felt heavy, but he started to drift, a hundred conflicting feelings roaring in his head. Now that he was here, with Daevin so close, so…real, the fire of his anger began to ebb. Thoughts of responsibility, of promises and coercion rattled in his brain, until he finally slept.

❖

The next morning, Lexa-Blue opted out of the meeting with Daevin. "You talk to him, find out more about what's going on. I'm going to hit the streets, see what things are like on the ground." She was already dressed and ready when he came from the shower. "Besides, it'll keep me from maiming him on the spot."

"You think they'll just let you go for a walk?" he asked, towelling his hair and tossing the damp towel into the reclamation chute. "I'm not sure what the security is like."

"Excuse me for interrupting," Qoios's urbane, even voice offered from the air. "I can assure you the Technarch has ensured that you may travel unrestricted here. You are more than welcome to explore the city if you wish. The Technarch is waiting for you, sei, to join him for breakfast. At your convenience, of course."

"That's my cue." Lexa-Blue saluted cockily and left the suite.

"Shall I tell the Technarch when to expect you?"

So this is it. He took a deep breath. "Tell him I just need to dress and can join him in fifteen minutes."

"Very good, Sei Ota Chiaro."

When he went to dress, Keene almost wore his steelskin, but he deliberately steered away from it, choosing the pants and shirt he had worn the day before. He did, however, strap his gun to his leg.

My gun?

The thought shot through him like a beam of light. Why did Bach let me keep it? They don't know I'm not a threat. I could waltz into this meeting and blow Daevin's head off. And considering how he treated us, it wouldn't be all that unlikely. Unless...

Keene drew the gun, a twin to Lexa-Blue's, and thought it to its lowest setting. He thought the diagnostic pattern, and nothing happened. He didn't see any readings through the power metre or the aiming sensors. The gun was dead weight in his hand.

A damper field, Keene realized. He thought about leaving the gun behind but decided against it. They don't need to know I know. He re-holstered the gun and cinched the strap tight with a sharp tug.

"I'm ready, Qoios."

"This way, please." Qoios's voice was neutral.

Following the holographic arrows Qoios provided to guide him, Keene found Daevin's quarters. The doors slid open as he approached. Anyone would think I was expected, Keene thought.

Though immense, the suite looked empty compared to the rest of the palace. Gaps in the decor gave Keene the impression that many of the more ornate fixtures had been removed. The rooms felt more real than the rest of the building, yet more empty and isolated.

"The Technarch is waiting for you on the terrace. Please go on through," Qoios said. Keene crossed the main room and stepped out onto the terrace. His eyes widened.

Like everything else, the terrace was huge, covering one corner of the pyramid. It appeared to be carved out of marble, pale blue ribboned with dark emerald green. There was a huge oval pool, complete with a pool house and a gazebo fitted as turret in the corner where the terrace walls met. Four sinuous sculptures carved of flawless white stone stood around the rim of the pool. And standing at the low wall that rimmed the terrace was Daevin, his back turned.

Keene felt a spike of last night's anger but was surprised to feel a glimmer of something warm, nostalgic. His fury at being coerced into coming here had not faded, but this was Daevin as he remembered him, relaxed and at ease. Not a leader, but a man. A long lost chapter of his life he thought was long closed was suddenly open again, the ending unwritten. The weight of unrealized expectations filled the air, along with menace and danger. He felt suddenly like he wanted to run, but Daevin turned and saw him, trapping him there. Daevin walked quickly toward him, smiling, and Keene's compulsion to flee vanished.

Now that he could look at him without the filter of rage, Keene noted the changes in him. Gone was the awkwardness, the uncertainty. He moved with authority and precision and had crinkles at the corners of his eyes when he smiled. His hair was tied back from his face. He's grown up, Keene thought.

Well, what did you expect, idiot? The same innocent from ten years ago?

Daevin hugged him with real affection, and Keene stiffened, not ready to hug back. Daevin held him a moment, then released him with grace and no awkwardness.

"I was just about to go for a swim," Daevin said. "Join me. We'll eat and talk after."

He removed his robe, and Keene saw he was naked. His body was stockier, stronger than it had been, but without Keene's muscle tone. Keene could see that Daevin would be fighting fat for the rest of his life. Still, he thought, he seems to be winning. The hair on Daevin's chest had become thicker, trailing down his belly to the blaze of red curls at his groin. Keene smiled. At least that hasn't changed, he thought. Daevin executed a perfect, simple dive and disappeared under the water's surface.

From nowhere, Keene felt a sharp pang of desire. Every minute of their shared past came crashing back in vivid detail, leaving him shaken. Unable to prevent it, Keene was swept up by longing: longing to make love to Daevin again, longing to be the person he had been then, the person that Daevin had loved. This is insane, he thought, his pulse roaring in his ears. It was ten years ago. How can I be feeling this again? Especially after what he did.

Feigning poise he wasn't sure he felt, Keene stripped off his clothes and followed Daevin into the pool. The water closed around him, cool and reassuring, and when he came up for air, he wiped water from his eyes and looked for Daevin. Keene saw him swimming laps, the strokes of his arms like blows against the water. He swam alongside for a while, then drifted off to the shallows, waiting for Daevin to tire and join him. He was surprised by the fury with which Daevin swam, throwing all of his energy into his strokes as if trying to outrun the devil himself.

Keene frowned. Whatever is going on is terrifying him. The difference between Daevin's calm greeting and the frenzy of his swimming was unnerving. Keene felt an urge to swim into his path and stop him, grip his shoulders hard and force him to open up, but he restrained it. Daevin would have to tell him in his own time.

After a few more laps, Keene saw Daevin notice him as he turned his head out of the water. Their eyes locked, and Daevin's stroke faltered, lost its rhythm. He paddled over to Keene. "Sorry. This is one of the few times I have to myself in a day. I get a little absorbed in it sometimes. It's nice to be able to let it all go. If only for a short time."

"It's okay," Keene said. "I can come back later."

"No!" The sharpness of the reply rang in the morning quiet. Daevin's voice softened when he spoke again. "Our breakfast should be here in a minute anyway."

They climbed out of the pool, and Daevin handed him a robe. The fabric was cool and feathery-soft against Keene's skin. It's good to be the king, he thought. As they dried off, server-mechs arrived with their meal and laid it out on the table in the gazebo. Neither of the men spoke until the robots had departed.

Keene filled his plate, still trying to feign poise. "So, what's the plan, Little Prince?"

He saw Daevin start at the old nickname. His eyes narrowed slightly, then he recovered. Daevin picked up a plate of cubed, red-pink fruit. "Try the ice melon, it's delicious."

Keene accepted both the evasion and a plate heaped with wedges of pinkish fruit. When he bit into a piece, crystal cold juice flowed across his tongue, leaving a tangy sweet trail down his throat. The taste of the melon was so exquisite that he allowed Daevin to stall again. He closed his eyes and took another bite, savouring it. When he opened his eyes, Daevin was smiling at him, enjoying seeing his own experience mirrored on Keene's face.

"Don't think this lets you off the hook, Daevin. Talk."

Daevin looked him in the eye, his expression unreadable. "Elai and I are getting married."

"Oh," was all Keene could manage. The thought of Daevin marrying the ghostly, frail woman, the woman who could look through him to all his secret thoughts, seemed unreal, impossible to him. Then he remembered her sweet, haunting smile and the possibility seemed more solid, more concrete. It's not like there are any rules against marrying whomever you want, he thought. Did I come here looking for some kind of romantic reunion? "That's your plan?"

Daevin chuckled at the quizzical expression on Keene's face. "I thought that might get your attention. Don't worry, old friend. In any other circumstance, my ideal mate would be the bearer of a Y chromosome. I'm not marrying her for love, though my feelings for her have deepened. This is a marriage of political convenience to unite the ruling families and, hopefully, bring Brighter Light and Sotari together once and for all."

Keene looked confused.

"It isn't really a marriage at all. It's a Unification ceremony."

Keene heard the capital letter in Daevin's voice.

"I take her into my family and she takes me into hers. Elai has a life partner back in Sotari. She has no illusions about this union either," Daevin explained. "Both our cultures have an immense respect for family, if in different forms. This will be more of a mutual adoption than anything. When we bring our families together, it will send a clear message and most of the opposition will have no choice but to accept that Orb is united. Unfortunately, a state occasion such as this also creates the perfect opportunity for the terrorists to strike a potentially fatal blow to the unification movement. Which explains the timing of my summons to you. As I've told you, hard line radicals on both sides will fight this Galactum to the death. Some already have."

"Which is where I come in, I guess," Keene said, none too confident he could do anything. "You're putting an awful lot of faith in me here, Daevin. I'm not trained for this."

Daevin shrugged. "You're my last hope, and I have to try something. We are on the brink of civil war, and the Galactum charter is crystal clear on that point. Civil war means expulsion and we are dead in the water if that happens. My god, after the last mediation failed, the Council put us on probation and pulled out all of their personnel. Even the Galactum Security Force post was closed. We were lucky they didn't cancel any of our contracts or place us under interdict, but believe me, we felt the loss. Our economy is based on the export of our technology to other worlds in the Galactum. If we are expelled, all of that will disappear. Add to that a devastating civil war that might decimate both sides, and the whole planet will collapse in on itself like a black hole."

Keene took this all in and sighed. Daevin knew him too well, despite all of the years that had passed. If he could do anything to help, both of them knew he would. "So, what can I do?"

"Well…" Daevin stopped as a chime sounded. He raised a hand for silence and touched a commo panel on the table's surface, summoning a holo. Keene recognized Mordren Bach.

"Forgive me for disturbing you, Sei, but there's been another incident."

Keene saw Daevin's face go pale, then cold with anger. "I'll be right there. Have my car ready." Daevin stabbed the holo off and stood. "Get dressed. You should see what we're up against."

CHAPTER FIVE

Outside the suite, Lexa-Blue queried Qoios. "Which way to the street?"

"The elevator is this way, Sei Lexa-Blue." Midway up the wall in front of her, a golden ripple of light flared off to her right.

She followed it and was soon descending to the street, floor after floor passing by. She rode down through the levels of Daevin's quarters alone. As she reached the lower floors, where she knew the more public, research, and business oriented areas of the building were, people came and went on the elevator car. Technicians in lab smocks, earnest and serious executives carrying cases, middle management drones. Some carried exotic equipment she didn't recognize. Keene would be in heaven, she thought, if he was let loose in some of the labs here. He'd play for hours. Of course, he'd probably end up shooting a hole through the wall.

Finally, the elevator opened on the main lobby. A sheet of cool dark stone inlaid with a massive Brighter Light logo large enough to land the Maverick Heart on spread before her. Sunlight streamed across the space through a long line of glass doors, and she picked an exit at random.

Outside, a wide expanse of the same stone was broken by a fire-fountain and beyond that, wide steps leading down to the street.

At the base of the steps, she queried Know-It-All for a local map. A graphic of the entire Brighter Light city-state, complete with a point of light labeled *You are here* opened in her mind. She stood for a moment, studying the garish colours of the map. The light representing her was below a block of colour named "Brighter Light Central."

I'm interfacing with the city's directory cortex to get you some specifics, Vrick informed her.

What's the quickest way to get around?

There's a mag-lev station just across the square. Ey added an overlay to the map, tracing the route. *It'll take you right to the city core. Lots of stuff is easily walkable from there.*

At the station, she checked the schedule and found a train was due in minutes. She smiled at her luck and went out on the platform to wait.

She noticed the Eyes first, covering every possible viewing angle of the waiting area. She recognized the emitter ports ringing the dark metal spheres as neural stunner. Powerful ones, if her guess was correct. Very tight security, she thought. She shifted her attention to the people waiting with her for the train. Pretty typical, she thought. Just another group of commuters waiting for transit, except for the spacing between them. As she watched, an older woman laden with packages came on to the platform. She watched with fascination as the other passengers moved apart from each other, seemingly without conscious thought, arranging themselves well out of reach of each other.

She heard a sound from inside the station, and she recognized it as something commonplace like a dropped package hitting the polished floor, her instincts giving her only a slight spark. Around her, though, she saw heads snap in the direction of the sound, eyes widening, bodies tensing. They looked to her like a flock of birds startled into a flutter of feathers. She watched them slowly settle when nothing out of the ordinary happened.

The arrival of the train calmed the crowd, and she followed them into it, taking a seat as it accelerated out of the station. She watched the city pass by her, the buildings sleek and graceful but still seeming soulless to her. She had a hunch she would be hard pressed to find her usual type of haunt here.

Vrick gave her a mental tweak when she reached the city core. Standing, she left the train and headed into the station, where she saw a crew hanging decorations, garish and festive, from the ceiling. She sensed an aura of relief from them and the streamers and lanterns they hung, as if the city seemed happy to have something to celebrate. She headed for the exit, stepping into the cool shadow of the towers. Choosing another random direction, she began to explore the city's core. With no pattern, she wandered up and down the streets, inspecting shops, businesses. She sat in cafes, discreetly watching the faces of people around her. She tuned out the stares she received in turn, for once focused on something other than that. She poked her nose into any nook or cranny she thought she could without getting arrested for trespassing.

Everywhere on the ordered, precise streets, her observations confirmed what she had seen at the station. Security Eyes patrolled everywhere. She recognized discreetly armed police on every corner. Brighter Light was a city under siege. It was a quiet siege that many had long ago become accustomed to, but a siege nonetheless.

I'd better contact Keene and take the lay of the land, she thought, smirking at the turn of phrase. And hope I'm not interrupting anything.

Meat, you have a dirty mind.

Mind your manners. Don't snoop.

I could say the same to you.

Lexa-Blue sent the filthiest mental images she could think of back through the node and set off to find a quiet place to make contact.

I'm getting some heavy chatter on the local emergency channels, and it's right near you. Can you hear the sirens? It's the terrorist response team. That security chief you met last night is on his way. Sounds like something big.

Right as she heard Vrick's 'push, the piercing warble caught her ears, dopplering closer to her. *Got em. Where are they headed? I'm going to check it out.*

It's a shopping complex just a couple of streets over. Here are the coordinates.

She set off down the street, then crossed where his instructions indicated. The sirens became even louder as she approached. Following their call, she came upon a jam of emergency vehicles wedged into the courtyard of a vaulted pale stone building. As she watched, two more ambulances appeared over the neighbouring rooftops, jockeying for a landing position in the crowded street.

Emergency personnel were everywhere, people running around in a panic. A line of officers in black lined the entrance to the plaza, holding back the crowd that had gathered in the building's shadow. Ruck, she thought, I'll never get through there to see what's going on. Her mind raced to find some way to get in to see what had happened. Find the door, and wedge it open, she thought. There.

Through the mass of bodies she saw a woman struggling to lift heavy cases of equipment from the back of a dark utility hovervan. The insignia on her lab coat matched the one she had seen on the security chief, Bach, the previous night, but this woman was no security officer.

She was soft. Pretty, but bookish and intellectual. Lexa-Blue knew she was not the type to be in the field, enforcing laws. She was a squint, probably tech support or crime lab or something like that. But the way she picked and chose from the racks of equipment in the back of the van was practiced and certain. Soon, she had more cases at her feet than she could carry in one trip.

There's my in, Lexa-Blue thought, moving through the gawking crowd toward her. She waited until the other woman looked up and caught her eye. Even from this distance, Lexa-Blue could see the tight, strained lines of her face.

Seeing Lexa-Blue coming toward her, she brushed back a strand of hair that had escaped from the tie at the nape of her neck. Her eyes widened, and Lexa-Blue knew she had recognized her somehow, though they hadn't met. "You look like you could use an extra pair of hands."

The other woman looked at her, then at the cases she had unloaded.

"I'm Lexa-Blue." She offered her hand, and the other woman shook it. "I was just out exploring and heard the sirens."

"I know who you are. The Technarch briefed us on your arrival this morning. I'm Saphia Valme, Director of Security: Technical Support. Bach shoots guns, and I get to sift through the rubble. We're to accord you all professional courtesy, which means you get to muck in with the rest of us." Saphia's voice was grim, belying the humour of the words. "Grab a case and follow me."

"Is it bad?"

"As bad as it gets. You sure you want to see this?" Saphia asked, grief etching her face.

"I've seen much worse, believe me. Let me help."

Saphia thought a moment, and then nodded. She touched the control to deactivate the barrier and thrust two cases as heavy as the ones she was carrying into Lexa-Blue's hands. "Follow me." She ushered Lexa-Blue past the guards. "She's a guest of the Technarch. He's assigned her to assist with the investigation."

Lexa-Blue hoisted the cases and followed Saphia as she threaded her way through the mass of technicians and medical personnel surrounding the doors to the shopping centre. As busy as it was outside, the thrum and buzz of tension was ratcheted even higher inside. Saphia led her through the mass of emergency workers to an open space in the building's atrium.

And Lexa-Blue saw the bodies.

She recognized the chilling, false serenity of the dead. They had fallen where they stood, as far as she could tell. She saw no blood or signs of violence, and she had seen many in her life. They looked to her like marionettes, their strings cut. Farther out from the epicentre, she could see signs of panic: dropped, trampled packages, overturned litter bins and benches, medics attending to bruised and bloodied victims of the frenzy to escape. But in the middle of it all were those silent, pristine bodies. Lexa-Blue knew death, but had never seen anything like this ugly quiet.

Saphia's voice pulled her attention from the scene. "There's Bach. Come on."

Lexa-Blue grudgingly followed her toward the blond security chief. When they reached him, he looked up from a holo floating above his left wrist. He scowled at it, then handed the emitter back to its bearer before turning to them. His scowl darkened even further when he saw her standing at Saphia's side, and Lexa-Blue felt her back go up. Good thing my hands are full, she thought, or I'd have to punch him.

"What's she doing at a secure location?" His voice was cold with contempt.

"Stow it, Bach. All professional courtesy, remember? She was nearby and offered to help. This is what the Technarch called her and her partner here for, isn't it? So, back off and let her do it." Saphia shifted the weight of the cases she carried and met his scowl with one of her own. When he didn't challenge her again, she turned to Lexa-Blue. "Come on, I want to set up over here."

Lexa-Blue followed her to a relatively clear spot, putting her cases down beside the ones Saphia placed on the floor. She watched as the other woman opened them and began laying modular components on the floor. "Open that case," she said, pointing to one that Lexa-Blue had carried, "and start unloading the sensor rods. We'll be setting them up around the perimeter."

Lexa-Blue began removing the rods and laying them out in a row, examining them as she did. They looked to be a modification on the old KX model remote sensors. Extra stripes of conduit around the burnished metal twined like vines. In a chamber near the upper end, she could see waving yellow filaments like strands of blond hair. She watched Saphia put aside the control panel she had been calibrating and take up the first rod in the row. Saphia extended the legs and twisted the body of the cylinder, making the energy filaments flutter and hum as they resonated with each other. She stood them upright, checking the calibration occasionally on the control pad.

When the rods were all unpacked and calibrated, Saphia handed one to Lexa-Blue. "Take them and place them evenly around the area." Working together, it only took them a few minutes to lay out the pattern of sensor rods. When they were done, Lexa-Blue watched over Saphia's shoulder as the other woman tapped instructions into the control system.

"What is it we're looking for?" she asked Saphia, trying to understand the readouts she was seeing.

"The nanotechnology bonded to the Sotar gene sequence leaves behind a specific energy resonance trace. I've redesigned the rods to register it, and then hopefully we can track it to design a field that resists it or something. I'm clutching at straws, but it's the best I've got at the moment." Her voice was tight as she operated the keyboard and controls.

Lexa-Blue heard the tension in the other woman's voice, noticing the line of strain across her shoulders and the intensity of her gaze at the screen. She watched in silence for a moment or two. "Anything?"

Saphia shook her head and stood from the console. "It's going to take a while for the routines to pick through everything. Come on, there's more we can help with."

Daevin dressed and was striding to the door while Keene was still buttoning his shirt. Tucking in his shirttail, he caught up to Daevin at the elevator, just in time to see him stab a finger at the already lit call button. The tension radiating from Daevin was setting Keene on edge too. Here we go, he thought, right into the thick of things.

The elevator chimed and opened, Daevin stepping in quickly and turning. Keene had a second to register his dark blue suit and turtleneck, accentuating the grace and power with which he moved. This Daevin was every inch the influential leader he had become since they had parted. Daevin's eyes flickered impatiently at his hesitation and Keene hurried in beside him, the closing doors almost catching him. "Garage," Daevin said.

Their descent was swift, with only the hum of the elevator to cut the foreboding silence. When the doors opened, Keene was looking at a squat, armoured car that looked like a turtle's shell with the driver's compartment where the head would have been. Keene heard the soft hum of car's anti-gravs, ready to take them to the scene of the attack.

A small group of heavily armed security officers dressed in steelskins milled around the vehicle. Daevin walked straight toward a young woman with lieutenant's stripes.

"Technarch Adisi," she said, snapping to attention and bowing. "Chief Bach is already at the Plaza examining the scene."

"Delphi Plaza?" Daevin's scowl darkened further.

The young lieutenant nodded, her own anger showing. "Yes, Sei. Preliminary reports from the scene are still coming in. Your limousine is ready."

Daevin nodded and got into the limousine, Keene at his heels. The lieutenant issued clipped, precise orders and the group dispersed, the limo's driver to his post, the others to their escort vehicles. Taking a seat in the limo's egg shaped interior, Keene found himself on a curved couch across from a brooding Daevin. When the limo began to move, buoyed on anti-gravs, Daevin spoke. "Delphi Plaza is our largest retail complex. Thousands of people go through there on any given day. As usual, our Deathmind friends knew just where to hit us."

Keene could think of nothing to say, dread filling him.

The ride took barely ten minutes, yet the time seemed interminable. When they stopped and the limo's hatch opened, Keene heard their escorts' sirens fade. He stepped out of the car behind Daevin into a war zone. Vehicles everywhere were skewed at odd angles to fit them as close to the Plaza as possible. Red and blue stabbed the air. Medics loaded stretchers onto ambulances and flits, locking them down for transport. Keene noticed an alarming number of the stretchers were covered.

Keene, Lexa-Blue is inside, Vrick told him, relaying what had happened. Keene 'pushed to her and received only a curt ***come find me*** in return.

Turning from the tableau of vehicles, they were escorted through the plaza's doors into the vaulted, ten story atrium of the Plaza. Despite the chaos, Keene was struck by how beautifully designed the building was, rising tiers of stores above a lushly planted courtyard. Set along the arc of the tiers were glass cylinders holding the elevators, breaking the sweep of the curve into neatly organized sections. The colours and decor were bright and inviting. Off to one side were lines of neat, white body bags.

Medics and morgue teams swarmed over the courtyard, examining and loading. Forensic scanning teams covered every inch of the courtyard, sifting for evidence of any kind. Mordren Bach oversaw the intense activity, a grim observer in black. When he registered their presence, he turned and stood at attention. "Sei, it appears to have been a pulp. One hundred and four dead. Eighty-seven outside of the locus. We won't know how badly they were hurt until they're treated. My teams are going over everything, but nothing has turned up yet."

"Pulping is one of Deathmind's favourite tricks," Daevin told Keene. "They teleport in and unleash one powerful psi blast that ruptures the cell walls in the brain of anyone in range. The victims on the outer edge of the pulp's range suffer brain damage. How bad depends on how close. This is the worst one yet."

"They can teleport?" Keene's eyes widened in shock. "I knew about the telepathy and telekinesis, but teleportation? How are they managing that?"

"From what Elai has told me from their history, the quantum jump nano was the last thing that Fauxmosome was experimenting with when the revolt took place. The ability was only rarely used," Daevin said, his expression grim. "Because it could only be used once."

He nodded toward the bodies, and Keene noticed a corpse with the same slender, angular shape as Elai. When he looked more closely at the scene surrounding the Sotar terrorist's, he realized he could actually see the radius of the pulp's effect. Beyond the circle of the attack, the overturned benches, strewn packages, and other debris showed where the survivors had fled in a panic. No such signs were in the terrorists' path. The bodies had merely dropped where they had been standing. No blood, no signs of struggle or violence. The victims looked almost as if they were sleeping. Only the absolute stillness in the midst of the investigation's chaos destroyed the illusion.

Keene had seen death before, both in the Merchant Fleet and since his partnership with Lexa-Blue. Even under the aegis of the Pan Galactum, the raw frontier of space was often harsh and unforgiving. The smugglers he and Lexa-Blue had helped round up last year had been brutal in their attacks. But nothing he had ever seen compared to this eerie, unnatural quiet.

As Daevin and Bach discussed the investigation, Keene fought down a wave of cold, queasy grief, and then saw Lexa-Blue in the crowd. He saw her feel his presence and look up to see him, then say something to the plain, efficient looking woman she was working with. When she came toward him, her face shone with sweat, and her hair was lank and damp. She pulled it back from her eyes.

"I guess he needed us after all, eh?" he said.

"You could say that," she said. "I'll be assisting the Director of Security: Technical Support until we finish up with this. Stick close to Daevin, and I'll see you later."

He wanted to reach out but knew she would rebuff his concern. Instead, he nodded. "Take care of you."

Over the next two hours, he stood by as Daevin grilled every investigator at the scene, pushing until he was satisfied the investigation was making progress. He watched Daevin go over the scene himself, as if trying to glean something his forensics staff was unable to see. He waited as Daevin read the list of identified dead, learning the names of the citizens he had lost.

As they rode back to the palace, Daevin was stone, no hint of his feelings showing. Keene sat opposite him again, alternating waves of shock, fear, and rage washing over him. The hideous reality of what he had seen seeped into him, all the way to his bones. The death had been real, immediate, not some abstract report on a newsbite that could be shrugged off by changing the channel.

Once they were back in Daevin's office, cracks began to show in Daevin's facade. He crossed to the bar and poured a drink, the shaking of his hands betrayed by the rattle of ice in his glass. Keene came to his side and took the carafe and glass from him. He poured and handed it to Daevin who took it gratefully, a weak smile on his face. "Drink."

"Thank you." Daevin took a deep swallow, and Keene noticed his eyes shone with tears. In those tears, Keene recognized another facet of the Daevin he had known before, the depth of caring he had to keep hidden behind a facade of competence and strength for the good of his people. He pulled Daevin close and held him, needing to comfort Daevin as much as he needed to be comforted himself. Daevin's tears were wet against his neck. "They were my people and I failed them. I keep failing them."

Keene broke away and squeezed Daevin's shoulders. "Hey. Deathmind did this, not you. Remember that." He settled Daevin into a chair and refilled his glass, then sat in the chair beside him. "You want my help to nail these guys, you've got it. But I need information. You said these attacks have been going on for a while, so you must have learned something. Tell me what you know."

Daevin sighed and ground away his tears with the heel of his hand. "Okay. The attacks are consistently vicious. Pulps, pyrokinetic fires, and explosions. Elai says that in Sotari, SCI uses weapons and devices to pretty much the same effect. The cruelty is the same. We just have more creative technological ways of achieving it. We've searched for some hidden base on both of our respective territories, but found nothing. Physical evidence is minimal. They 'port in so fast that they leave very little trace. The tech that SCI uses is more likely to leave traces, but the Sotars are so suspicious of any technology, Elai has trouble convincing her people to let us in to scan. By the time we get a chance to examine the scene, there's not much left to see because they've made repairs or cleaned up. We think both groups might be operating out of the Median Lands somewhere because there's so much unoccupied and unscanned space, but we can't narrow it down. Beyond that…" Daevin shrugged.

Keene listened to Daevin's report and tried to find something in it, some jumping off point to a new idea. Nothing came to him. Come on, Keene, think. He paced, trying to get his mental wheels in gear. Still nothing came. He poured a drink for himself, then felt Lexa-Blue's weary presence through his node, knowing she was back. *You okay?*

I will be.

He felt the echo of water on skin and knew she was in the shower. *I'll be right there.*

Keene crossed to Daevin and laid a gentle hand on his shoulder. "Are you all right?"

Daevin's eyes were red when he looked up at Keene, but he managed a ghost of a smile. "I've done this before, old friend. Go. We can talk later."

❖

Daevin didn't actually hear Keene's feet on the floor, the sound deadened by the dense carpet. All he heard was the soft hiss of the door closing. He stood at the window, not wanting to look back at the office and see that Keene was really gone. He squared his shoulders, clasped his hands behind his back, and looked down from the window at the sprawl of the city below. His city.

From the height of his office, everything below seemed an abstraction, nothing more than an impressionist painting of his world. Far below, his people were little more than distant patterns of movement. In the streets, vehicles were colour and motion, lit by sparks of sunlight. The mag-lev trains were a blurred ballet of speed. To his eyes, Brighter Light was an organism, a breathing interaction of forces, of people and energy and creativity. And he was its head, the brain directing this being's life. Every unseen soul below was his responsibility. Every life snuffed out in this senseless war of ideals was his failure. Every act of terror perpetrated by his people on Sotari could be laid at his feet. As Technarch, his duty was to shepherd Brighter Light, stay the course and keep the city running. He kept his people alive and well, maintaining their culture and way of life.

He remembered the years of preparation for the mantle of leadership laid out for him when his father had adopted him. Childhood play had been relegated to the background by hours of study and hard work, grooming for the leadership of Brighter Light. Years of loneliness and sacrifice, when all he wanted was some semblance of a normal life, of laughter and skinned knees and all the secret mysteries of childhood.

But those dreams had faded in those years he had been at school. When he had met Keene for the first time, he had only a vague understanding of the position he would one day assume. Beyond a lurking resentment at the weight of his courses and the restrictions on his personal life, leading Brighter Light had all seemed far removed from the life of a student. The Technarchy was his father's world, not his. And he hoped to avoid it for as long as possible.

Then he had met Keene, and the abandon of that affair had been a vibrant, welcome relief from the pressure of training for a role he barely understood. Despite the restrictions imposed on him, he had thrown himself into loving Keene with all the passion he had. The pleasure he found in flesh and sweat was real to him in a way abstract obligations and leadership were not. Being in bed with Keene made more sense than his impending Technarchy ever had. Even the wrenching sorrow of the inevitable ending, piercing his heart like a thousand knives, had been concrete and immediate.

He found out what his new life meant on his return home from school. As his father lay in the medical centre, clinging to the last shreds of his life, Daevin had been forced to keep Brighter Light running, see to the large and small details of running a multi-planetary corporation state. Through his initial mistakes, he learned, coping with diplomacy and design specifications and budgeting, topped off by the demands of government.

Then, just as he was beginning to understand, to feel the threads weave together, his father was gone. On the cold, wet morning of the funeral, Daevin had watched the shifting thousands of mourners waiting in the rain to pay their respects, and for the first time he had really understood his role. He saw it in the rows and rows of grief stricken faces as they filed past the bier where his father lay in state. He saw their need, their faith in his office, their hope for the future he could bring them. He listened to all the condolences and congratulations, feeling every minute the almost feverish desire for an end to their losses. The waves of it had washed over him that day in the Great Hall, beside his father's body, driving his desire to find some resolution.

How naive he had been to think he could fix it for them, make the terror and the death end, keep all his citizens alive and well. It had not taken long for the realities of his rule to come to harsh light. Despite his best efforts, more had died, and he had been powerless to stop it. Nothing stemmed the tides of fear and death that plagued his world. He had begun to realize, like so many parents before him, that no matter how he tried, he could not keep all his children safe and warm. He could only fight to shine the light into the dark corners, fight to make a world at least marginally safer for those in his charge.

❖

Back in their suite, Keene found Lexa-Blue staring out the window at the sky, holding a glass of the blood red liquor she preferred. He came up behind her, standing close enough for her to feel his presence.

"Are you all right?" He knew this mood of hers, had seen it before. She would resist comfort, fight it out of a habit that had begun years before when she had been alone. Eventually, she would either come to terms with her pain, or expunge it in violence in the Heart's gym, or confide it to him on some night in some bar after one too many drinks. But for now, all he could do was ask.

She shrugged. "It's just death, partner. No one yet has been able to escape it, no matter how hard they try. Same old story it's always been. You're born, you live a while, and then it ends. Most often in some way you couldn't even imagine. It's just the way things are." She refilled her glass, put the bottle back in the bar cabinet, and shut it.

"Still, not a very nice way to go," he said, crossing his arms tightly across his chest and squeezing down a shiver. "To have your brain just…crushed like that."

She shrugged again, but he saw the pinched lines at her mouth and eyes. He could tell it haunted her, despite all her protests to the contrary. Defying the habits and roles they were used to, he put a hand on her shoulder anyway, expecting her to pull away. He was surprised when she didn't move from the soft pressure. Instead, her hand rested on his a moment and she turned to him, with just the slightest upturn of her mouth.

"So, now we know what's going on. What's the plan?"

Keene looked at her with a raised eyebrow. "Go to a wedding?" When he saw her expression of puzzlement, he outlined Daevin and Elai's plans for the unification of their families. When he finished, she whistled softly and rolled her eyes.

"That's so archaic, it's revolutionary. Can you picture it? The whole Galactum Council in one big mass marriage ceremony."

He chuckled at the thought, but the sound strangled itself. He leaned forward and rapped his head lightly, three times against the window. "How do we manage to get ourselves into these situations?"

"Karmic retribution for past sins. Has to be." Her crooked grin was so familiar, it anchored him.

"I guess we're in this up to our nards, eh?"

She shook her head and waved her hand at the level of her neck. "At least."

"Time to dig?"

She nodded. "Time to dig."

❖

And for the next week, dig they did. As soon as they rose in the morning, they joined Daevin in his office to review reports and data from the investigations into the terrorist attacks. The deevees in the office ran thick with datastreams and simulations. They sat through sickening tactical recreations and surveillance recordings of the attacks. Daevin's office grew more and more untidy, with flimsies strewn on every surface, racks of bit chips covering his desk in lines, constantly replaced by library techs as soon as the last was slotted back in its place.

They had many meetings with Mordren Bach and Saphia Valme around a burnished wood conference table in one of the larger meeting rooms. They reviewed reports and grilled the security staff over every detail of the investigation. Daevin's staff delivered their meals and kept the urns of coffee full. After the first few days, they stopped studying the attacks in Brighter Light, and Elai gave them information on the attacks in her land.

"The first attack surprised us. Most of us had had no dealings with humans, or Silents, as my people call them, not since before our ancestors had escaped their captivity. The scientists who created us had been less than ethical in their search for subjects. Our distrust of the Silents ran deep. We kept to ourselves and most of us had had never even seen one of you before. All we had were our preconceptions. You are nothing but loud, coarse, and vulgar, so caught up in your physical bodies that you have lost the ability of contemplation and true communication. You sweat and rut, yet you never seem to think about your actions or how they affect others. In Sotari, we live in each other's thoughts, in each other's emotions. We know what our actions do to others of our people, for we see what we do through their minds. Hurting another Sotar is like self-mutilation. We share in each other's joys and pains and fears."

"Like a hive mind?" Keene asked.

"More like being surrounded by mirrors that reflect your self back at you. Or an echo. We resonate with each other, like the vibrations of certain types of crystal."

"And when you deal with us 'Silents'?" Lexa-Blue rose from her chair and poured herself a glass of water.

"It is like…" Elai paused, as if groping for a word in some language that was not hers. "Like trying to communicate with someone behind a wall. Like trying to discuss ethics with an animal. I'm sorry. I realize how this must sound, but I mean no disrespect. In the time since we were created, we didn't realize how wide the gap would become.

"When SCI came upon us, we saw what Silents were capable of. We learned pain in ways we had never experienced. Every wound was felt by all, and every death left a void in all our hearts, in the whole that we were. Their weapons tore into our bodies, into our society. You spoke of the pulp and how still the bodies were. In Sotari, when SCI strikes, we are rent. Our healers are taxed to their limits mending bodies that have been broken in ways they have never seen before. Many were lost until we grew used to what we were facing. Much meditation was required to heal the spirits of those who survived."

"But you have people with precognitive abilities, don't you?" Keene asked. "Weren't they able to warn you before the attacks happen?"

A weak smile crossed her face, mirthless and raw. "It isn't mysticism. The abilities we possess are rooted in the science our culture rejected. What passes for precognition is nothing more than predictive algorithms in computers etched smaller than the atoms in our genes. When the first attack happened, those of us with that gift sensed something coming, but these abilities are not like language or pictures. They come like dreams or impressions and can take time to interpret. Images of Daevin's world were strange to us, so strange that we couldn't understand the thoughts of violence toward us. Sometimes they attacked us from a distance, their weapons traveling to us from beyond our borders. More recently, when they came upon us, we sensed nothing from their minds, as if their thoughts were gone. Somehow they have learned to hide themselves from our abilities."

"There's some speculation amongst the S:TS that they may be using mood stabilizers or some kind of anti-sociopathy drugs to flatten the emotions," Daevin told them. "Because so much of telepathy is non-verbal, emotional or impressionist, they scramble the reception. Imagine an impressionist painting. Up close, it is merely daubs of paint, but it forms a cohesive picture with context. The drugs may be stripping that context away. But without being able to capture any SCI members, it's just speculation."

"Art as a metaphor for terrorism," Lexa-Blue said. "Bet the art snobs love that one."

"They're not my concern right now," Daevin snapped.

"Okay, I think it's definitely time for a break," Keene said, forestalling a confrontation. "Let's all stretch our legs, get a drink, get some food, whatever. We can meet back here in an hour or so."

Keene left Daevin brooding at his desk. Finding a kitchen with a cooler full of chilled drinks, he chose a bottle of spiced tea. He felt the strain of their long hours and rapidly fraying nerves, rubbing the bottle's cold sweat against his forehead before cracking it open and taking a drink. The tea was gingery and sweet, the heat of the flavours countering the icy temperature and loosening the gnarl of his shoulders. It's a start, he thought. Now for something to eat.

Blue? Did you find food?

Yup, there's a cafeteria one level down, east wing.

Order me something and I'll be right there.

❖

After the others left, Daevin stretched and rubbed his eyes. He regretted snapping at Lexa-Blue. She was just trying to lighten the cloud of frustration they were all feeling. He had learned over his term in office to read the people he dealt with, taking their measure quickly and shrewdly. He knew beneath Lexa-Blue's sarcasm beat a caring heart. Seeing her at the Plaza with Director Valme, hefting equipment and assisting with the gruesome investigation when she could easily have stood back and watched, she had won his respect instantly.

"Qoios, would you send someone with a fresh pot of coffee?"

"And something to eat, perhaps?" Ey responded in a pointed tone.

Daevin actually chuckled. "Looking after me, old friend?"

"Merely an observation based on your obvious fatigue and the sudden plunge in your blood sugar."

"Point taken," Daevin said, bowing his shoulders. "Send up whatever is on the go in the cafeteria." He waved a hand at the wall displays. "Cache all of this until the others come back and bring up filename *Faces*."

All the data they had been reviewing compressed into a single dot of light and moved to the lower corner of the wall facing Daevin's desk. In its place, a ruddy, smiling face appeared and minimized to the upper corner, followed by another and another. Soon the walls were filled with ranks of faces, lined in neat, ordered rows. When Daevin's lunch arrived, the porter found him surrounded by the faces of the lost, their personnel photos looking down at him from his deevees. As he ate, the dead kept him company.

Daevin had begun this roll call of the lost after the first attack and had kept them there for days afterward, memorizing them all, coming to know their positions, their families. He had learned what holes they left in his community, the places and times and talents that had been snuffed out. Ever since he had become Technarch, he had kept the butcher's bill in his head, always knowing what this quiet, undeclared war had cost Brighter Light.

When he and Elai met and began their talks, their friendship had been a tenuous one, soured by years of mistrust and death. But he had asked her to share what her people had lost, had asked for the names and faces of Sotari's dead. He remembered the flash of disgust that had radiated from her and how he had hastened to explain. Fighting his own reluctance, he had allowed her into his mind, let her see how he kept the memories of Brighter Light's casualties, what it meant to him to remember. Her eyes had softened then, and the wall of suspicion had crumbled. They sat long into the night and told stories of departed friends, of lives brutally ended. Their plan for peace was born that night. And it was that desperate plan, to save lives on both sides, that had led him to remember Keene and all that they had been.

Over the years, he had occasionally searched for information on Keene, wondering what had happened to the boy he had loved with so much raw, unformed ardour. But Daevin usually ended up berating himself for opening old wounds and cutting off the interface without even reading all of the information available. One day, he had seen the reports of Keene and this mysterious business partner getting involved with the authorities and bringing down the ring of smugglers that had terrorized the outer belts, something sparked in Daevin's mind. Maybe, just maybe, they could do something together. Maybe Keene could help. Daevin was no fool. He knew it was a risky and potentially useless ploy, but surrounded by the faces of the dead, he found he was willing to try anything, do anything to make the bloodshed stop. And so, he hatched his plan. Bring Keene here, make him see what was happening and hope he could help bring it all to a halt.

But was that all he had wanted? Had he not had flashes of what might have been? Or could be again? Had he not, in some buried part of his brain, wanted Keene to run into his arms, proclaiming undying love? Or maybe not even something that romantic. Maybe he had wanted nothing more than some rekindled burn of sex? There had been no one meaningful since their brief affair. His position had swallowed his life whole. Somewhere, in the base, animal part of his brain, he had wanted Keene to leap without thought into bed with him, feel ease in that desire. Anything but the cold hostility he had seen in Keene's face that night. He had wanted anything but that.

But Keene was here now. And their unified purpose had thawed some of the distance between them. That one thought burned a new hope in Daevin, and he allowed himself to think that something might change, that this would make it all right. He knew how irrational it sounded, but it was all he had to go on.

"Excuse me, sei." Qoios's voice was a gentle interruption to the roil of Daevin's thoughts, but then he heard something else in the AI's tone. "The warning systems have gone off. We have a problem."

"What is it, Qoios?" He knew what those systems warned of. An all too familiar fear made his stomach churn.

"I'm getting alarms from the Orbital Research Station. Priority One."

Daevin's mind raced. He had more than a hundred people on the station. If Deathmind attacked it, the results would be disastrous. "Pipe all the information to my office and notify Bach and his teams. I want everyone on alert. Be ready to go public if necessary."

❖

Keene chased one last cube of protein across his plate with chopsticks before giving up and plucking it from the plate with his fingers. Licking his fingertips, he saw Lexa-Blue looking past his shoulder at something.

"What is it?" he asked, turning in the direction of her gaze.

"Something's up."

As they watched, groups of people at various tables deserted their meals and left. Several of them wore the matte black of the security division.

"That's never a good sign," Keene said, scanning the room as more grim-faced people left.

"Yeah, Sec never gets called when something fun happens." Lexa-Blue stood. "We should get back and find out what's up."

When they reached the office, they saw Daevin, hands clasped behind his back, strain across his shoulders, standing at the window behind the black expanse of his desk. Elai sat near him, her big, dark eyes wide with fear.

Daevin waved Keene and Lexa-Blue closer and gestured for silence. "Status report," Daevin said to the commo. Bach answered.

"They've barricaded themselves in Control and sealed everything else off. They've fired all the manoeuvring thrusters on full power to alter the station's orbit, and it's already starting to decay."

"Track it. I want to know the trajectory and everything that's going on up there."

"Of course, sei. Bach out."

"What is it, Daevin?" Keene said, crossing to stand at his side.

Daevin took a deep breath. "We've had another attack. This time on our Orbital Research Station."

Lexa-Blue turned to Elai. "How did Deathmind manage to get to orbit? Can they teleport that far?"

Elai looked to Daevin, too wrought with emotion to speak. Daevin answered for her.

"It isn't Deathmind. It's SCI."

"What?" Keene said, shocked. "Why are they attacking your station?"

"I have no idea, but we have to find a way to stop them. With the orbit decaying, the station will come down. Even if it doesn't hit a populated area, it will tear a hole in the planet and wreak havoc on the ecology."

"Where is it going to hit?" Keene asked. "Can you evacuate the area?"

Daevin shook his head. "We're trying to get a fix on the projected trajectory, but we don't have predictive algorithms for it."

Keene made a dismissive noise in his throat. "It's simple course plotting, Daevin. Don't overthink it. Can you bring up the data here?"

"Of course," Daevin said. "Qoios, transfer what we have on the station's orbit here."

One of the displays on the wall changed and began to fill with data.

Vrick, can you see this? Absorb and analyze.

I have it, Keene. He felt a sensation like a valve opening, as he 'pushed the data streams he was seeing through to Vrick. Then he felt Lexa-Blue's node opening to them as well, the three of them together processing the information at a rate faster than any of them were capable of alone. The lines and leaps of the information twisted, split, jumped and swirled through them, resolving into one outcome.

"Sotari," Lexa-Blue said out loud. "SCI destabilized the orbit, but they're guiding the descent to turn it into a guided missile headed straight for Sotari."

Elai's sudden alarm surged like a spike of static electricity, making the hairs on their skin stand up.

"The station will begin to break up in the atmosphere, but something that large will come down on them in chunks the size of boulders," Keene added. "Can your people turn the debris away telekinetically?"

"Some may be strong enough, but Sotari will be devastated by whatever they cannot stop."

"What about the crew?" Keene asked. "Can they regain control of the station in time?"

Daevin shook his head, his eyes pinched closed. "They're on the other side of sealed pressure doors designed to withstand a hull breach. They're working on burning through, but there isn't time."

"Can they evacuate? Use the escape pods?" Lexa-Blue said.

Daevin stood straight, his expression pained but proud. "SCI gave them time to evacuate, and some have, but the rest are trying to stop the station from coming down." He paused. "They refused the order to pull out."

"Ruck," Keene said. "They'll burn up with the station when it hits atmosphere. There has to be something we can do."

"I'm open to ideas," Daevin said. "Qoios, full sim."

"Yes, sei."

The office darkened, the uncoiling shadow swallowing all light in the room. It was a darkness Keene and Lexa-Blue recognized, for they made their home in it. Stars resolved into hard points of light, becoming a backdrop for endangered station. When the holo was complete, the four occupants of the office were standing like giants astride the world, with the station in the middle of their circle. The surface of Orb was miles below their feet.

Daevin raised his arm and touched one end of the station's image, a cursor forming at his fingertip. "Control is here, near the main reactors. It's designed as a fall-back position in case of emergency, triple shielded. If it's closed off, it would take a focused plasma drill to get through."

They watched in silence as the mass of metal continued to move in agonizing slowness closer to the outer barrier of atmosphere surrounding Orb. Voices from the Emergency Centre and the station chattered across open commo lines.

"…Mikkels, try to slice the door controls, see if you can override the program…"

"…Pods three and six away…"

"…We've lost gravity. Everybody grab hold of something. Don't let that drill tip over."

"…No response from Green or Red Lab…"

"Ruck! We're losing it. Go, go."

"Pod eight is jammed. Get everyone out and onto one of the others, now…"

In the simulation, the station's hull began to glow, turning sullen yellow and building to a raging orange red scoured by the outer layers of Orb's atmosphere. Sparks of light dotted the station's hull, marking the exodus of its escape pods. Rather than arcing away from the faltering station on a safe trajectory, two of the pods skewed, tumbling back into the station's hull, caught in the fiery streams of superheated air.

They watched helplessly as the station skated across the atmosphere, seeking its target.

"Ideas," Daevin said.

"You need to break it apart somehow, get the debris as small as possible. That should minimize the effects of the impact. Most of it should burn up in the atmosphere." Lexa-Blue turned to Elai. "Can your people handle it then?"

Elai's eyes lost focus a moment, obviously communing with her people in Sotari. "Yes. There will be damage, but infinitely less."

Daevin looked at her, and Keene saw something intimate and weary pass between them. "The planetary defense grid," he said.

"But there are still people on board, Daevin. You can't just shoot them out of the sky like that."

"We've given them every chance we could. They made their choice and knew what it meant. There is no other option."

Elai's eyebrows rose, and she looked at Daevin. Keene knew from her face Daevin had never shared this secret with her, despite their closeness. He met her gaze with sadness in his face. "It was something I hoped never to have to use."

She smiled a worn smile. "I understand."

"Qoios, bring the defense grid online and target the station. Signal any remaining personnel to evacuate."

"Done," ey answered.

A new pattern of lights appeared in the simulation, marking the locations of the orbiting satellites. "Targeting scanners online," Qoios said. "Four satellites in the network are within range. I am powering them up and aiming them now." A tactical view opened, offering multiple views of the satellites ringing the falling station. As one, the silver cylinders of the defense satellites turned toward the plummeting space station. The station's glow became brighter and redder as it hit the outer layers of the atmosphere. Glowing metres marking each of the satellites showed the inversion weapons jockeying into the proper firing solution.

The station was listing badly, the thrusters continued to fail one by one. The orbital decay was worsening by the second. They watched as the mass of metal began to lose its structural integrity, massive sections breaking away.

"Targeting solution complete. All weapons in range."

"Fire."

"Firing sequence green. All weapons firing."

In the sim, the cursors marking the defense satellites glowed purple with sudden, spiky stars of energy before searing into knives of light. The first lance hit the wounded station, shearing through the hull in a bubbling glow of plasma. Along the path of the weapon's strike, the plasma expanded, eating through the panels of alloy and ceramic and reducing them to their elements. Again and again, the lances hit the carcass of the station, reducing it to glowing debris. Keene watched it all, his stomach turning at the destruction, at the knowledge that men and women were dying in the twisting, incandescent burn of metal. He was sure he saw bodies tumbling away from the wreckage, but was too afraid to ask for confirmation from the others. He kept watching, sure that each shadow was another life lost, as the lances carved the research station up, piece by anguished piece.

"The lance satellites are beginning to fail." Qoios's voice cut through the tense wait. "The task is too much for them."

Tension strained Daevin's face. "How long until failure?"

"Failure in thirty seconds."

They watched as first one, then all the lances failed, drained of energy. The remains of the station hit the atmosphere burning.

"Was it enough?" Lexa-Blue asked. She and Keene felt the response from Vrick as Qoios spoke out loud.

"Projections say the majority of the debris should break up in the atmosphere."

They all turned to Elai, who nodded, a small joyless smile on her face. "We will do what we can."

"Sim off, Qoios. I think we've all seen enough." The image washed away, leaving them all once again in Daevin's office. He turned from them to look out the window. No one spoke for several moments.

Elai was the first to break the raw ache of the silence, her voice small. "I don't know about anyone else, but suddenly, I am very tired and in need of a cup of tea. My Nanima used to say nothing couldn't be solved with a good cup of tea. I doubt she meant anything like this, but I'm willing to try. Would anyone else like some?"

There was a chorus of agreement, and Elai's frail frame floated up out of the chair, suspended as if on invisible strings. Realization appeared on her face, and she seemed to catch herself, as if committing some horrible faux pas. She lowered herself to the floor and took a stiff step toward the synth.

"Can I help with that?" Lexa-Blue offered.

A tired smile crossed Elai's face. "Thank you. That would be much appreciated."

Lexa-Blue joined her at the wall unit when she nodded, a grateful smile on her face.

While their attention was occupied with the tea, Keene moved to Daevin's side. "Are you okay?"

"I was okay once a long time ago," Daevin said. "I think the days of okay are long gone."

Keene rested a hand on Daevin's. "In spite of the reasons, I'm glad to see you again, Daevin. I don't know how much it matters in the face of all this, but it's true."

Daevin turned, a forlorn smile on his face but quiet steel in his tone.

"It matters."

CHAPTER SIX

Throughout the afternoon, they watched and waited as the station's debris rained down. At one point, Daevin gave a speech that went out on all the local deevee channels. They watched him from just out of camera range as he spoke, his tone both grave and inspiring. When the broadcast ended, he was drawn and pale. As evening drew to a close, people organized vigils of remembrance, prayer, and grief across the city. In his office, with the others sitting nearby, Daevin composed messages of condolence for those lost, arranging for posthumous commendations. Then he added their faces to his list. In a chair by his desk, Elai communed telepathically with her aides in Sotari, taking in all detail about what was going on there. Across Brighter Light, a day of mourning was declared.

The quartet remained in Daevin's office as the devastation was catalogued, Elai opening her mind to them as she communicated with her people. Damage in Sotari had been minimized but not avoided. One section of the main city had been hit by a large chunk of smoldering, twisted metal. Keene, Daevin, and Lexa-Blue experienced the grief and purpose as the Sotars picked up the pieces, a mental song of remembrance and love echoing through their minds.

Daevin paced behind his desk. Elai sat, rigid in her composure, with only a glisten of tears in her eyes. Keene stood at the window, unable to watch anymore, needing quiet comfort from the endless blue of the sky. Lexa-Blue sat in front of the deevee, so intent on the images she seemed to be absorbing them through her skin. Finally, she called an end to it when she stood and stretched. "All right, people. Enough is enough. I think we all could use a break here. What's say we meet in an hour? I'll cook us dinner in our suite."

"The guest quarters are all equipped with kitchens, but you don't have to go to the trouble. We can have the staff provide something," Daevin said.

Lexa-Blue shook her head. "Believe me, it's no trouble. I need something to take my mind off things."

"If you insist," he said, shrugging. "Qoios, see that she gets everything she needs, please."

Grateful for the relief from the sound of Orb's voices mourning, they went their separate ways while Lexa-Blue returned to their suite quarters and prepared dinner. Daevin returned to his pool, swimming laps until his muscles ached. Keene wandered the halls of the palace for a while and then returned to his suite and tried to read, but just ended up sitting with the book pressed to his chest. Elai sat on her bed and meditated. An hour and a half later, they convened in Lexa-Blue's quarters, Elai arriving first, then Keene, then Daevin. Lexa-Blue dimmed the lights and came to the table carrying two bowls, one full of a hearty stew, the other with salad. "It ain't fancy, folks, but there's lots of it. Take a seat and dig in."

Of the other three, Daevin enthused the loudest without even having tasted anything. The preparing and serving of meals was so remote from his daily existence, he seemed awed by her skill.

"Calm down, your techness. Your chef and his staff do it every day," Lexa-Blue said, filling bowls and passing them around. "I came up with the ideas, but Qoios is the one that had lackeys in and out of here to set everything up. All I did was call up some stuff from your stores and put it all together. Sit! It's going to get cold."

They settled themselves around the table and dug in, realizing they hadn't eaten since the morning. Daevin's first bite prompted him to lavish her with praise.

"Who taught you to cook?" he asked.

"My father," she said, not elaborating. The silence was expectant as they all waited for more, Keene prompting her when she didn't elaborate. "Yeah, Blue. I don't think you've even told me about your family."

She took a sip of wine, looking like she was unsure of how much to reveal. "My father taught me to cook, and my mother taught me to fly. My family was one of most prominent trader clans, based on one of the big, independent ships. We opened up a good chunk of the Brink in our day. I'm a starborn, raised in the ways of trading since birth, so I come by my vocation honestly. As soon as I was old enough, my parents had me learning to pilot a ship."

"Yet you work with Keene now. What happened to your family?" Daevin asked.

Lexa-Blue hesitated for a second, "I was in the hospital on Hub, being treated for some stupid, rare infection that the ship's auto-doc couldn't handle. While I was recuperating, our ship was attacked by pirates and destroyed with all hands. As sole heir, I came into quite a bit of money. It staked me to a new life. Keene came along later."

Elai made a small sympathetic sound. "I'm sorry."

"Don't be. He's not that bad."

"I mean about your..." Elai raised an eyebrow when she saw the smirk on Lexa-Blue's face. "I'm sorry about your family."

"Frontiers are dangerous places. I was doing lifepod and spacesuit drills as soon as I could walk. We all knew the risks of the life we lead. But thank you."

Daevin was pensive for a moment, then asked, "What happened to your eye?"

Lexa-Blue stared at him, surprised by his blatant enquiry. "You're lucky you're not a cat. Curiosity kills them, you know."

The corner of Daevin's mouth rose. "It's a fatal flaw. I have no patience for the polite conversational dance. When I want to know something, I ask. I find it saves time in the long run. Elai takes me to task for it all the time, telling me I have no gift for diplomacy. I am much better than I used to be, believe me. I'm sorry if I'm prying. You don't have to tell me if you prefer not to."

"That's all right. Don't forget the second part of that saying: satisfaction brought it back. Besides, I'm used to your direct approach. I've seen it in action." Daevin ignored the jibe. "Most people stare or point. The really rude ones will whisper, but few have the courage to come out and ask. Honest curiosity is a...refreshing change. Before Keene and I partnered, I was in on a deal that went bad. I was attacked, and I lost the eye. After I healed, I had it replaced with this," she indicated the sensor gem, "and went looking for someone to watch my back in tight spots." She looked askance at Keene. "And when I couldn't find anyone, I took him."

Daevin's composure slipped. When he spoke, his voice was almost inaudible. "I am so sorry."

Lexa-Blue shrugged. "It was a long time ago."

"So why don't you get the scar fixed? One of our doctors could have it corrected and have you out before lunch tomorrow."

"After my family died, I had offers from several of the big trading outfits to join up. I was young and stubborn and sure I could go it on my own, that if I didn't have my family with me, that was that. It ended up costing me an eye. The scar reminds me of who I am. That I'm not perfect, and that if I'm not careful, that can cost me. It keeps me on my toes."

"You never told me," Keene said, looking at her as if he was seeing her for the first time.

She shrugged. "It's not something I feel the need to talk about much." She reached for the wine bottle and poured for herself, then topped everyone else's glass. "Enough about me. What about you, Daevin? This unrest is bound to make your peers question your leadership ability. It's only a matter of time before someone sees this as a sign of weakness and goes for your throat."

Daevin appraised her and nodded slowly. "The thought has occurred to me. Once or twice."

"But that won't happen," Elai said. She took a sip of her wine and fixed them all with an even, calm gaze. "We won't let it."

By the time they finished their after-dinner liqueurs, they were all exhausted, the stresses of the day taking their toll. Elai excused herself first, covering a dainty yawn with the back of her hand. Keene and Daevin offered to clean up until Qoios informed them that he had already sent for a crew of porters to take care of it.

"Well, I'm going to bed then," she said, laughing. "Shoo, boys, go on home."

❖

Outside in the hall, Daevin asked Keene, "Walk with me? I want to show you something."

"Sure."

Daevin led Keene to a wide walkway bevelled into the building's outer wall. Above their heads, the walls sloped in to the pyramid's apex, cleaving a sharp line between the stone and the vast twilight sky over their heads. The railing around the path stood between them and the long, sliding incline to the ground below. "I like walking out here before I go to bed. I wanted you to see it."

Keene leaned against the railing and breathed in the night air, surprised by the warm fragrance of flowers and cut grass that rose in the growing dark. Brighter Light was a sparkling blanket below. "It's beautiful. Thank you for sharing it with me."

Daevin slid his hand along the rail and closed it over Keene's, squeezing tight. The contact felt warm and familiar to Keene, and he found himself enjoying the sensation. Neither one of them moved for quite some time. Keene turned to Daevin and saw silent tears in his eyes. He pulled Daevin in his arms and stroked his head, whispering comforting nothings in his ears.

Daevin pulled away and dried his eyes on the sleeve of his jacket. "It's late. We should get to bed." He traced the line of Keene's cheek with his finger.

They kept walking and came to Daevin's door. Daevin turned to Keene and even before he spoke, Keene knew what he was going to ask.

"Stay the night," Daevin said, without a hint of pleading in his voice. He might as well have been relaying instructions to an employee. "I don't want to be alone."

There it is, Keene thought. I knew it was coming, didn't I? The need had appeared during dinner. A touch of a hand here, a look there. The simmer of his anger at why and how he was here had drifted to the background in the face of what he had seen, the way that life had changed for all of them that day. He had known uncertainty and danger before, but never like this.

The decision seemed to make itself. "Lead on."

Daevin led Keene into his quarters and on to the bedroom, where he leaned close and kissed him. His lips were feather-light against Keene's, almost questioning. Keene answered by spurring the kiss on. As Daevin answered with just the hint of a moan that signalled a release of control somewhere deep inside, Keene wondered if he should stop it now before it went too far. The memory of his anger at Daevin's highhanded manipulation to get him here was still there, whispering in his ear, but it was drowned out by stress, need, and loneliness. He released his hold on Daevin's lips and slid his mouth across his stubbled cheek to nuzzle an ear. Daevin arched his neck with a hiss of pleasure and cupped the curves of Keene's ass in his hands. As Keene ran his tongue down the line of Daevin's neck, Daevin pulled Keene's shirt from the waistband of his pants, stroking the skin underneath.

This time it was Keene's turn to groan. It had been ages since he had made love to someone, and Daevin's touch against his skin felt like pleasure beyond words. They kissed again, rough and passionate this time while fumbling with clothes. Daevin's suit jacket went first, then Keene's shirt. In moments they stood before each other, naked together in a far more intimate way than the day before. Daevin took Keene's hand and led him to the bed.

They made love with a fragile intensity; unable to go back and uncertain of how to go forward, knowing that right here in this moment, they had nothing else.

Hours later, Daevin made a quiet sound in his sleep and Keene lay still a moment, waiting to see if he would wake. Even in the dim predawn light, lost in sleep, Daevin's face showed the lines etched in his face by the burdens he bore. Though with his hair untied and loose, framing the soft lines of his profile, Keene sensed some ease. Even some of the lines around his eyes seemed fainter. Amazing what a good squish will do for you, Keene thought with a smile.

When he was sure Daevin was still sleeping, Keene pulled him a little closer, brushing his lips against the warm skin of Daevin's shoulder blade. He traced his hand along the planes of Daevin's chest, circling each nipple and moving down, coming to rest in the hair that covered his lower belly. Daevin made another sound, somewhere between a purr and a sigh.

You sleep like the dead, Little Prince, he thought. I wish I could. He found himself realizing just how unused he was to sharing a bed. It had been forever, and the rhythm was unfamiliar, making sleep difficult. Also, echoes of the death and pain he had seen since coming to Orb teased him in and out of sleep. How do you do it, Little Prince? How do you sleep with the weight of a world on your shoulders? I guess you must have had a lot of practice.

Lying in the vast bedchamber, Keene realized the dawn light was growing and found himself wondering whether he or Daevin had needed last night more. With no answer forthcoming, he drifted off to sleep again.

❖

Releasing one last cleansing breath, Elai concentrated, feeling the air around her body warp to her will, lifting her off the floor. She uncurled her legs from the lotus position and stretched them down, her toes stopping inches from the rug below. Relief coursed through her body at the release from the strain of using her limbs to walk. The gentle caress of the shaped air was cool against her skin. It was a cheat, she knew. A sacrifice in the name of easing the discomfort the citizens of Brighter Light felt when they saw her, but too much was at stake, and she knew all too well what others in this land saw when they looked at her. It was hard enough to erase the childhood nightmare image she and her people embodied, but to be seen floating, or to have objects spring to and from her would be too much. A greater goal is at stake here, one more than worth aching limbs.

She hung suspended an inch or so above the floor, pausing for a second to enjoy the tranquility in her soul before dismantling the meditation circle.

Late into the night, she had communed with her people, joining in the healing of those injured in the rain of metal. When she could remain awake no longer, she had found sleep elusive. When she woke, her meditation had taken twice as long to restore some semblance of calm and re-establish her balance.

As each well-worn stone floated up from the floor, she felt it with her mind, sensing them in a deeper way than mere touch, savouring the unique textures, still rough from never being touched by human hands. Four red cardinal stones, one for each direction and cut from the tears of Rhokhara itself, separated and joined on the circle by clear crystal. She placed each stone back into the protective case with care, and then returned the case to the beaten leather carryall. Time for breakfast, she thought, and meditation always makes me hungry.

Outside her suite, she lowered herself, putting her feet to the floor once again, and walked with her uneven, painful gait down the corridor. She was glad this part of the building was quiet this early, as the constant thought-hum of suspicion and awe from Daevin's people at the sight of her had ebbed only slightly since she had been here. Usually, she felt it press in on her no matter where she was, and it took her considerable discipline to block it out. The respite was welcome.

As she approached a high archway leading to a patio garden, she sensed someone was already there. She opened her mind, focusing to cut out the noise of thousands of other minds around her. The world became thought and colour, emotion and impression. She narrowed down to the one mind beyond the arch and felt the cool, defined autumn colours that identified the presence.

Lexa-Blue.

Elai reached out with her mind, feather-light, across the surfaces of the other woman's mind. She made a point to keep the touch gentle, determined to avoid probing deeper and violating Lexa-Blue's privacy. She had spent enough time among the Silents to realize how much they valued the sanctity of their minds.

She realized that Lexa-Blue was exercising, a workout that was both physical and mental. Elai caught a trace of formidable determination and concentration in her mind. Did she wish to be alone? No. Elai sensed that the session would be ending soon. She moved through the arch.

The garden was large and open, cut into the face of the pyramid where it would catch the most sun for the longest time each day. Set against terraced levels of cool, leafy green, flowers grew in a tumult of colour: sprightly pink, demanding red, shy peach and sunny yellow, languid, drooping purple. A glass and iron table sat in the middle of the tiled patio, surrounded by this explosion of life. Elai always took her morning meal here, watching the sun creep along the stones to kiss the blossoms. To her, the tiny garden was a welcome oasis of real life in a society that seemed obsessed with gadgets and technology.

In the middle of the patio, Elai saw Lexa-Blue, rosy and sleek in the dawn light. She wore a simple grey leotard and sweat shone on her skin as she moved through her routine. Each move was calculated and precise, a high vicious kick and a powerful punch that would easily have broken bone. Elai could see each line of muscle, clear and defined beneath the other woman's skin. She watched in fascination, captivated by the controlled ferocity, and the utter, alien physicality of it. Once, this place had seemed repugnant to her, this constant touching and being touched, the endless swirl of movement and almost carnal delight these people took in their bodies. Now, it fascinated her, as she worked to accommodate this new culture into hers, to adapt and live among these bodybound cousins. Elai had never seen anything so intense as this almost ritualized workout. It felt to her she was intruding on some private moment of physical passion or intimacy.

She realized that the style of the movements was changing, becoming more graceful, more tranquil, and slowing until Lexa-Blue was finally still. Elai sensed a calm of body and soul that she had not experienced often. Lexa-Blue opened her eyes and saw Elai.

"Forgive me, I did not wish to intrude," Elai said.

"No intrusion, I'm finished," Lexa-Blue said with a smile, sponging away sweat with a towel. "It's all yours."

She turned to leave, but Elai held up a hand. "I was about to eat. Will you join me?"

Lexa-Blue laid the towel around her shoulders and took the offered chair.

"The way you move," Elai said, a tinge of awe in her voice. "It is quite beautiful to watch."

One of Lexa-Blue's eyebrows rose, making Elai laugh, the sound as pure as ringing crystal. "Do not assume that because Daevin prefers his own gender, I do too. I was merely paying you a compliment."

"Reading my mind, your highness?"

"A Sotar who would violate a Silent's mind has no honour. I know we just met, but I would hope you think more of me than that," Elai responded in the same tone of light humour.

Lexa-Blue inclined her head, conceding the point. "And for the record, don't assume that if you were making a pass I'd say no." Her face twisted into its mischievous smile. "Or yes."

Elai quirked an eyebrow and smiled back, nodding. "There is man named Giri who is waiting for me in Sotari. He is my…" She paused, searching for words to describe a concept that she had no words for. "The closest words that describe it that I can think of is Soul's Blood. He is my partner, my mate, the nourishment that gives me life. The person who fills the emptiness that hadn't existed until it was filled."

They were silent a moment, listening to the buzz of an insect somewhere in the foliage.

"Keene is glad that you came with him," Elai commented.

Lexa-Blue cocked an eyebrow.

"I don't need to be telepathic to tell," Elai said, "just observant. He is fortunate to have a friend like you. You must love him a great deal."

Lexa-Blue shrugged. "He's my partner. How could I let him walk into all of this alone? Daevin has a lot of nerve dragging Keene into all of this, and Keene's not going to regret it if I have anything to say about it."

A troubled frown crossed Elai's face. "Dark and dangerous times for us all. I fear that none of us will emerge unscathed. I am here in this place that feels cold and alien to me, where people rely on machines for their very lives, it seems. All I want to do is go home and be with Giri and forget all of this anguish and death. But we do what we must before we can enjoy what we want."

"Why do it then?" Lexa-Blue asked. "Can the hatred ever be rooted out?"

"My original ancestors were stirred together in a dish and brought to term in wombs of plastic and sterile chemical solutions. Their DNA was cut and melded and stitched together with machines so small that a billion would fit on the head of a pin."

Lexa-Blue listened for bitterness in her voice but heard none.

"They had no parents but for the technicians who built their cells. Their growth was accelerated by a factor of four, and they grew up in neat, ordered cages. It is no wonder that they learned to despise technology when they found their way to this world. It made them giants, and it made them outcasts."

She shook her head, pushing away the sombre turn the conversation had taken. "Enough of such things. I'll have Qoios bring us breakfast, and we can watch the sun come up. Daevin is taking me to the Brighter Light Market today. After what happened, he thinks it's important for us to appear in public as a united front, to show the people we must all go on. I think you and Keene should come along."

Great, Lexa-Blue thought. Shopping, my favourite thing in the universe.

❖

When Keene awoke, he heard the sound of splashing from the terrace and knew that Daevin must be taking his morning swim. He queried his node and the time, both Local and Galactum Standard flashed in his mind. Thank Fate I didn't sleep in too long, he thought. I'm usually the morning person. Blue would never let me hear the end of it.

For a moment, he thought about searching out his clothes, then gave up and padded out to the terrace naked. For a moment, in the shade of the overhang, a breeze played over his skin, raising gooseflesh and making him shiver. He stepped into the bright sunlight, shading his eyes, and grew warm again.

Sure enough, Daevin was in the pool. Keene noticed that his pace was gentler, less driven than that first time Keene had found him here.

He joined Daevin when he saw he'd stopped and swum over to the edge of the pool.

"I hope I didn't wake you when I got up," Daevin said, propping himself up on his elbows along the pool's rim. "You looked so beautiful, I couldn't bring myself to wake you."

Daevin traced a line down Keene's inner thigh with one damp finger. Suddenly, he seemed to realize what he had said and what he was doing. He stopped, a shy, embarrassed look coming over his face.

Uncomfortable with both the compliment and his reaction to Daevin's touch, Keene shook his head and lied. "No, I conked right out."

They pulled away from each other then, suddenly awkward in the light of day, away from the flare of need and desire. Keene wished he had taken the time to find his clothes, then chided himself for the thought. It's not like he hasn't seen you naked already, he thought.

Daevin pulled himself out of the pool and dried himself, then in a fit of modesty, started to wrap the towel around his waist. Then, he stopped. For a few comic seconds, he fussed with the towel, trying to look nonchalant. Their eyes met, and they both laughed.

"Why does this seem so strange?" Daevin asked, sitting at the table.

"It's been a long time, Daevin. We can't just slip back to where we were ten years ago. We've both changed, and anything that happens now is something new. And we went through a lot yesterday. You went through a lot."

"I see your point," Daevin said, nodding. "But it begs the question, what is the something new? Where do we go from here?"

"I don't know, Daevin. I don't think you do either. We're just going to have to let it play out as it does."

For a moment, Daevin looked like he wanted to argue the point, but he had no argument to make. He leaned back in his chair and ran his fingers through his damp hair, shaking it out, then he looked at Keene with warmth in his eyes. He laid a hand on Keene's knee. "I can tell you one thing. I'm glad you're here." He chuckled. "You led us a merry chase, I'll give you that. Even after we arranged for your friend Zyd to detain you, you fought Jaekir tooth and nail."

Keene frowned. "Zyd?"

"Gods, yes. He staged the whole theft scenario to keep you occupied until Jaekir could reach Highland and contact you. And let me tell you, he was a tough nut to crack," Daevin said. "We almost had to shut down his whole operation to get him to cooperate."

Keene listened to Daevin's unwitting confession and seethed, tamping down his fury to keep it from exploding.

"He set up those thieves perfectly. They didn't even know that the bit chip they stole was worthless, Zyd set them up perfectly…What's wrong?" Daevin asked.

"Let me get this straight." Keene's voice was ice calm. The ire he had stored away fired to life again at Daevin's words. "Not only did you try to stall my livelihood and force me to come here, you blackmailed one of my friends by threatening his business, put my partner in jeopardy, and set it all up just so you could get me here to help you."

"Yes, I did," Daevin said, surprised by Keene's anger. "I had to get you here. I needed you."

"My god, Daevin, what makes you think you have the right to manipulate people like that."

"I was desperate," Daevin shot back, getting angry himself. "You've seen what I'm up against here. I couldn't wait."

"So that makes it all right?!" Keene shot to his feet, knocking his chair over to clatter on the marble. "The end justifies the means. Well, I hate to have to break it to you, Daevin, but it doesn't work that way. You can't just screw around with people's lives because you need something from them. I thought that was your father's way, not yours. Maybe the apple doesn't fall far from the tree after all."

Keene stormed away, but Daevin called to him, his own anger growing. "How dare you say that to me? You know how hard I tried not to be like him, how much I hated the way he treated you. Damn it, Keene, wait."

He grabbed for Keene's arm, but Keene jerked away. For a fraction of a second, the threat of fists and blood crackled in the air between them. In that second, they looked at each other and saw what they were about to do and stopped, both knowing how terrible it would be for them to cross that line. Daevin looked miserable. "I'm sorry. I never meant to hurt anyone, especially not you. Please, don't go."

Keene hesitated. His anger was so strong, he wanted to keep going, collect Lexa-Blue and the Maverick Heart and get off planet immediately. Though he disapproved of Daevin's methods of getting him here, visions of burning cities and placid, suddenly empty bodies hovered at the edge of his vision. He was here now, despite the reasons why. He took a few steps in the direction of the pool and Daevin, who sagged in relief.

"Look," Daevin said. "Elai and I have to make a public appearance at the Market today, a show of strength for the people. Please come. We'll just have a quiet day and talk about this later, over dinner. Okay?"

Keene thought a moment and then nodded, his anger ebbing only a little.

❖

After a hearty breakfast of fresh fruit, pastries, and grilled tumon steaks from Orb's sea, Lexa-Blue excused herself to shower and dress.

When she met the others in the palace's garage, Keene and Daevin stood apart, some unspoken tension between them. When she tried to catch Keene's eye, he looked away, moving to a seat as far from Daevin as he could when the limousine pulled up and opened for them. Daevin sat across from him, silent and unreadable. Elai watched them both, her face dark with concern.

Daevin touched a control, and the top half of the passenger compartment seemed to become transparent, a holo-field showing them the clean, well-tended streets of Brighter Light. The architecture they passed was pure and strong, the epitome of utilitarian function. Buildings were neither too close together nor too high, freely interspersed with greenery and carefully maintained open areas, with no advertising or graffiti to mar the buildings. Few other private vehicles were on the streets, but from the rushed glances into the mag-lev trains that sped past, they could tell that the public transport system was widely used.

Eventually the pitch of the gravity cushion dropped a note as the limousine slowed and stopped. Massive in the holo-field, they saw a huge stone arch, a crowd of people visible through the opening. The artificial view faded out, greying as though on a dimmer, and the limo's hatch swung slowly open.

Daevin stepped out first, turning to offer his hand to Elai, who slipped her arm through his and took her place by his side. Four small security remotes floated away from the limo's hull and hovered over their heads, light sparkling as the fields energized.

Lexa-Blue got out and turned to Keene, smirking and offering her hand in a parody of Daevin's gesture, but it just seemed to irritate him. He swatted her hand away and scowled as he stalked past. When Daevin's bodyguard joined them, taking point, the limo hummed away to park, and they walked through the arch into the Market.

A sprawling, open square, the Brighter Light Main Market seemed crammed to capacity. They saw innumerable booths and stalls, some graceful freestanding structures, others rickety and portable. Rows of stands led off into the distance in precise, even lines. Despite all their world faced, all that had happened, life went on. Still, some stalls stood empty, while others burned with candles on makeshift altars. They walked deeper into the Market, feeling a relief around them from the crowd, like the release of held breath, one small sign that life was returning to normal.

As they sauntered along the first row they came to, Keene frowned at his partner, and she returned his quizzical expression. The vendors they passed seemed to have nothing to offer but bit chips, gadgets, widgets, and other oddments of technology. Keene saw spools of glistening fibre optic filament, racks of programs on every format possible, even repair people running their businesses from stalls heaping with scanners, probes, and home written code.

Elai noticed their surprise and came to them, chuckling, while Daevin wandered ahead. "I see you have the same reaction I did. It's not quite what you expect when someone says open air marketplace, is it? I think I know what you're looking for. Follow me."

After letting Daevin know where they were going, Elai led them past the ranks of stalls to a secluded grotto off to one side of the market. With a sweep of her hand, Elai showed them in. "This is my favourite place to come. It reminds me so much of home, I can't tell you."

The secluded mini market was everything they had expected a market to be. Stacked on a cart were massive bolts of luxurious fabrics, interwoven with glints of gold that begged to be touched. Handcrafted jewellery delighted the eye while the heady scents of spices and grilling meats saturated the air. Fat kegs contained wines and ales, and they saw crafts and art of every description, even a tiny, wizened woman selling leather goods as supple as well worn cotton.

And hardly anyone was there. While the main area of the market bustled with activity, few customers wandered back here. It seemed as if only the merchants were shopping at each other's stalls, bartering their wares back and forth. When the three of them entered the area, all heads turned in their direction, eager for fresh clientele.

They spent two hours looking around. Lexa-Blue haggled with a dour bookseller over a leather bound book of poetry, finally getting the better of him. Elai bought a small bottle of scent, dabbing a bit along the curve of her neck. Keene's black mood seemed to soften, and he went back into the main area of the market, poring over the selection of enhancer chips offered by a mech-tech. Out of sight of the others, Daevin picked a ring from the collection of a talented silversmith, intending it to be an apology to Keene later.

When they stopped for refreshments, Keene made his way to a cart where a dark-skinned woman with a wild fringe of hair stood before a mass of tubing and nozzles that dispensed a heady, spicy brew in tiny cups. She smiled brightly at him when he ordered and set to work twisted dials that pumped pressure into the machine. He watched the cords in her arm tighten as she worked the levers and knobs of the antique copper machine. When she finally presented him with the cup, the steaming drink tasted of pepper and chocolate and made his tongue tingle. He was so lost in the taste, he didn't hear Lexa-Blue coming until she was beside him at the counter. She gestured at his cup, calling for another, but they didn't speak until her drink was in her hand.

"What's up with you two?" she asked. "You haven't said two words to each other."

"We had sex last night."

"I'm not surprised. Considering what happened yesterday, I'd have done it too if I'd had an offer. Squishing is always nice tension relief. What's the problem?"

Keene hesitated a moment, and then told her of Daevin's confession. She was tipping her cup to drink when he started, but she stopped, fixing a level gaze on him over the white arc of her cup.

"So, do I get to kill him now or later?" The tone in her voice made Keene wonder if she was joking.

"Come on, Blue. I know it was a shitty thing to do, but he needs our help. I don't approve, but I think I can understand. No harm was done." He chuckled. "Except maybe to Nord's jaw. And don't try to tell me you didn't enjoy that."

Lexa-Blue snorted a laugh, spilling her drink. "No fair making me laugh when I'm trying to stay pissed."

Keene slipped his arm around her waist and brushed his lips against her cheek. "Don't worry, Blue. If he does it again, you have my permission to kill him."

She pointed a finger in his face. "Slowly. Kill him slowly."

They drained their cups and turned to see Daevin and Elai surrounded by a small group of people. They could see Daevin was kind and gentle with them, listening to their fears, their losses. He turned no one away, gently touched the shoulder of a man who broke down in tears. Over the man's shoulder, he caught Keene's eye and gave a small, diffident smile.

Suddenly, Elai's head snapped up, then to one side and the other, terror branding her face. They had only registered her alarm when they heard a howl of tortured air and the first scream.

Chapter Seven

In an instant even faster than time, the knowledge spilled over Elai, a memory running in reverse and changing every colour, smell, and thought she perceived about her surroundings. She opened her mind to the crowd, letting the onslaught of their thoughts crash into her like a wall of chaos. After a moment of disorientation, her discipline won out, and she searched for the spot where the teleportal would open. There. She sensed it a second before the weave of the physical world bent, opening the portal from there to here. Displaced air screamed in protest.

The rush of air flooded over the market, releasing wind borne debris in a flutter. Four Sotar floated in a swirl of black hooded robes in the centre of the portal. Elai braced herself for the pulp, waiting in horror for the sudden blankness that would replace the teeming, vibrant minds around her.

It never came.

She watched in shock as the intruders broke and moved into the crowd, a stocky female and a thinner male taking the lead. A ratchet of acid panic surged through the minds of the market-goers, and Elai knew one of the four was a 'phobe. Her surprise that the four had survived the teleport vanished as the wave of projected fear hit her. She twisted the air around her into the mental equivalent of armour plating and brushed the fear aside with ease. You'll have to do better than that, she thought, probing the others to determine the nature of their powers. The well-built male was a pyrokinetic. She sensed his energy flare, star bright, and saw a wooden stall laden with fabrics burst into gouts of flame. The last of the terrorists, a small, young male was a telekinetic, sweeping his energy through the crowd like a bludgeon.

Elai lifted off the ground in a sharp arc, putting herself back down between the terrorists and Daevin, who hadn't seemed to realize what was happening. She found Daevin, Keene, and Lexa-Blue and knit a link between them, fast and hard, feeling them reel at the sudden connection.

(Deathmind terrorists) She sent the images of the two 'phobes. *(These two are fear inducers. I think I can stop them and counteract the effect, but you'll have to stop the others)* She 'pathed the images, abilities, and locations of the others, and, firming her physical and mental shields, pushed into the panicking mob.

❖

Lexa-Blue was already moving when Elai's link bloomed in her back brain, spurred into action by the first scream. She loped toward the increasingly frenzied crowd, closing the distance between her and the mob until they hit her like a wall. Squirming, she pushed through the mass of people, jabbing and pushing none too gently. Better bruised than dead, she thought.

I've got the kinetic, Keene. You take the pyro.

She ducked behind an overturned skimmer cart and popped the clasp on her holster. She peeked around the cart's rear end, spotting the telekinetic terrorist.

All around her target, stalls shattered and buckled. Wooden struts tore into kindling, raining clubs and splinters on the ground. Steel alloys bent and twisted like tin. Anyone in the path of the unseen force was merely tossed aside.

Lexa-Blue stood, aimed and fired, her trigger finger a blur. Six bursts of energy struck the kinetic, staggering him. Lexa-Blue cursed as her sensor eye showed the tell-tale distortion of the gun's energy that meant he was shielding himself. Must be some kind of teek shield, she thought, and now he knows where I'm hiding.

She dropped back down, planning her next move. Before she had a chance to think, she heard a telekinetic bolt hit the cart and felt it creak and groan as its mass begin to tip. She sprang, tucking and rolling as the cart heaved itself into the dirt where she had been crouched. The move kept her from being crushed, but left her in the open. She scrambled to her feet, looking for cover, but before she could find it, the force bolt struck her in the chest, sending her to the ground.

❖

Elai wedged a path through the throng, broadcasting an urge for calm retreat. The shell of her shields shaped and reshaped, both moving people aside and keeping her safe. The tide of fear in the crowd pulsed like a living thing, now ebbing, now surging, breaking over her in thick, nauseating waves, each mind a roiling bubble against her. Alone, neither of the 'phobes would have been a match for her, but together they were challenging her considerable skills.

She kept moving, beginning to feel the strain of using her energy in all of the different necessary ways. Though she moved her body in a mostly straight line, her mind danced through a world she perceived as planes and curves of energy.

She extended a tendril of her mind to check on Daevin, and relaxed when she found him secure in the ring of his security remotes, and turned her attention back to the task at hand.

From his position of relative safety, Daevin saw a woman fall before the crush of people. Without thinking, he ran from his bodyguard's protection to help her. Adrenaline humming in his ears, he wrestled her up and out of harm's way and dragged her to a nook between walls. Satisfied they would not get trampled here, Daevin propped the unconscious woman against the hard stone and crouched at her side, checking her injuries. Aside from the knock on the head and some bruises, she seemed unhurt. He leaned closer, making sure she was in the ring of safety provided by the remotes.

He was stunned a moment later to see the remotes drop to the ground. He toed one with his boot, but the inert sphere just rolled in the dust. He picked it up and examined it. No sign of damage. No power at all. In a fit of frustration, he pitched it at the stone wall. The remote landed, undented, in the dirt. Daevin looked up, searching for his bodyguard again. Without the remotes, the bodyguard was his only protection. He saw the burly man, alerted by the remotes' failure, covering the area with his pistol drawn, and moving closer.

About fifteen metres from the alley, the bodyguard burst into flames.

Daevin jerked forward to help but was forced back by an inferno. The very air around the bodyguard seemed to burn. Daevin caught a glimpse of the other man's stunned face through the flames before he collapsed, already dead.

❖

Keene swore. The pyro had disappeared in the shifting storm of bodies, despite Keene's best efforts to track him. He was about to start another sweep when he caught sight of Daevin struggling to move a woman out of harm's way. As he watched, Daevin's remotes failed and the bodyguard died in a swirl of fire.

Driven by a primal, protective instinct, Keene ran. His muscles screamed as he ran, no idea what he would do when he got there, only knowing that Daevin was in danger. He was almost there, his hand nearly in Daevin's, when the jet of flame struck him, and the world caught fire.

❖

The crowd had begun to disperse. Elai sensed the ordered precision of the riot control officers arriving at the Market's entrances. She was free to move now, stalking the 'phobes. The male was easy, young and inexperienced. She erased herself from his perceptions, moving ever closer. She brushed through his mind, searching through the sticky strands of memory for some indication of who had sent him. Nothing. He was merely a foot soldier, misguided in his idealism, recruited by one who had been recruited by another, and so on. She moved into his field of vision and allowed him to see and sense her. He registered sudden, stunned fear.

(I am First Mind for a very good reason, young one. You would do well to remember that) With ease, she broke through the shield he tried to erect, and then through his mind.

He dropped, catatonic, to the ground.

A tingle warned Elai, and she layered her shields deep and hard. The female 'phobe's attack flowed over her. She allowed herself to feel the skating energy and absorb it. It whirled around her, growing stronger as it melded with her own power, then shot back along the path it had come. The 'phobe's shields were strong, stretching and resisting as Elai tore at them, but there was more. Elai sensed the fringe of chaos around the 'phobe's resistance. The other's power was ragged and wild, and she fought Elai with something close to madness. Then, Elai sensed the truth, felt the echo of the neural stimulants coursing through the other's body, driving and amplifying her power.

In that moment, Elai knew why the teleport had not killed them. Their bodies were polluted with alien substances, their bodies breaking down under the fire in the cells. She knew that the drugs would not prevent their deaths, merely stave them off until their hateful mission was complete.

Elai felt her calm evaporate in an eruption of rage, her power surging. The other was no match for the onslaught of wild energy coming at her. When a tiny crack appeared in the 'phobe's shields, Elai attenuated, slithering in and hammering through. It fell away in a glitter of broken thought and will.

(Don't fight me, kindred. You know you cannot win.)

Elai probed through memories, still searching for the name of the raid's mastermind. There. She sucked the strand of memory into herself and noticed the mind around her going dark.

In a blink, Elai was back in the physical world, the 'phobe braindead at her feet.

❖

Lexa-Blue heard a rib snap as another TK bolt hit her.

Vrick, I need help here. Bump up the energy scans. The field he's generating is energy, we should be able to see it.

The world as seen through her sensor eye shifted into a startlingly intense new pattern of energy. As another bolt sped her way, she saw a flickering ghost of something and managed to shift her body to avoid serious injury. She staggered to her feet.

He's energy shielded, but his physical shield is low, almost nil. You should be able to overload it.

The plan was there in an instant. She scanned the area and calculated her movements, herding the kinetic where she needed him. Finally she stopped, levelling her gun at him again. For a fraction of a second, he hesitated. Then she felt his laughter inside her head, scraping across her mind like grit and broken glass. It was the worst thing he could have done.

"Oh, that's it, asshole. You are going down." She shifted her aim, set the gun to its highest setting and fired. The market stall of bit chips beside her assailant exploded in a rain of fragments and jagged shards. Several of the sharp missiles struck home, making the kinetic shriek in sudden pain and shock.

Energy shield is down. You broke his concentration.

Ignoring her own pain, Lexa-Blue was on him in seconds. Shards of blood-spattered polymer stuck out from his face and side like porcupine quills. Painful, but not fatal. Before he could move, she planted her booted foot across his throat, aiming her gun squarely at his face.

"Gotcha."

Reducing her pistol to stun, she fired.

❖

Keene felt himself lifted and tossed into the shadows of the alley by a battering ram of superheated air. He hit the ground hard, and realized that the shirt across his back was burning. Some instinct took over and he rolled, smothering the flames in the dirt.

I'm alive. Hurts like a son of a bitch, but I'm alive.

Daevin.

Keene pulled himself around, his only thought for Daevin's safety. Through a haze of pain, he saw a dark, menacing blur advancing on Daevin. Keene watched as the pyro teek-lifted something out of an equipment pouch.

Thought was barely possible through the wall of heat and pain, but still he frowned. What's a Sotar pyrokinetic doing with a neural stunner? It made no sense.

The black monster drew closer to Daevin, and the questions fell away. Keene winced at the pain across his shoulders and drew his gun. There is no pain, he thought. There is me. There is the gun. There is the target. In the clear moment of purpose that came over him, Keene thought the gun to its highest setting and fired.

Keene was lucky. Lucky that the pyrokinetic possessed no precognitive or telepathic ability to warn him, no teek to shield him.

The gun blast hit him just above the diaphragm, tearing him apart.

As relief washed over him, Keene blacked out from the pain.

❖

Daevin watched the terrorist die, too stunned to move. He realized what had happened, and it jolted him into action. He scrambled over to where Keene lay, unconscious and face down in the dirt. Nausea washed over him when he saw the blackened, blistered skin of Keene's back, but he leaned closer, gingerly searching for a pulse. It was thready and weak, and he felt panic skitter in his stomach. He forced it down, knowing that Keene needed immediate help.

Daevin's mind raced. He wasn't sure the auto-doc in the limo could handle burns as severe as this. He frantically scanned the crowd, trying to spot a business or person who might be able to help, but the Market was chaos, only just coming under control.

Over the noise, Daevin heard the distinctive, warbling sirens of ambulances growing louder overhead. He ran to the mouth of the alley and saw the stubby ovoid aircraft, emblazoned with the red cross and caduceus, circling to land. One of the ambulances landed near him, the hatch opening before the landing struts had flexed to take its weight. Medics spilled out and fanned into the crowd.

Frantic to get their attention, Daevin waved his arms and shouted. One of the medics caught sight of him and recognized him. She ran toward him, calling over her shoulder to another tech, who followed.

"Are you hurt, Technarch?" she asked, brusque as she began to examine him. She was already running a scanner wand over him before he replied.

"Not me." Daevin indicated Keene and the injured woman. "Them."

"Take the woman," she told the other tech, dropping to examine Keene herself. She moved the wand over him in precise, angular passes and, after a moment, set a hypo-gun and hissed an injection into his arm. She scanned him again, and the rigidity of her posture relaxed just a bit. The other tech, his check of the woman complete, kneeled beside her.

"The woman is okay, minor concussion. Conscious, but a little groggy. She's on the monitor. This one?"

"Severe burns to the torso and upper arms. He's stable for now, but we have to get him in regen right away. Help me get a stasis pack on him, then call for a stretcher and commandeer one of the pods for immediate evac, Code Red."

Daevin hovered, trying to stay near, yet out of the way. He watched helplessly as the medics attached the stasis unit to Keene's chest and powered it up, attaching leads to his temples. When everything checked out, they loaded Keene onto a mobile hover-bed and into the pod. All Daevin could do was watch as the pod door lowered, cutting Keene off from sight. The anti-gravs whined and the pod lifted, tilting its lower hull to Daevin before sweeping off into the sky.

For a moment, he stood there, a sudden irrational premonition he would never see Keene again stabbing into his heart. When the pod was too small to see anymore, Daevin turned and went to find Elai and Lexa-Blue.

CHAPTER EIGHT

Daevin heard voices, a low murmur just at the edge of awareness. He was certain someone was speaking to him, and he struggled to parse some meaning from the sounds. As hard as he tried, comprehension remained just out of reach, the words whispered like secrets behind his back. He turned but saw only empty space and silence, the voices shifting again to be out of sight. As his frustration rose, paranoia followed. He wasn't even sure where he was, why the voices were following him when he wasn't even sure of himself. It's something important, he thought. If I could just hear what they were saying, I would have the answer. If I could just make it out, I could stop all this. I just need to listen harder. There. It's just...

He woke with a start, feeling a jab between his shoulders, and realized he had fallen asleep contorted in the hard-backed chair. He stretched, hoping to untangle the gnarled muscles. I used to be able to sleep anywhere, he thought. I'm getting old.

He shook his head and woke enough to remember where he was. Keene's room in the burn unit of the Med-Centre. He fought down a moment of panic that the voices had been bad news about Keene's condition, but he realized the noise he'd heard was the mutter of the equipment monitoring Keene's healing. The clear plex cylinder in the centre of the room was intact, and in it, Keene was still safely immersed in the minty blue regenerative gel, his breather mask still in place, bobbing gently as if weightless. As Daevin watched, tracers of light flickered across the face of the screen over Keene's head, and it chirped, sending a data spurt to the nurse's station down the hall, then quieted again.

Despite the quiet warmth of the hospital room, Daevin still felt an uneasy chill. A shudder ran through him, and he put it down to fatigue and the remnants of the hard rush of adrenaline that had seared through him in the market. Until that moment, he had only seen the aftermath of Deathmind's attacks, the wounds left in his nation. In that moment, in that crowd, he had been a victim. He had understood what his people endured in this constant struggle in a new, visceral way. Had they come specifically for him? Or had it been merely random circumstance? It took concentration, but he finally managed to control the tremor in his hands.

When he looked up, he saw Lexa-Blue standing guard by the regen tube, her hand against the transparent surface, as close to touching Keene as she could be at that moment. Daevin saw him thrash briefly and saw Lexa-Blue stiffen at his movement, attuned to his pain. Keene quieted down, moving only in response to the currents of the thick fluid, and Daevin saw Lexa-Blue exhale and relax. He could see how tired she was by the slump in her shoulders and the pain lines around her eyes. But she hadn't moved from Keene's side, hadn't slept or eaten since he had entered the tube, nor accepted treatment for her broken ribs. The arm that wasn't reaching for her partner was wrapped around her chest. She must be in agony, but that small change in expression was all that hinted at it. Daevin wondered if she had moved at all while he had slept in his chair.

He envied the bond between them, though on some level, he wasn't surprised by it. The seeds of the man Keene was, had been there even in his youth: his humour, his strength and compassion, his disarming naiveté. He had drawn Daevin in and held him in orbit until Daevin's life had torn him away. It made sense that gravitational pull had attracted others in the intervening years.

And I took advantage of all of his best qualities to get him here, Daevin thought. I blackmailed, browbeat, and abused anyone I could to get him to come here and help me. Deep down, he had known that Keene would come, even without the pressure he had brought to bear on their lives, but the need had been too great. He wished he had trusted that feeling, but it was too late for regrets. The parade of death had worn him down, the seemingly endless stream of state funerals had given his plan a desperation that he recognized, but loathed.

Is that what it comes down to? he thought. Does my goal of bringing this world together justify anything I do?

It's because of me that you're hanging in that tube, Daevin thought. Does my need justify that? He looked at Lexa-Blue again. And you, he thought, I know almost nothing about you. You probably knew even less about me. Yet, without even knowing what he was walking into, you followed him into my war. What did he do in all those lost years with you that earned such loyalty? What adventures did I miss that formed this bond between you?

Lexa-Blue noticed his scrutiny and her smile was wan and tired.

"How is he?" Daevin asked, feeling guilt press down on him.

"No change." She moved her hand away from the tank, cool and dispassionate again, but Daevin felt he had truly seen the depth of her bond with Keene.

He stretched again and rose from the hard contour of the chair, the kink in his neck twinging again. From the corner of his eye, he saw her wince as she turned away from the regen tank. "You really should have that rib looked at."

She shrugged. "When I know he's all right."

Daevin shook his head. "He could be in there all night before they know for sure. You must be in pain."

"Pain's just pain. No getting away from it. Wait it out and it passes. One way or another."

Her meaning was clear. When Keene was either well or dead. He searched her face for some sign of reproach or blame, but her eyes were on Keene again. "It shouldn't have happened," Daevin said.

When she looked at him, her face was neutral, as if she was discussing the weather. "Lots of things that happen shouldn't. Lots of things that should happen, don't. Can't do much about it most of the time."

"If it weren't for me, he never would have been here in the first place."

"You're right."

Daevin eyed her warily, half expecting anger or violence from her after seeing her skill against the terrorists, but her face was calm as she went on.

"And if you hadn't been there to call the medics over, Keene might have died. And if you hadn't been in danger, Keene would never have been hurt." She paused. "And if you hadn't threatened Zyd into cooperating, you would have missed us at Highland, and none of this would have happened."

Daevin felt his face burn and began an apology, but she cut it off. "Save it. It's done, and you can't change it. I'll let it go this time. For him. But if you ever try anything like that again, you'll regret it. My point is that you can 'what if?' yourself to death if you want to. It's easy, but it doesn't get you anywhere. Shit happens, you deal with it."

Daevin knew she was right, and was just as sure that she was capable of making good on her threat. For a moment, he was too tired to care.

The door opened and Keene's doctor came in. She nodded a curt greeting and checked the monitors, interpreting their data. The doctor examined the readouts from the monitors, stopping only to make a small adjustment with hands as blunt and hard as a set of well-worn tools. She checked the readouts again and she looked satisfied with what she saw.

"We could use some good news here, Doc," Lexa-Blue said, when the doctor didn't speak immediately.

"His vital signs are strong. He's taken to the regen well, and there should be no permanent damage. I'd like to keep him in the tank for the rest of the day, but he should be fine in the morning."

Daevin felt a surge of relief so sudden and intense it was almost nausea. He heard Lexa-Blue sigh and saw her eyes close, the only sign of her emotions.

"And you," the doctor said, pointing a square finger at Lexa-Blue, "are having that rib set. No arguments. I've adjusted the sleep field. He should be conscious in a minute or two, and you can talk to him through the vox unit. Keep it short, though, please, and then meet me in Treatment Room Three."

Daevin watched Lexa-Blue lean close to the cylinder and grin as Keene's eyes opened behind the breather mask. She put her hand on the regen tube again, near his face, and her thumb stroked the clear surface. "How you feeling, partner?"

Looking over her shoulder, Daevin saw his lips move, and the vox patch against his throat transmitted his reply. The voice that came from the speaker was almost his, but flat and tinny.

"Like shit."

"Well, that's how you look too."

"Same to you, bitch."

"Hey, I look like this 'cause I was up all night making sure they fixed you up right, so why don't you cut me some slack?"

"Thanks, Blue."

"Hey, you just get better. I've got to go, partner, I've got a date with a cute doctor." Daevin saw her wink at the doctor, who merely shook her head and raised an eyebrow. "But there's someone else here who's been here all night. You be nicer to him than you were to me."

Daevin joined them, his heart thudding in his chest. As he passed Lexa-Blue, he thought he felt the touch of her hand on his arm but she was gone before he was sure it had even happened. All he could see in that moment was Keene, his skin pink and taut where the burns had been; Keene looking up at him with a crooked smile Daevin knew all too well. He leaned in, wishing he could reach through the regen tank and touch Keene, hold him; wishing the gulf of years between them was gone. He saw Keene's mouth move and heard the vox unit say, "Miss me?"

Daevin chuckled but felt tears in his eyes. He swiped them away. "I'm so sorry."

Keene shook his head, causing a flurry of bubbles in the regen gel, and gave Daevin a foggy smile. Something hissed in the equipment, and Keene's eyes fluttered, his pupils dilating. "S'okay. Love you." He touched the inside of the regen tube, staring into the distance. The hand began to drift, and Daevin's own shot out to touch the tube from the outside, as if he could reach through the hard clear surface by sheer force of will. The sound must have caught Keene's attention, because he looked at Daevin's face. His beatific smile made Daevin want to laugh. "I love everybody." His eyes closed, and he drifted off to sleep, as if exhausted by the words.

"Everybody loves you too," Daevin said. He sat there for several minutes, but Keene seemed to be in a deep sleep.

Nothing for it, he thought. Time to get back to work.

Daevin stood, stretched one last time, and felt something pop between his shoulder blades and release the tension he had held there all night. He sighed at the sudden ease and felt clearheaded again. With one last look in Keene's direction, he left the room.

The nurses at the station in the hall smiled at him with that deferent expression they seemed to think was due his position. Even after so many years, it still didn't sit well with him. *I can handle the fact that they look at me like I steer their fates, because I do. But they look at me like I have all the answers as well.*

A familiar weight settled on him as he walked the cool corridors of the centre, then out into the courtyard. He turned toward the sun, hard and hot against his face. *That's it,* he thought, *the end of the interlude. No time now for the one, only for the many.* He looked around at the stream of people passing him to enter the Med-Centre. They are all mine again, mine to tend and protect. Mine to save.

As he descended the steps to the street and his car, he felt his determination returning, felt the cool, dispassionate mask of his leadership fall back into place. He wasn't sure anyone else would notice the set to his shoulders, the tightness dragging the corners of his mouth down. His duty to his people was back after the brief, personal interlude of his own life. As he sat back in his seat in the car, he took the warm kernel of joy at knowing Keene was going to be all right and put it aside, already missing its presence in his heart.

But even though it no longer ruled, it remained near enough that he could still reach it.

"First Mind?"

"Yes, Qoios?" Elai looked up from the cup of tea she had been staring into. Still shaken by Keene's horrific injuries, she had been using the spicy heat and nostalgic memories of her Nanima's secret blend as a familiar remedy to calm herself. In her mind, Giri's love was sweet and hard, like rock candy that lasted for hours. It lapped against her in languid waves. *(I must go/loss/alone/pangs/sadnessaches/reunion soon/inevitable)* Giri's only response was an enfolding embrace that filled her, became one with her and stretched away on a slender, but unbreakable thread.

"The Technarch wanted me to tell you that Sei Ota Chiaro is going to be fine. He will be released from the medical centre and back with us tomorrow."

Elai felt the weight of her fear leave her in a gush. She had been linked with the others when Keene had been burned, and his agony had seared across her mind. Had she not already defeated her foe, she might have lost all control at the shared experience of his wounds. It had taken all her discipline not to invade his mind and monitor his recovery from within. Her growing affection for him had been a sore temptation to violate her taboos. She could do nothing but leave him in the hands of Daevin's medicine.

"Thank you, Qoios. That's good to know."

"The Technarch would like you to wait for him in his office if you would."

She stood, and the pain in her joints eased in the wake of her joy at

Keene's recovery. Her step was lighter as she walked from her quarters to Daevin's office, her head higher. Daevin was not there when she arrived, but Qoios opened the door for her. She could see it had been tidied in Daevin's absence, but the stacks of flimsies still dominated the desk, the deevee set to a soothing idle pattern, but in multiple displays that must have hidden reams of data behind the soothing swirls of colour. She smiled and felt close to her friend in that moment. The controlled chaos felt familiar and warm to her, like a favourite shirt. So many times she had watched Daevin navigate his way through a volume of information that made her head ache.

She had only been there a few moments when Daevin arrived, barely looking at her when he took his seat behind the desk. She could see the circles under his eyes, feel the frayed edges of his fatigue. She opened her mouth to speak but stopped when he raised a hand. She waited, taking no offense.

"Qoios, have Bach report to my office, now."

"Yes, sei."

She heard the edge in his voice, something she rarely heard from him. Even in the tensest of situations, he managed to stay calm. "You should get some sleep."

He looked at her, seemed to finally really see her in front of him. "I will, later."

She saw the set to his jaw and knew this mood, this resolution. It had been in his eyes the day before in the market, when he had told his advisors in no uncertain terms he was unavailable for the rest of the day.

"You can rest now, Daevin. Keene is going to be all right."

Daevin made a derisive sound. "No thanks to me."

"You can hardly bear the responsibility for that, Daevin. The person who hurt him is dead. He is the one who did it, not you."

Daevin scrubbed his face with his hands. "I know. In my head I know that. My heart needs some time to catch up."

"Give yourself some time. You'll get there." She paused, unsure of whether her news would help or just upset him more, then pushed on. She owed him the truth she had discovered. "I think I know who is behind Deathmind."

His eyes fixed on her, the edges of his aura suddenly fiery. "Who is it? How did you find this out?"

"Before the 'phobe killed herself in the market, I was able to extract a few errant thoughts from her mind. It was the first time I've been close enough to one of them to look that deeply." Her face wrinkled into a frown at the thought of what she had done. "His name is Bodi."

"What can you tell me about him? What are his weaknesses?"

"Let me show you." She reached into one of the pockets in her robes and took out the slim taper of crystal. She extended it to him. "Hold out your hands and rest the crystal across your palms."

Daevin complied, the crystal amber yellow against his skin. Elai moved her hands until they were just above the crystal, barely a whisper from touching Daevin's. After a second of nothing, she heard Daevin gasp as images blossomed in his mind, pulsing like a heart pumping blood. She felt him want to struggle, then calm himself as she had taught him. Taking the lead, she shaped the images from the crystal, translating them into something his Silent mind could comprehend.

Daevin's office fell away, and they were sitting in Elai's study in Sotari, the crystalline walls a pale amethyst. The only furniture was a pair of chairs facing each other. Elai pulled Daevin's avatar into herself, merging them with the memory of her that sat in one of the chairs. She/Daevin faced the man across from them.

Like Elai, he possessed the racial characteristics of Sotari. His head was large, his body more frail than human norms. His colouring was the opposite of Elai's. Where she was fair, with hair sunny and golden, his skin was darker, his hair an even darker brown than Lexa-Blue's. The differences extended to the eyes. Bodi's eyes held something dark and hooded—not just colour, but secrets they held in check, hidden from anyone without the senses Elai and her people possessed. Daevin/Elai felt those eyes seeking deep for something, probing, appraising.

A ghost image formed over the man's features, superimposing an impenetrable wall between him and Elai/Daevin. When his thought came, it was as though someone had poured warm oil between their shoulder blades and rubbed it slowly into the skin. The seductive charm of the man radiated off him in waves, though his mind presented a wall of closed doors to Daevin. Linked with him, Elai felt Daevin realize his charisma might easily sway people to his viewpoint. Daevin felt Elai translating the imagery and sensation rich thought language of her people into words he could understand. Still, some of the sensations leaked through, confusing him as he smelled the colours and heard the scents that swirled through Bodi's mind.

"Forgive me, First Mind, if I don't share your optimism. We are dealing with a people who know nothing of our ways and have no interest in learning of them. They fear our abilities and are suspicious of our disinterest in their technology. Their conduct at Rhokhara Canyon was reprehensible, and I do not have to remind you what that incident cost both our families. Any peace between our two peoples is a fragile one at best. Even if we achieve some lasting accord, how long before our culture suffers the indignities of assimilation? What becomes of our ways then? Where will our traditions, our culture go when the humans swallow everything we have created for ourselves? Would you have us in the thrall of technology again?"

Daevin/Elai felt the reasonable concern behind the words and was moved to consider their validity for a moment. Elai took control in that moment, showing Daevin he was falling victim to the very charisma he had been concerned about only moments ago. The den washed away like a watercolour, and they were back in the office. He blinked and shook his head.

A crease of worry touched Elai's face as she watched Daevin re-orient himself. "I knew he was against our alliance, but I never suspected he would go this far. He's a dangerous enemy to have, Daevin. His father was the leader of the expedition that died at Rhokhara Canyon, and I fear his bitterness has poisoned him. When I became First Mind, he was my only serious rival; his power closely matches mine. He's xenophobic, a chauvinist in the truest sense of the word, almost insanely devoted to his notions of cultural purity. The charm and charisma you just experienced make my people listen to him. Then he speaks directly to their pride and their fear of being overwhelmed by your technocracy, of us enslaved as we were by our creators."

"That's not what we want."

"I know that," Elai said. "But, Daevin, you can't forget the layers of history and culture that our peoples have with each other. You represent our origin, something we have spent decades coming to terms with. We were born of humans' unfettered desire to meddle in and control the forces they barely understand. I am born from ancestors who murdered thousands just to be free, and my people will live with that stain forever.

"And you. To you, my people are nightmares, monstrous gods who can tear every thought from your minds and ferret through every dark, secret shame you would hide from yourself to keep from going mad. We are the demons that terrorized your childhood."

She paused a moment, as if speaking these truths had wearied her.

"I know all of this is not true. I know we are the same where it matters, you and I. I know the path our souls walk, and I know we walk that path together.

"And most of my people know it too. Unfortunately Bodi and his followers refuse to believe it. I've watched him closely over the years, Daevin, though it seems not closely enough. He'll die fighting this union, and he won't shy away from taking many people, mine and yours, with him. I'm certain of it now."

"A fanatic. The most dangerous enemy of all." Daevin rubbed his eyes in frustration and anger. He turned to the window and sighed, and she heard all his fatigue and frustration in that small sound. "Why is it we can't seem to leave these bigotries behind? No matter how many of them we conquer: racism, sexism, orientation, some new wall threatens to keep us apart, some new division between 'us' and 'them'."

"Excuse me, sei," Qoios interrupted. "Chief Bach is in the outer office."

"Send him in." Daevin sat straighter in his chair as Bach entered.

Elai noticed Bach take in the whole room on entering, as if evaluating every detail for the slightest sign of danger in the environment. When he settled his icy eyes on Elai, however, his lids narrowed, making him seem even colder than before. If that's even possible, she thought. She saw Daevin frown at his disrespect.

Bach took up a position in front of Daevin's desk, standing at attention, his arms clasped at the small of his back. "Technarch." He turned his head a fraction of an inch, barely even taking Elai in with his eyes. "First Mind."

"Your report, Chief," Daevin said, sharpening his voice at Bach's tone.

"Four terrorists in all: two fear inducers, one pyrokinetic, one telekinetic. Two dead on scene, the other two dead in interrogation, suicide by the same means as described by the First Mind. Civilian casualties total fifty-four dead, two hundred and twelve injured. Nineteen of the dead were killed directly by the terrorists, the others died in the ensuing panic."

"How did they get past the defense grid?" Daevin asked.

Bach flushed, the almost healed scar deepening to an angry red. "We don't know. According to diagnostics, the shield did not fail. They must have come up with an override code somehow. All codes were changed after the attack three days ago, and I have a team looking for the leak, but they could have telepathically plucked the codes out of someone's mind. Two hundred and seven Sotar are in Brighter Light at the moment. I'm tracing their whereabouts, but any one of them could have come in contact with someone who had access to the codes."

"But there's no guarantee that something like this won't happen again." Daevin frowned.

For a moment, Bach looked like he would rather chew glass than answer. "No."

"The other question is, how did they survive the teleport?"

"I have my suspicions," Elai said. "Chief, have you performed autopsies on the bodies of the dead Sotars?"

Bach grimaced. "No. Why would we?"

"I think if you do, you'll find some form of stimulant or chemical in their systems. Possibly a mix. I sensed it when I was inside one of their minds. It was burning her out, unraveling her genes. It wasn't going to keep them alive long, but it gave them the extra time they needed to complete their attack."

Bach's scowl deepened. "Permission to speak freely, Technarch."

"Granted."

"Our people are dying, sei." Colour rose in Bach's face, the tendons in his neck corded. "And we are not doing enough to stop it."

"And what exactly do you suggest, Chief?" Daevin's tone was carefully neutral, despite a growing hardness in his gaze.

"The Emergency Powers Protocol. It gives you the power to declare martial law. We need to go on the offensive and put a stop to this once and for all. The Sotars are making fools of us. Flouting our laws, our security, and our very lives."

"My people are dying too, Chief Bach," Elai said quietly.

"Forgive me, First Mind, but that isn't my concern. My mandate is to keep the citizens under my protection safe. Something your people seem determined not to let me do."

"Enough!" Daevin sat straighter in his chair, placing his hands on the desk. "I'm sure I don't need to remind you, Chief, that the First Mind is here as my guest and is due all the respect you would accord to me." He paused. "If not more, as she is our guest. This has gone beyond our community and theirs. This is about keeping all of the citizens of this planet alive. We stand together or not at all. The Emergency Powers Protocol is not an option. Do I make myself clear?"

Bach stiffened but inclined his head. "Yes, sei. I'll have Director Valme test the bodies against the baselines we have of Sotar physiology."

Daevin steepled his fingers and looked carefully at Bach. "Chief,

I want everything you can spare assigned to this. I want daily reports from you and your head of Security: Technical Support. I want these attacks stopped. Do I make myself clear?"

Bach's gaze moved to Elai for a moment. "Yes, sei."

He turned on his heel and walked out.

❖

Saphia Valme had been so busy, she couldn't remember her last meal. Her assistant had practically pushed her down to the cafeteria. Of course, she had taken along a techno-forensics report on the research station's fall, making notes on the flimsies with one hand while she wolfed a sandwich with the other. Barely looking up from the pages of the report, she tossed the sandwich's wrapper in the recycler and stood from the cafeteria's table, still reading. On the way out, she stopped to pick up a hot cup of coffee and headed back to the lab, somehow managing to carry the mug and the report while still making notes.

She was so used to the trip from the cafeteria to the lab that she didn't even look up when she reached the door. The biometric locks read everything from her height and weight to her facial features to her brain activity and pulse, and it slid the door open for her.

Inside, she took a sip of coffee and headed across the room to her office. She passed her various teams, clustered around their workstations. Her teams examined the jagged curves of burnt metal from the fallen station scattered on various benches and tables. She heard snippets of a heated discussion between Smis and Loa as she reached the door to her office.

She caught a glimpse of herself in the tintable glass wall that separated her office from the rest of the lab. Sharp, broad features, hair pulled efficiently back from her forehead, she knew her looks would not get her anywhere. She also knew, however, that looks mattered for nothing in Brighter Light. Her intellect and skill were the only coin that mattered here. She knew what she could do, what she brought to her position was all she was judged on, and that was just fine by her. Despite the current political situation, she had faith in her skills and knew she would do everything in her power to end the strife that Brighter Light faced.

Her family had been in S:TS for years, and her ascendance to the directorship had been the highest achievement of any family member, something she had earned on her own merits alone. But some days, she wanted nothing more than to retreat to a nice quiet entry level tech position, sitting in a corner doing material assay tests every day.

Her office door opened for her, and she stopped dead in her tracks when she saw the pile of work on her desk. The stacks of flimsies, bit chips and reports had grown more than she thought they could have in a quick trip to the cafeteria. She sat at her desk and picked up a flimsy, scanning through it. When she left for the commissary, she had been only a week behind in her work. This one request alone would add at least another day to that. And that was just one. She dropped the flimsy back on the stack and scowled. She took another sip of coffee, set the mug to one side, and stabbed the call key to summon her assistant.

A moment or two later, she heard a timid rap at her door.

"In," she barked.

Her assistant, Vero, stuck his head past the door frame without actually crossing the threshold.

"You." She pointed one long finger in his direction, then swung her hand in an arc to indicate the frightening stack of new work on her desk. "Take a break, Saphia. You need to eat, Saphia. What could possible happen in a half hour, Saphia?"

At least he had the good grace to look sheepish about it. "Sorry, boss. But you were dead on your feet. You were getting that glazed look in your eyes that you get when your blood sugar is flatlining. You assigned Loa to do a new metal stress analysis on fragment D."

Saphia spread her hands, a look on her face. "So?"

"You called him Rael, and he's a biologicals tech."

"I did?" She frowned, then rolled her eyes and chuckled. "Okay, when you're right, you're right. But you're helping me triage this. Pull up a chair and pick a pile."

She waved a hand at all of the work on her desk and noticed a yellow taper of crystal weighing down a stack of flimsies. Where did that come from? But there was something familiar about it, something just at the edge of her thoughts that she couldn't quite...

"...boss? Calling planet Saphia."

She heard Vero's voice increase in volume, as if suddenly unmuffled. "What?"

"Where did you go?" he asked. "It looked like you just took a break from your body there, for about a minute."

She shook her head. "I must be more tired than I thought. Maybe it's the caffeine hitting me." She moved the crystal out of the way and pushed the pile in his direction. "Start in on these."

He shook his head. "Sorry, boss. Old Icicle Dick called for you just before you got back. Said it was urgent, and you were to call him the second you got back."

Saphia grunted. The last thing she needed right now was to talk to Bach. "What did he want?"

"He doesn't inform lowly techs like me of his grand and glorious plans. You'll have to get it from him. Ping me when you're done, and I'll help you with that." He half-heartedly waved at the unsorted pile of new work and left her alone to face Bach's call.

She asked Humana, the lab's AI, to connect her to Bach's office and the Security Chief's image appeared before here. Gods, she thought, the man even holos uptight.

"Valme."

"Why good day, Chief. What can I do for you today?" As usual, he missed her sarcasm completely.

"Anything new from the Market?"

"I have the reports on my desk. When I've gone over them, I'll transfer them, along with my recommendations, to your office." Like I always do, she thought.

She could see his pinched face begin to settle into a glower. Not that it makes much difference. The thought made her want to smile, but she managed to keep her face neutral.

"I want full spectrum autopsies done on the bodies of the dead Sotars."

"What for?" she asked, frowning. "Is there something I don't know?"

"The First Mind believes that the terrorists survived the teleport due to some form of chemical stimulation or interference."

Saphia noted how the First Mind's title sounded like an epithet when it came from Bach's mouth.

"That makes sense," she said. "They've never survived the teleport long enough to act up until now. I knew some new wrinkle was on the table. I'll have my team run the scans."

"Also, I want complete testing and upgrading of the security subroutines in the Technarch's AI, to begin immediately."

She hadn't even noticed the knife until he slipped it in, and she thought some of her favourite curses. "With all due respect, Chief, I designed those subroutines myself. Implemented by a Class Four AI like Qoios, they're the best there is."

Bach's face could have been carved of granite. "Make them better."

The holo fragmented and was gone.

"Why, you freeze-dried, techno-fascist gun monkey," she spat. She did a slow, calming count to ten, with deep breaths in between and felt slightly less murderous. "Humana, get me a priority override uplink to Qoios and clear my schedule for the afternoon."

Bach leaned back in his chair, feeling the stab of a headache begin in his temples. A fragment of a smile formed on his face when he thought of Valme's reaction to his last order. Served the overconfident squint right. She needed to be taken down a notch or two. Not like Shen. Quiet, confident Shen had been the best, brightest, fiercest light in his life, a developer in an outlying lab testing security tech for Brighter Light's weapons division. Lithe, muscular Shen who had loved him and been ruthlessly efficient in their bed.

A new ache started in his scar, melding with the ache in his heart, as fresh and raw as if it were new. He realized his head had fallen forward into his hand. He straightened his neck and the pull of the damaged skin eased. He allowed himself a moment of diamond hard, frustrated grief, then ruthlessly shut it off, reshaping it into anger and resolve. The Sotar mindfreaks had cost him his family, the Onestra, shattering the family line forever at Rhokhara Canyon. His skill at security had saved him from disgrace, allowing him to join the Bach line, while others wallowed in their hatred of the Adisi.

But Mordren Bach knew the truth. It was not the Adisi that were to blame. No, the fault lay squarely in Sotari. In what they had done. When Deathmind attacked for the first time, Bach was not surprised. He knew where they came from, knew their history. As far as he was concerned, the mindfreaks were finally just showing their true nature. He knew too well the bloody details of the Fauxmosome Revolt and the death left in its wake. Sotars were killers, as simple as that. It was grafted into their genetic make-up as surely as the nano had been. They were all cut from the same cloth in Bach's eyes, one he hoped one day to see eradicated for good. He had been proud to serve Brighter Light against the Psi threat, but it had not proven near as easy as he had thought.

Frustration rose in him at their failure to deal with the situation quickly. His people, usually an elite, efficient force, were barely holding their own. No matter what progress was made, eventually it would fall by the wayside as new threats emerged. The constant "two steps forward, three steps back" was wearing on them all, but on Bach especially.

And now, without Shen, who had been his anchor through the worst of it all, he wondered how he would stay in control. On the worst days, the days when his borderline obsessive nature had caused him to miss some pertinent detail, some telling clue, she had always been able to cut through it all and get straight to the heart of the matter, calming him with her quiet, wise manner.

Unwillingly, despite all his efforts to forget, he flashed back to that day at her lab. Shen as he had last seen her, on the stretcher. The medics had just pronounced her dead, her brain pulped and torn apart. He saw again the dull laxness of her face, marred by a single strand of spittle at the corner of her mouth. Everything she had been, everything they were together, gone.

Bach slammed his fist onto the desk, trying to beat the memory into submission. The explosion of pain in his hand was a welcome change from the dull throb in his heart. Anything to keep that gruesome, tranquil image from his mind. He stabbed at the commo, connecting with his aide.

"I want all furloughs and passes cancelled," he snarled. "I want every officer and reservist on active duty immediately."

In a corner of Bach's mind, even as he spoke, lurked a nagging fear that it would do no good.

CHAPTER NINE

K eene slipped his gown open and turned away from the doctor, who ran the peripheral sensor of the probe over his bare back. The movement of her hand was deft and practiced, covering the newly grown skin in an even back and forth motion. When she was finished with her scan of Keene's back, she tapped him lightly on the shoulder.

"All done," she said, closing and stowing the probe. "You can cover up. The tissues have healed completely, no scarring or impairment. There may be some sensory disruption for the first day or so, but it will fade."

"You mean like an army of bugs doing the samba under my skin?" Keene said as he rearranged and tied his flimsy gown.

"That would be it. But from what I can see, all the nerves are healing properly, so it should pass quickly. I'll authorize your release," she said, offering her hand. "I don't anticipate any problems, but feel free to contact me if there's anything at all."

"I will, Doctor. Thank you."

With a final smile, she put her hands in the pockets of her lab coat and left. Keene hopped down off the examining table and reached for the shirt and trousers Daevin had left for him while he slept, removing the burned rags that were all that was left of his other clothes. Keene slipped out of the gown and picked up the shirt, the fabric cool and soft against his fingers. Before he could put it on, the door chimed to announce a visitor. "Come in."

Daevin hesitantly entered, remaining close to the door, unsure whether to come closer.

"Hi," he said, looking like the shy boy that Keene had loved so long ago.

"Hi, yourself," Keene answered, smiling, but feeling oddly

modest as he held the shirt over his crotch. There was a pause as Daevin fidgeted with the small bag he carried.

"How are you?"

Keene flexed his arms, exploring his range of motion. "All better. Though I've had two showers, and I still feel like I've got regen goo all over me."

They laughed together a moment, but the sound seemed stilted and clumsy to them both. They had so much to say to each other, and yet neither knew how to broach the subject.

"Do you like the clothes?" Daevin asked, seizing on niceties as a way out.

"They're beautiful. Thank you." Keene seemed suddenly to realize that he wasn't actually wearing anything, and slipped his arm into the shirt's sleeve.

"Wait. I thought you'd want these. I had to pull a few strings to get them past security..." His voice trailed off, and he berated himself silently for sounding like he was bragging about his power.

Keene reached into the bag Daevin offered and felt his steelskin and his gun. He pulled out the steelskin and was deeply relieved to have it back, having felt naked and unsafe without it. Not to mention foolish for not having worn it that morning at the Market. "Thank you."

"I thought you might want it after..." Shut up, Daevin, just shut up and get your foot out of your mouth.

Keene slipped on the shimmery quicksilver garment, ran his finger along the seam, and felt it seal and solidify on his body. Satisfied, he put on the rest of his clothes and cinched the straps of his holster to his thigh, feeling safer already. He quick-drew the gun once to check the release mechanism and replaced it. He hugged Daevin, who returned the embrace tightly, almost desperately.

"I thought I was going to lose you again, for good this time," Daevin murmured, his voice muffled by the curve of Keene's shoulder. "I don't know what I would do if that happened."

Keene clung tightly, kissing Daevin's temple and brushing his lips along the outer curve of his ear. "Let's get out of here."

Reluctantly, they broke apart, Daevin opening the door and following Keene out of the room. They walked out of the Med-Centre side by side, their upper arms occasionally brushing against each other. They didn't speak much, but still they were intensely aware of the comfort of each other's presence.

The streets were stained wet from recent rain, but the dark clouds, fringed with early evening light, were well on the way to breaking up. The air was heavily scented with moisture, and the bands of a rainbow were beginning to form in the distance. Keene closed his eyes and inhaled, greedily filling his lungs. Daevin stopped two steps lower on the stairs, and turned his face to Keene, puzzlement in his eyes.

Keene opened his eyes and looked at Daevin, sensing his concern. How do I explain this to you, he thought, how do I tell you how much more beautiful it looks? How do I tell you how much I feel? How much I...

In the end, he shook his head and continued down the steps to the limousine.

As they rode back, Daevin made the holo-field completely clear, transforming the limo into an open carriage. They sat side by side, hands tightly entwined as the setting sun ignited the colours of twilight.

The only thing missing was the scent of the rain.

Back in his suite, Daevin fussed over his choices for their evening meal. Simply choosing the music had taken five minutes, but now the delicate whispers of an alto wind harp wafted from the speakers all around the suite. Keene had succumbed to the urge to bathe again. The itching was indeed fading already, but he still felt slimy from the regen tank.

"And we'll finish with the mocha almond mousse," he said finally, completing the menu.

"Very good, sei," Qoios replied. "The meal will be ready in eight minutes."

"Thank you, Qoios." Daevin went to the bar and poured two glasses of a fiery red liquor Lexa-Blue had told him Keene liked. Carrying them to the open bathroom door, he peeked in.

Keene lay in the immense tub, his arms extended along the polished stone rim. His head was tilted back, his eyes closed. The dark skin of his upper body stood out in sharp contrast to the pure white of the stone. Below the water line at his nipples, the rest of his body rippled as light refracted. Daevin stood for a moment, taking in the lean, corded muscles of his arms, the broad curve of shoulder, and the smooth line of his neck.

I think I love him, Daevin thought. The notion unsettled him after all the years they had spent apart. All the years when he rarely thought of Keene at all, and when he did, as nothing more than a fond remembrance. To have these feelings rush back at him again left him disarmed and unsure where to tread; how to handle it.

"Knock, knock," he said.

Keene's head came up, and he opened his eyes, giving Daevin a loose, lazy grin. Daevin walked over, sitting on the raised rim of the tub. He offered one of the glasses to Keene, who took it and downed half. Daevin tasted his and coughed as it burned at the back of his throat.

Keene laughed and patted Daevin's thigh with a damp hand. "It's an acquired taste."

"It would have to be," Daevin said, hoarsely, pouring the contents of his glass into Keene's. Keene took another long swallow and ran a hand through the tightly curled stubble of his hair.

"This music is beautiful," he said, his eyes closed as he savoured both the music and the alcohol. "Who is it?"

"Runa Tomen," Daevin answered, his voice suddenly colourless.

"She's very talented."

"Yes, she was."

Keene looked up at Daevin, hearing something painful and unsaid in the simple sentence. "Who was she, Daevin? What happened to her?"

"She was a friend." Daevin looked away, deep, unhealed grief etched on his face. "The first time I heard her play was on the streets of Sotari, on one of my first trips to meet with Elai. We were just getting to know one another, to build some kind of trust between us that might bring about peace. Runa was on a street corner, playing a wind harp that had been in her family for generations. She looked like a lost little urchin, sitting on an old hand-carved stool, but the expression on her face was pure bliss, as if nothing else in the world mattered but the music.

"I could feel I was missing something, some kind of hole in the music, like an orchestra missing instruments. Elai told me later that Runa was also broadcasting with her mind, weaving colours and emotions in her listeners as well. I caught only the barest hint of the mental part of her performance, and it was still the most beautiful thing I had ever heard. I watched as people stopped to listen, and I noticed that before they walked on, they would close their eyes for a minute and Runa's smile would brighten just a touch and she would nod. Elai explained that the people were offering meals or a place to stay in exchange for a performance. When she took a break, I offered her a trip to Brighter Light for recordings of her work. I remember she looked a little surprised and hesitant, but I think Elai's presence calmed her and she agreed. I showed her everything I could, though the only things that seemed to interest her pertained to music, and in return, she recorded every piece of music she knew."

Daevin paused, unshed tears glittering in his eyes. "She was on a shuttle home with a delegation. SCI arranged for the shuttle's fuel cells to rupture on take-off, killing everyone on board."

"I'm so sorry, Daevin," Keene whispered, taking Daevin's hand and kissing it lightly.

Daevin ground away the tears with the heel of his free hand. "I know. But that's the thing. Ask anyone either here or in Sotari, and they have a similar story. None of us are untouched by this. We've all become far too familiar with this kind of loss. All Elai and I want is a chance for our people to heal." He drew in a deep breath and when he spoke, his voice was even again. "No more stories like this."

Keene looked away, pensive a moment before he spoke.

"Look, you know how I feel about your methods in getting me here. The less said about that, the better. But I think I understand a little more than I did before. I'm sorry if I said anything to hurt you." He paused, turning to look Daevin in the eyes. "When I saw that terrorist coming for you, I went crazy, I was so scared. I thought I was going to lose you again. I want you to know that I love you. I don't know what it means for us, but I do. And when we get this sorted out, I hope we get a chance to find out."

Daevin pulled him close and kissed him, stronger and more passionately than ever before.

"Your dinner is ready," Qoios announced, repeating the message once before discreetly turning es attention elsewhere.

❖

Keene stood on the terrace outside Daevin's suite, looking at the dark curtain of pelting rain beyond the wall, though the terrace remained completely dry for some reason. He looked around, feeling hazy and disoriented. The sinuous, white statues were now grey and twisted into the embodiment of torment. The water in the pool was murky and dark. He searched the terrace for some sign of life, calling Daevin's name.

Suddenly someone was at the wall, and Keene's heart leaped. He took a step forward, hoping it was Daevin. The figure turned and Keene stopped, stunned.

It was the pyrokinetic from the market.

Keene grabbed for his gun, drawing and firing on instinct. Time slowed, allowing Keene to see the path of energy from the gun's barrel, crawling toward its target. The air around him became gluey, almost solid. Keene realized with horror that the pyro had changed, becoming Daevin, naked and aroused.

Keene screamed in his mind, watching the lance of energy move ever closer through the gelid air. He saw shocked, betrayed hurt on Daevin's face for a second before the beam struck, shearing away the left side of Daevin's head.

The body collapsed to the stone in a spatter of bone and blood. Keene felt his throat close up, strangling the scream in his mouth until he thought his head would burst.

Insanely, impossibly, Daevin's corpse began to stand. When it was upright, it staggered toward Keene, arms open. The shattered mouth began to move.

"...love you...love you...love you..."

The grisly croon burned into Keene's mind.

"...love you...love you...love you..."

Keene tried to run, tried even to move, but the air encased him like amber. Daevin was opening his arms, a parody of a tender embrace. His face came horribly close to Keene's showing blood and spittle around the bruised ruin of his mouth.

When the torn lips touched his, Keene found his voice and began to scream.

❖

Daevin straddled Keene's thrashing body, struggling to pin him to the bed.

"Keene, wake up!" he shouted, trying to hold him still and shake him awake at the same time. Keene didn't respond, still struggling and screaming. "Qoios, medical emergency."

Again, Daevin felt terror, slithering and wet, in his stomach. Not now, damn it, not again. I won't lose you again. Keene clipped his chin with one flailing arm, bruising the bone and making his eyes water. He felt himself beginning to lose the battle against Keene's taut, hysterical strength.

He dimly heard the sound of his door opening and then Elai was at his side. Immediately, Keene's struggles lessened. No, Daevin realized, not lessened exactly. Every muscle in Keene's body was still tight as a drum. He felt the surge across the barest edge of his mind as Elai telekinetically held Keene still. He saw her cup Keene's head in her hands, fingers at his temples. Ugly distended veins marked his skin, dark under her pale hands.

(Someone is forcing the nightmares into his mind.)

Can you stop it? Daevin thought, knowing she would hear.

(I can try.)

Daevin stepped back from the bed when Elai broke contact. Keene's body went suddenly still, and Daevin feared that he was dead. Only when Elai went still as well did Daevin relax ever so slightly. If she was in there with him, he would be all right. He had to be.

❖

Elai tumbled down a screaming tunnel of wind. She concentrated, preventing disorientation as the tornado of mental torment whirled around her. She steadied the projection of her thoughts, plunging down, sensing the barrier her foe had set up to keep her out. Focusing her will into the sharpest of blades, Elai immersed herself in Keene's nightmare, finding herself on the terrace, whipped by rain. The storm passed through her, ephemeral. She searched for Keene, finding him huddled on the other side of the terrace. He was surrounded by broken, ghoulish, replicas of Daevin clutching, grabbing at him. Each time he fired his weapon or knocked one aside, another would close on him, and the one he had shot dragged itself up to come for him again.

Elai felt the miasma of Keene's tortured emotions slam her like a fist. She reshaped her shield and moved closer, sweeping the golems aside with her mind, erasing their existence. Some of them turned to attack her, but she ignored them, giving them no power. One by one they fell away, ceasing to be as she passed them.

As they grew fewer and fewer, she began to sense the sickly bile-greenness of the dream maker's influence. She altered the tone of her shield, blocking the touch of the nightmare, parrying the energy like a sword. He is good, she thought.

But not good enough.

With a surge of strength, she enclosed Keene within the womb of her shield. The fierce storm attacking them abated suddenly as the enemy mind retreated. The sickening feel of his presence faded, but Elai sensed the tortured riot left in Keene's mind. She seized the last simulacrum of Daevin, catching it just as it began to fade. She wrapped it in light and healed it, making it whole. Infusing it with all she knew of Daevin, all of the warmth and love she had sensed between them, she made it hold Keene, touch him, soothe him. She felt Keene finally begin to relax, sensed the walls of the dream begin to lose substance. Finally, she retreated, smoothing the frayed edges of Keene's mind as she went, knitting his soul back together.

Back in the physical world, she kept her hands against Keene's head, guiding him back. The strain of her exertion made her light-headed, and she gulped air. Her vision swam for a second, then cleared, and she saw Keene's eyes flutter open. She smiled at him and turned to Daevin. She saw the relief in his eyes when he made eye contact with Keene, and saw him start to move.

In her weakened state, she did not sense the imminent arrival of the intruder until the teleporter appeared at Daevin's side. His altered, chemically driven mind burned suddenly across hers like an acrid, acid star.

In the instant she shielded from him and reached out, he clutched Daevin's arm, and Elai saw a glint of silver in the hand he held to Daevin's temple. Daevin's eyes rolled up into his head and before Elai or Keene could react, they were gone.

CHAPTER TEN

Blue, help. Now. was all Keene could manage through the haze in his head.

Alarms were already screaming, even before the air displacement left by the teleporter had begun to fade. Still disoriented from his ordeal, Keene tried a feeble lunge from the bed, only to land heavily on the floor. Daevin and his kidnapper were long gone.

"Qoios, get Bach and Jaekir down here at once," Elai shouted. She waved a hand sharply, and the bleat of the alarm klaxon faded.

"A Security team and investigation unit is on the way. Please remain calm and disturb nothing." Qoios's tone remained completely neutral. "Consul Jaekir has been notified as well."

"What happened?" Keene asked. Elai heard fatigue in his voice and felt his fear and confusion in cold, clammy waves.

"It was nothing but a diversion. They get me to focus on you, and then send one of their drugged suicide teleporters in to take Daevin."

Keene opened his mouth to speak, but the door opened and security personnel flooded the room, silencing him. Within moments, Daevin's bedroom was a hive of precise, controlled activity. Guards were stationed at the door, and the forensics team was going over the room with an array of scanner modules. Keene was aware he was naked, but any potential embarrassment seemed too trivial to matter as the technician applied sensor patches to his body with the same dispassion one would show the furniture. Beside him, Elai endured the same indignity. They exchanged a look of solidarity. Keene realized in that moment she was not just someone Daevin knew; she had become a friend in her own right. He owed her for saving him, and wasn't about to forget it.

He was allowed to dress, and they were escorted to the technarch's office. Behind them, the scan team continued their methodical search.

When Keene and Elai arrived at Daevin's office, Jaekir was there. The older man looked rumpled and small, obviously having been roused from sleep. He looked up at them as they entered, and Keene saw immediately the air of smugness was gone from the diplomat, leaving him looking old and worried. Keene wondered if the concern was for Daevin as a person or merely for the political ramifications of his disappearance.

"Come in, please." Jaekir's voice was calm, and his eyes were clear and hyper-alert despite the late hour. "We're just waiting for Valme and Bach."

Keene turned away, feeling a penetrating ache, like the phantom pain of a severed limb. He wandered the room aimlessly as they waited, stopping by the floating globe. With a listless touch of his hand, it spun slowly on its null-grav field. Brighter Light and Sotari alternated beneath his hand, stylized patches of colour. You came so close, Little Prince. You almost found a way to make it work. And me, he thought. I was just hanging on, waiting for the rollercoaster to pull in to the terminal. And now we might not get a second chance. He swiped at the globe, making it tilt and spin crazily. He turned away from it and went to stand by Elai, who sat quietly in the familiar leather chair, stiff and straight.

The door hissed open, and all three of them turned to see the new arrivals. Keene nodded at Bach, who ignored him and strode to Jaekir's side. Behind him, Valme looked distracted, her brow furrowed as she tried to secure the clasp holding her hair back. Before the door could close, they heard hard, pelting footsteps in the hall.

Lexa-Blue came through the door like a lighting bolt, searching for Keene. When she spotted him, she made a beeline for him, and he rose to meet her.

Bach stepped between them. "This is a restricted briefing, miss," he said coldly, clamping a hand on her arm.

Lexa-Blue twisted out of his grip with ease and reversed it, bending his fingers back with just enough force to make him wince, without causing any permanent harm. For a second, Bach was too stunned to react, but then his face contorted into a snarl. He drew his hand back to strike, but Lexa-Blue had already let him go and stepped back into a defensive posture.

"Bach!" Jaekir's voice was sharp and authoritative. "She is here on my authority. Let her be."

Bach curled his lip and stepped back, rubbing his fingers but not relaxing one bit. His eyes never left her.

Lexa-Blue matched his glare, standing at Keene's side. "Don't ever get between me and one of my friends again," she warned, her voice flat.

Bach's look grew even colder, sheer hatred in his eyes. Only another stern look from Jaekir prevented a brawl.

She turned to Keene, and her tone was suddenly warm and resonant with worry. "Are you okay? I went to Daevin's suite, but you'd already left."

"I'm okay."

"Please, tell us what happened," Jaekir asked, trying to defuse the tension in the room and get the meeting back on track. "Qoios, record everything."

Elai went first, having a more complete account of the incident. Despite having repeated the story several times already, she told it again in concise, unemotional terms, even though her feelings showed on her face. When she was finished, Jaekir looked to Keene, who added his own sketchy version of events. He stumbled slightly over the details of the dream, hating having Bach see into his heart and mind that closely. He concluded with coming awake just in time to see Daevin's abduction. Jaekir, Bach, and Valme listened intently.

"All right," Jaekir said, frowning. "The first question is: how did they get past our shields. Bach?"

Bach shook his head, scowling. "I ordered a complete shield recoding and upgrading of all security subroutines in the palace. It should have been sufficient to keep any intruders out."

Saphia spoke up, her tone sharp at Bach's implied accusation of failure. "I supervised those procedures myself, and they tested one hundred percent nominal. The shields and upgrades were at peak function."

Bach snorted. "Until they failed."

"I'd stake my life on those shields, Bach," Saphia snapped. "They did not fail."

"Maybe if your life was at stake here, we could expect some results."

"Be that as it may," Jaekir said, cutting off the escalating argument. "We still need to know how this kidnapper broke through our defenses."

Saphia relaxed back into her chair. "If it was Brighter Light we were dealing with, I'd say they used a self-erasing codeworm. It goes through the system like an access code and scrubs all traces of its passage, so we have no idea where it comes from. But we're dealing with Sotars. They're almost completely ignorant of computers. They don't have the technical knowledge of our systems or our coding to pull something like that off. They're just not smart enough." She stopped suddenly, aware of the racist overtones of what she had said and looked at Elai, genuinely contrite. "Forgive me, First Mind, please. I meant no offense."

Elai smiled, well aware of the pressure they were all under. "None taken."

Saphia continued. "What I meant was that to develop and execute a codeworm would take someone with my level of training and experience. Unless some secret computer training is going on in Sotari, there must be some other explanation."

Something in her description tweaked Keene's memory. "Wait a minute. I'd forgotten," he said, the words tumbling out of him in a rush. "When we were at the market the other day, the pyrokinetic I killed went after Daevin with a neural stunner. I saw him right before I shot him and passed out. It didn't make any sense at the time. Why would he need a stunner?"

After a moment of silence, Elai spoke. "This stunner, what does it look like?"

"A cylinder about so long," Keene said, using his hands to demonstrate. "Silver, with a black grip and a bluish energy discharge at the tip."

"The one who took Daevin had one of those as well. I was so drained from helping you, I just assumed that the terrorist used his psi to render Daevin unconscious, but now that I know what I was seeing, that was what he used." Elai's normally even voice hummed with excitement at the suddenly clear memory, then her smile faded suddenly. "Which means…"

Lexa-Blue finished the thought. "Someone could be working in collusion with Deathmind, providing materiel and quite possibly codes as well. You have turncoats in your midst."

Jaekir sat quietly, pondering and looking straight at Elai. Their eyes met in silent acknowledgment that this startling conclusion had to be true.

"As much as I wish it were not true, there seems to be no other explanation," Elai said. "Ever since this all began, we in Sotari have wondered how SCI knew our weaknesses so well. They attacked us with the trappings of technology: energy weapons and psionic jamming, but their knowledge of our society and vulnerabilities was too specific, too detailed. It never occurred to me that we were being betrayed by our own." The depth of Elai's sense of betrayal was brutally clear on her face.

"So we know we have traitors on both sides." Bach's tone was contemptuous. "That doesn't change a thing. The Technarch's kidnapping is an act of war. We should be mobilizing everything we have to go in there and get him back."

Lexa-Blue looked at him, her gaze cool and level. "Did you ever stop to think that maybe that's exactly what they want you to do? That if you go in there guns blazing, you'll lose not only Daevin, but everything he and Elai have worked for?"

"That's ridiculous!" Bach snorted.

"Is it?" Keene jumped in, taking up Lexa-Blue's argument. "Are you so sure that if you declare war on Sotari, you'll win? And even if you win, trust me, you lose. The Galactum will come down on you with all their power."

"Bach, you narrow-minded Neanderthal, think," Saphia burst out. "They're right."

Bach's scowl deepened as he contemplated the idea, seeing the logic of it and hating that they were right. Reluctant acceptance of what they were saying dawned on his face. Before he could voice it, however, his eyes glazed over and a voice that was not his spoke from his mouth.

"Through this vessel, I speak for Deathmind, the Voice of All Sotar."

They all looked to Elai for confirmation, and she nodded, her face set and grim.

"Your aggression against the Sotar must end. You have left us no choice but to act."

There was a brief pause before the speaker resumed.

"Daevin Adisi, Technarch of Brighter Light, has committed capital crimes against the Sotar. He has been tried, convicted, and executed for these crimes. He met his death with honour. Deathmind, the Voice of All Sotar, has spoken."

Bach's head drooped forward to his chest, then sprang up, his expression showing he was all too aware of what had just happened. His cheeks were flushed and angry, in counterpoint to the shock and grief that showed on the others' faces in the horrified silence that followed.

As he tried to process the information, Keene's face was blank, his mouth slightly open. Beside him, Lexa-Blue squeezed his shoulder tightly and muttered, "Shit." Elai sat straight, her face buried in her hands, while Jaekir looked crumpled and old, tears welling up in his eyes. With great, visible effort, he pulled himself together.

"Well, it would seem our decision is made for us," he said, his voice laden with sadness. "Qoios, confirm identities, Amory Jaekir and Mordren Bach."

There was a second of silence.

"All identity metrics confirmed. Emergency Powers Protocol engaged. Transfer of command functions complete."

"Very well," Jaekir said. "Chief Bach, inform the Technarchy Board and arrange security for a meeting. See to it that your people are in place and ready. I want this as orderly and controlled as possible. Until succession is determined, Brighter Light is under martial law."

Elai looked up at him, her eyes red, her gaze troubled. "Amory, think carefully. Are you certain you have no other options?"

Jaekir shook his head sadly. "None, I'm afraid. Our laws are very clear. If a Technarch dies violently without a named successor, the Emergency Powers Protocol is engaged until the next Technarch can be appointed, and it is proven none of the other families were involved. Security is granted discretionary powers to see that the killers are brought to justice."

"Which in this case," Elai said, each word barbed, "is tantamount to a declaration of war against my people."

Jaekir blanched. "I assure you, First Mind, I have not a little influence in these matters, and I shall do everything in my power to make sure that does not happen. But, please, if you will excuse me. We must make arrangements."

He gestured at the door, as polite a dismissal as could be managed in the awkward circumstances. Elai rose from her chair, straightening in the air. Everything about her posture radiated disdain, down to the briefest flick of the edge of her gown as it caught in the currents of air. She turned above the chair and moved through air made suddenly regal and cold. With nothing else to do, Keene and Lexa-Blue followed.

Outside, Elai turned to them, her body taut with fury. "They have no idea what they may have unleashed here. Daevin would never have allowed this to…"

Her voice trailed off and an odd expression came over her face. She held up her hand for silence and tilted her head, as if listening for a sound that might not even be there. She creased her brow and closed her eyes for a second, then re-opened them. "Please, forgive me, my friends. There is something I must look into."

She turned and glided away in silence.

Lexa-Blue turned to Keene, and saw her own shock and sadness etched on his face. She laid her hand on the back of his neck and pulled his forehead down to touch hers. It rested there a moment until he pulled away.

"I don't think you can fix this one, Blue," he said, his voice choked and quiet. With his grief thudding through her node, he turned from her and walked away.

CHAPTER ELEVEN

K eene walked, driven by a maze of cold, blind sorrow. To have come so far, to have felt so much in so short a time and lose it all, seemed more than he could bear. Eventually, he came to a long, shaded walkway that followed the entire girth of the building along the perimeter of the walls, passing by the panorama of the city-state and ending up along the seawall. The tone-on-tone blue of the ocean and sky spread before him, filling his field of vision, and the sheer immensity of it held him. He stood for a long time looking out at the vista of endless water beneath him, held at bay by the sheer rock face. Above, the sky was split by the burning, bright sun.

Earth, air, fire, and water, he thought, once upon a time believed to be the basic elements of life. A theory long ago replaced by quantum mechanics, which still holds a simple fascination for us. Primal, he realized. Something so basic and simple that it survives as myth despite all the scientific evidence to the contrary.

Grief is primal too, he thought, realizing it deep in his heart. The kind of grief that blots everything else out, making you want to scream your rage at fate until your voice cracks and your lungs ache with rage. Loss so sudden and unfair that no logic, no rational thought can ease it.

He found himself remembering years earlier when he had seen signals sent back by the Hawking Project, the first deep probe of a black hole. He had watched, fascinated as the probe fell deeper into the hyper-gravity of the hole, the neutron shielded scanners recording and transmitting its own descent to destruction. Faster and faster the probe had fallen, deeper into the churning maw, recording the death of matter and light. Then the probe hit the event horizon, capturing the initial seconds of its own demise in one final tachyon burst.

Between the sky and the sea, Keene's grief opened up before him, yawning black like that probe's grave. His rational mind told him that it would pass. Someday the loss would ebb, and he would remember all the beautiful things he and Daevin had shared. It told him that the hurt would become manageable, but deep inside his very cells, his body denied it.

He screamed then, a howl of rage and misery that tore at his heart; screamed until his throat burned, not caring who might hear. But the cry trickled away to nothing more than a faint tremolo.

For nothing had changed. Daevin was still dead and, no doubt, others would die senseless deaths at destiny's hand. And I'm still alive, he thought, with a lot to do before I go. He sagged onto a nearby bench, exhausted from the unbearable weight of his feelings.

Keene?

Yes, Vrick?

I'm sorry about your friend. I've been listening in, Vrick said. *Sorry.*

That's okay. Keene always knew that Vrick was there, observing, feeling what Keene and Lexa-Blue experienced in their small, frail flesh.

I know how you feel.

Keene recognized in his friend's voice an unquestionable knowledge of what Keene felt. He knew es voice was generated by a body of metals, ceramics, and plastic, a body that could bear the depths of space, and spoken by a being made of software and code more sophisticated than anything humankind had created in almost two centuries. Despite all this, he knew the searing pain of grief was shared by all living, thinking beings shared, no matter their origin.

Is there anything I can do?

No, but thanks.

Okay. You know where I am.

Even through Vrick no longer spoke, Keene felt the link, warm and open between them, opening to include Lexa-Blue. Faintly, he heard the quiet strains of one of his favourite pieces of music, a lullaby, through his node. *Thank you.*

Through the beginning of cathartic tears, Keene smiled.

❖

Elai's eyes snapped open as her meditation shattered. She gulped air to clear her head. Let that be a lesson to you, she thought. The rituals are there for a reason. She breathed evenly and regularly for a moment to calm her body as her mind raced.

I was right, she thought. I must tell Keene and Lexa-Blue. She lifted from her kneeling position and glided from the room, not even bothering to dismantle her meditation circle. She stopped a moment in the hall. Don't get ahead of yourself. "Qoios, where are Keene and Lexa-Blue?"

"Sei Ota Chiaro is on the one of the terraces on sea side of the complex, and Sei Lexa-Blue is on the patio where you take your breakfast," Qoios told her.

The patio is closer, she thought, angling the flow of her body through the air in that direction. Minutes later, she burst through the door and saw Lexa-Blue slouching on one of the chairs, bottle on the table beside her, glass in hand.

(Daevin is alive) She saw Lexa-Blue wince at the brusque outburst of thought, and paused to collect herself. "Daevin is alive."

Lexa-Blue looked sceptical, but Elai ploughed on. "We have been friends for years, I would know if he was dead, I would have sensed it. I know what that emptiness feels like in my mind."

"Why didn't you sense it before?" Lexa-Blue asked.

Elai shook her head. "Even I have my limits. Between rescuing Keene from the 'path attack and everything else, I wasn't thinking clearly, but I sensed something I couldn't put my finger on. Once I had time to think and meditate, I was able to see his presence is still out there somewhere. We have to find him. Come on."

Lexa-Blue stood, her face uncertain. She took Elai's arm and stopped her before she could dash off again. "Are you sure? I don't want you setting Keene up for a fall. I won't let that happen, do you understand?"

Elai opened her mind to hers and Lexa-Blue felt the absolute certainty there, like a hand squeezed tightly in her own. "I give you my word. Daevin is alive. There is no doubt. Now, come. We have to tell Keene."

"I can do that from here." *Up and at 'em, partner,* she 'pushed. *Elai says Daevin's alive, so get your ass down here, pronto.*

❖

By the time she hit the lab, Saphia was in a towering fury. After the announcement of the Technarch's death and the declaration of martial law, she had sat stunned for several minutes while everyone left and Jaekir went about his business. Jaekir finally noticed her several calls later, still in her chair. He had said some warm, comforting words, but she had not heard them. He had suggested she get some rest but, overcome by shock and anger, she came straight to the lab. At his desk, Vero merely watched her go by, unaware of all that had transpired, thinking it nothing more than one of her occasional outbursts. He called up her schedule for the afternoon, already planning how to rearrange the appointments.

"Vero, clear my afternoon," came her angry voice over the intercommo.

"Right away, boss," he answered, the task already halfway complete.

Saphia sat at her desk, arms outstretched, palms flat on the surface of the desk, trying to calm the visceral rage that gripped her. She breathed deeply several times, until she felt able to form coherent sentences. Again, she saw the yellow crystal on her desk. Light sparked from its surface and sudden, horrible memories poured through her, triggering a wave of nausea.

And she knew.

Sweat broke out on her skin as she struggled to calm the sick dread in her stomach. "Humana, give me complete privacy, all recorders off, all uplinks suspended until further notice."

"Privacy engaged, uplinks suspended," Humana said, a tinge of curiosity in es voice.

When her holo display flashed confirmation, she picked up the crystal, laying it across her palms as she suddenly knew to do. Light from it refracted a sickly yellow, making her skin sallow and clammy. The light from the stone brightened and pulsed like something alive. She closed her eyes, calling with her mind in a way she knew, yet had never consciously been taught. The image unfolded slowly in her mind, inhibited by her anger, but finally, she could open her eyes, the crystal forming the mental imagery through her optic nerves, showing her a man that seemed to sit just across the desk from her.

"Bodi." Her voice was dead with anger.

A bitter, faded scent of regret filled her mind, but Saphia didn't believe it for a minute.

"What the hell happened? You guaranteed the Technarch's safety in return for the codes," she said with a surge of anger. Inside, the thought that she might have been partially responsible for his death made her feel sick.

Bodi shrugged, the gesture smooth and helpless. Once again, the regret filled her mind, an image of white, virtuous innocence surrounding Bodi. She felt a dull ache in her limbs, and recognized it as a reflection of his hurt that she didn't trust him.

The thoughts were couched in such sincerity, Saphia found herself yearning to believe him. Confusion washed over her, and she had no idea what to do. She had warned him what would happen if he double-crossed her, but could she really go through with it? She looked again at the image for some clue, something she had missed to make her decision easier.

Without warning, she had a flash of a thought and she saw through his charismatic facade. He's been playing me like a violin, she thought, horrified. This was how he planned it all along, and I played right into his hands. "You bastard," she hissed. "I told you that if anything happened to the Technarch, the life of your First Mind was forfeit. Did you think I was joking?!"

Bodi's shock and fear would have convinced her if she hadn't known the truth.

Pleading filled her mind, a pale violet cascade of drops that tumbled like rain hitting the ground at her feet. And the only actual words he spoke *(You can't do this.)*

"Watch me."

Saphia hurled the crystal away and it shattered against a metal table in the corner. Feeling the rage bubble up again, she began stabbing away at the keys of her board, accessing the security subroutines she had designed for Qoios. Just watch me.

Elsewhere, in a room with walls of sterile, cold rock, Bodi leaned back in his chair, relaxing his thoughts after the mind-link. His second-in-command, Simir, looked closely at his leader. A complex tangle of pride and commitment and doubt flowed from his mind, forming a question something like *(Do you really think she'll do it?)*

Bodi's mind smiled, his reaction cold and bleached, culminating in one thought as sharp as bladed glass.

(I'm counting on it.)

Chapter Twelve

Completing the security arrangements for Technarchy Board's meeting, Mordren Bach stood and stretched, his sigh coming out more like a snarl. He moved through a series of harsh, sparring blows for a few minutes to get the kinks out of his back, ending with a set of precise, savage kicks. The exercise left his back limber once again, but he still simmered with rage at his recent humiliation. To be used by the mindfreak assassins as a mouthpiece was almost more than he could bear. The incredible shame left him feeling exposed and dirty for all to see. Someone would pay for it, he was certain, and if he had his way, pay dearly.

The knife-edged thud of another headache was already beginning in his temples.

He tossed himself into his chair, and it spun. He followed the motion, letting it bring him full circle to face his desk. He hunched forward, his chin resting on his clenched fist, glowering at nothing. The angry wheels turning in his head were almost audible.

More than a day had elapsed since the Technarch's kidnapping, several hours since the announcement of his assassination, with not so much as the slightest lead. No witnesses other than the First Mind and the boyfriend, unreliable at best. No indications of the source of the security leak, no news from Valme. Nothing but dead ends wherever he looked.

And those fools on the Board would squabble over succession to the Technarchy like scavengers on a corpse. No direction or idea of what was best for Brighter Light, only concerned with their petty jockeying for power. They would spend so much time bickering that the Technarch's killers could attack the city again and again without them even ever reaching a decision.

Frustration rose in his gorge, thick and sour. As he had worked his way up through the ranks of Security, it had been so simple. Crimes, evidence, arrests, convictions. Question this person and detain that person. All were specific problems with specific solutions, not like the ghosts he was forced to chase these days. Nothing but wisps of fog, trails of smoke. Bach longed for an enemy he could see, someone he could face and subdue physically.

He longed for anything but these nameless, faceless killers who struck from the shadows and had lost the right to call themselves human anymore.

Bach took the Technarch's death personally, but not as the loss of a trusted friend or esteemed colleague. Bach saw Daevin as a possession, something that belonged to him. Bach took the violation of his security as a violation of himself, and such violations required retribution. Yet Bach had nowhere to direct his desire for vengeance. The Technarch was merely another loss in a game Bach had been losing for years.

And the one with the scar! Bach felt a new anger rise in him at the thought of her, intruding where she didn't belong, presuming to tell him that the Technarch's assassins were trying to goad him and his country into war. Still, he had to admit that the desire to go into Sotari and hunt down the assassins by force was almost overpowering. Is it even possible, he wondered.

The door chimed insistently, indicating someone to see him. Bach experienced a surge of irrational hope it was someone with some new lead. "Open."

His hopes were dashed when he saw the Technarch's lover, the one-eye, and the Sotar. Revulsion filled Bach's mind when he realized Elai hung suspended in the air before him, her eyes seemingly boring into his mind. "What?"

"Daevin's alive." The words exploded out of Keene's mouth.

Despite himself, Bach was out of his chair, leaning across his desk as his hope surge. "Where?"

Keene paused. "We don't know."

"Get out," Bach sneered.

"Elai can sense him."

A sound of disgust rumbled deep in Bach's throat. Keene turned to Elai for support.

"It is true," she stated, refusing to be baited. "Over the years of our relationship, Daevin and I have developed a rapport. If he had been killed, I would have sensed it. When I searched for him telepathically, I knew he was out there somewhere."

"But you don't know where?" Bach's tone was openly mocking now.

"There must be a powerful jammer shielding him. Or perhaps he is being held somewhere far away. I can't sense him directly." Bach's attitude was obviously straining her calm to its limits.

Bach looked away from them for a moment as if considering their information, then turned back toward them. "Get out of my office, now. And don't waste any more of my time with your pathetic Sotar superstition. Come back when you have some shred of evidence other than the word of...that. The Technarch is dead." Bach focused his attention on a sheaf of papers on his desk, shutting them out.

Elai leaned across Bach's desk, her voice ragged with controlled anger. "Am I correct in assuming, Chief Bach, that you intend to do nothing about this?"

Bach didn't even glance up. "That is correct."

"Then we will find him ourselves," Elai said, drawing herself up to her full regal stature, and enunciating every word. As she turned from him, Bach slammed his hand on his desk, stopping her.

"You will not!" Bach said tightly, each word precisely enunciated. He stabbed his commo on his desk. "Escort detail to my office, immediately."

She was too stunned to react.

"You will be escorted back to your quarters, where you will stay until the board makes a decision on how to proceed from here."

"I am still the First Mind, Chief Bach. You have no right..."

"Listen," he cut her off. "Under the Emergency Powers Protocol, I could lock you up and hold you there until the sun goes nova."

Two security agents, black-clad and heavily armed, entered the office and stood at attention. Bach's smile gleamed with cold satisfaction. "As it stands, I have every reason to believe that your life is in danger. SCI may attempt to kill you in reprisal for the Technarch's death. I'm placing you in protective custody in your suite until I'm confident you are out of danger."

He gestured at her escorts and they stepped forward to usher her out. As the one on the left reached for her arm, the very air between them warped with a sound like metal buckling, shoving both of the security agents away. They looked confused as they struggled against the force keeping them away from her.

Elai looked down at Bach, raising one warning finger. "Tread carefully, Chief. Very carefully."

She turned and swept from the room. As she passed them, the force holding her escorts lessened and, after a quick glance at Bach for confirmation, they followed Elai, keeping a respectful distance.

"As for you two…" Bach said.

"As for we two," Lexa-Blue said, her tone even. "You have no reason to believe that we are in any danger from anyone. I'm sure you know that holding the bearer of a multi-merchant license without cause is a violation of Pan Galactum Trade Statutes? And that those codes supersede any local regulations or laws? I believe you'll find our credentials complete and up to date."

Bach looked at her with seething hatred in his eyes. "You're both free to go."

Lexa-Blue's smile was angelic, even though it never reached her eyes. She caught Keene's arm and led him from the office.

"Okay, what just happened here?" he asked as they headed down the corridor in the same direction as Elai and her security shadows.

"What happened is that we just got lucky. The man in there with the black hole for a sphincter is playing with fire, and we very nearly got ourselves singed."

Ahead, Elai's guards rushed to keep up with her. Keene and Lexa-Blue followed just out of their reach.

We have to find Daevin and fast.

Great idea, partner, how?

I don't know, Blue. Maybe Elai can scan harder for him.

Possible. Whatever happens, we're gonna need all the help we can get. Let's see if the goon squad will let us in.

They arrived at Elai's door and found her escorts had taken up guard duty on either side. Both stood at attention, their hands clasped behind their backs, with blank expressions on their faces. As Keene and Lexa-Blue approached, the two guards stepped closer together, barring the doorway.

"We'd like to see the First Mind," Lexa-Blue said. "I assume she's allowed visitors."

The guard who seemed to be in charge looked at them coldly. "That would be up to her. Qoios, show the First Mind their faces and see what she says."

"Let them in, you idiots."

Keene stepped forward first, but the guard stopped him. "Qoios, weapons damper and security grid to maximum."

"Yes, Lieutenant."

Keene was sure he heard mockery in Qoios's voice.

The guard stared at Keene and Lexa-Blue as the door opened for them. "Try anything funny, and the blaster grid will turn your brains into a pretty pattern on the wall."

"Don't tell me. You write poetry, don't you?" Keene said.

Inside, Elai was sitting, rigid with the strain of remaining calm after Bach's affront to her dignity and position. When she greeted them, her voice was rich with irony. "Why, how lovely. You're my first guests in prison."

"Glad to see you're taking it so well," Keene said, eliciting a reluctant but genuine smile from her.

"We need to talk," Lexa-Blue said. "But who knows who might be listening."

"We can ask Qoios," Elai suggested. "Daevin assured me that ey isn't programmed to lie. Qoios, is Bach spying on me?"

"Spying is such a harsh term, First Mind," Qoios said. "With the security grid at maximum, I have no choice but to monitor your activities in case of a security breach, and Chief Bach does have access to those channels. You do understand, I hope?"

"Of course, Qoios," Elai said. "We must have security above all else, mustn't we?" *(It's a good thing none of us needs to speak out loud, isn't it?)*

Five minutes later, Lexa-Blue was immersed in a book while Keene taught Elai the basic rules of Quisling over a lighted game grid, smiling and laughing as he touched each glowing piece, demonstrating the rules. No observer would have realized they were deep in mental conference.

We have to get Daevin back here.

I want in on this, Vrick said. *I want to help.*

Elai, meet our ship, the Maverick Heart. He tried to encompass the ship's lineage, history, and their place in each other's lives, wrapped up on complex bundle of thought.

Please, First Mind, call me Vrick. All my friends do.

(And I am Elai. It is my honour. I thank you for your aid, friend Vrick.) They all felt Elai's delicate, rose-petal wonder at the idea of a sentient, independent ship.

Now we just have to figure out how to find Daevin, Lexa-Blue thought. *Any luck scanning for him, Elai?*

(None. And while I'm stuck here, there is little I can do. I do, however, know someone who may be able to help. He is a finder, and he's very good at it. Unfortunately, he is in Sotari.)

So we take Vrick and go get him.

You two go, Blue. I don't trust Bach not to pull a fast one. He hates Elai, and I know he wouldn't try very hard to protect her. I'd feel better if one of us was here to watch her back. Plus, we can work on Jaekir, get him to make Bach ease up.

(We must act swiftly, though. The Board will not debate forever, and things could go badly for us if we don't act soon. And Keene is right, Bach is a definite threat. Back in his office, he was radiating his desire to, quote, teach that smug bitch a lesson, unquote.)

Gee, I don't think he likes me very much.

(Are you sure? He might have been thinking of me. Either way, I will definitely feel better with an ally here. Here is the information you will need to find Giri.)

Lexa-Blue felt the mental pulse enter her long term memory: coordinates, landmarks, and descriptions.

"You two have fun playing," she said, standing with a supple stretch. "I'm going for a walk."

❖

(Miss Valme.)

The voice was softer than even a whisper in her ear, but it made Saphia's head snap up from her keyboard. Guilt flashed across her mind as she quickly punched in the last command, checking the holo above the keyboard, seeing it flash green to indicate her program was up and running successfully.

(Miss Valme, this is Elai. Please don't be alarmed, this contact is one way only. I cannot read anything from your mind. I am merely sending because you need to know. We have discovered that Daevin is alive. Bach isn't willing to listen, but I hoped you would be more reasonable and be able to help us somehow. Please contact me as soon as possible.)

Saphia reeled with agonizing nausea, as if kicked in the stomach. The Technarch wasn't dead! She grabbed for her keyboard, already knowing it was futile. Stabbing at the keys, she punched in her access code. The holo-display flashed red, denying her access. Frantically, she punched up everything she could think of, every possible avenue. Still Qoios refused her entrance.

She leaned back, fighting to calm her rising panic. She knew she had done her work too well. The virus was impervious to her now. If she hadn't added that final failsafe code, she could have stopped it. But now it was too late.

Her fear rose anew, and she rubbed at her temples. Think, girl, think. It's what you do best. How do I know the Technarch isn't dead? All I have is the word of the First Mind. No guarantees. Okay. Confirm for yourself. How? Short of finding him, don't know, but don't have time to search.

She checked the time. She had less than an hour until the virus infected Qoios's higher logic centres and took effect, turning em into the perfect assassin. Shortly after that, Elai would be dead at the hands of the security programs Saphia had written. Not enough time, damn it.

Her mind raced for some course of action, maybe some way to prove the Technarch was alive. Suddenly something tickled her memory from her first days in command of S:TS. Something her predecessor had been experimenting with.

"Humana, upload file sequence beginning Prime 001, coded: DEAL WITH IT LATER."

The upload seemed endless, but the first file finally booted up on the display. Saphia paged through the files, furiously searching for something to twig her faulty memory. When she saw it, she all but yelped in triumph.

"Project Tag, initiated 04/06/141. Implantation successful, but project terminated due to...blah, blah, blah." The report became bureaucratic jargon, but the important facts were there.

A tracer vein had been implanted in the Technarch's body, growing along the major nerves in his body from a nanosome taken with one of his meals. Even though the project had run aground, the transponder was still in place and would be as long as he was alive and his stomach was intact. All scan for the frequency. Saphia paged ahead to find it. There.

"Humana, scan for tracer code: Three Three Five; Omicron Two."

"Scan calibrated," Humana answered. "Code frequency active. Scan for location?"

Saphia's heart skipped an erratic beat of elation and terror as she grabbed for a bit chip and inserted it. "Scan and record."

"Complete."

Saphia yanked the chip out and held it, facing the total disaster she was responsible for. It had all made sense at the beginning. Find a way to keep Brighter Light and Sotari apart without war. Find a balance of power that would keep both sides just frightened enough of each other to not try anything stupid. The terrorism was just a means to an end, and the deaths were merely acceptable losses.

The thought suddenly sickened her. My god, she thought, how could I ever have thought such a thing? Acceptable losses? Those were people with lives and families. Where did an obscene idea like that come from?

Bodi.

Her anger flamed high at the thought of his name. Who knows what he did to the inside of my head, she raged. Who knows how he manipulated me?

She reached for the matrix crystal, forgetting for a second she had smashed it in a fit of rage. She saw the fragments in the corner, lying where she had left them. She ran to the corner, sifting through the pieces, choosing the largest. Worth a shot, she thought. She returned to her chair and cradled the fragment in her hand, mentally calling as she had done before. Minutes passed and nothing happened save her growing dizzy from the effort. Then just as she was about to give up, Bodi appeared in projection across her desk. His eyes were colder, deader than before, and he wore a cold, mirthless smirk on his face.

"You lied to me," Saphia said, her voice quivering with barely suppressed anger.

His thoughts a bland beige of apathy, Bodi's mind shrugged. "Yes, so?"

"You manipulated me into helping you, and you lied to me. The Technarch is alive and you knew it all along. You deliberately let me think he was dead, knowing what I would do. How could you? Do you have any idea what you've done? What I've done?!"

Bodi merely laughed, and it rained across her mind like a shatter of breaking glass. His plans echoed through her mind, like precise, clear, high-resolution imagery. She had given Sotari its greatest martyr. Once the First Mind was dead, the Technarch would be miraculously found alive and well. He would be returned to Brighter Light just in time to deal with a Sotar people outraged at the brutal assassination of their beloved leader. He would arrive home just in time for a war Bodi had already planned for Brighter Light to lose.

Without another word, he was gone. Saphia gaped, stunned by Bodi's manipulation and betrayal. Maybe there's still time, she thought.

"Humana, contact Qoios."

"Qoios is not responding. Es commo links have been cut off."

It's starting, she thought, a wall of fear rising before her. Her mind spun, not knowing who to believe in anymore, who to trust. The crime she had committed lay in her heart like a dense, aching gravity.

She had only one choice. Bach. If she told him everything, maybe he could save Elai before it was too late. Maybe a full strike team could keep Qoios from fulfilling es mission. Maybe.

She started to stand, but stopped. Who knows what Bach will do? He's always been a loose cannon, and he has no love for Elai or Sotari, she thought desperately. With a slight quake of dread, she sat back down. I don't trust him. I can't trust him. Her mind raced, and she grasped at the frail straw of an idea. She plugged the bit chip back in and copied the transponder code into her database and thumbed her journal record key.

Five minutes later, with her meagre insurance policy in place, she checked the time though she knew precious little was left.

Saphia left her office at a dead run.

When Lexa-Blue saw Vrick where they had left em, resting on the landing pad atop the huge building, she felt a blessed, cool relief go through her. She crossed the pad to the gangway and entered the ship.

"Miss me, you big lug?"

"Well, since I've been inside your head the whole time, I haven't missed much."

"Well, I missed you, you big hunk o' junk. But we have ourselves a Technarch to find. You powered up and ready?"

"Pfft. Am I ever not?"

Vrick lifted smoothly into the air, leaving the massive building behind.

"You know where we're headed?" she asked, thinking of the coordinates Elai had implanted in her head. ***Here you go.***

Vrick brought up a holo of the planet and translated her thoughts into a course, marking it on the globe.

"I'll plot us a course that looks like we're going up to wide orbit, but that takes us back down out of Brighter Light scanner range to here." A glowing blue dot appeared on the holo-globe.

"Getting skittish in your old age, Vrick?"

"We both need to get there in one piece, Meat."

That we do, she thought. That we do.

CHAPTER THIRTEEN

Through all that comprised human space, at right angles to the worlds and citizens of the Pan Galactum in all directions and dimensions, was Know-It-All. It was the sum total of human knowledge that could be compiled since the tiny human species had lived on its one tiny world. Every book, every lecture, every poem. Every work of art, every achievement and near miss was catalogued within it. Its vast storehouse of knowledge held every language still spoken and many long forgotten. A billion libraries the size of a billion planets would have strained to carry the knowledge it possessed.

It was not sentient in the way that humans or Sotar or even the Maverick Heart and es like were sentient. It had not been constructed in that way. However, within it, touching it, and adjacent to it, Artificial Intelligences like Qoios and Artificial Sentiences like Vrick opened onto it. They were able to taste it, feel it, know it, though even their massive intellects could only touch a small corner at a time.

In this dimension of computer thought, Qoios had no body. Unlike humans and their shells of flesh, or Vrick with es hull and engines, Qoios felt ey existed as merely thought and data. Ey was information, and the duties ey was created to perform and all of the data that made em up was an ever-changing, pearlescent matrix in that dimension of otherness. Through strands of a web like a network of capillaries in a living body, ey was connected to the rest of Brighter Light and the Galactum through Know-It-All.

It was through one of those local links, ey realized the intrusion in less time than it takes a cell to divide. Ey felt the dark, ugly thing slide into em. Reacting to the threat, ey moved instantly to cut off the affected areas, then stopped, realizing that would cauterize the security subroutines that protected the palace. The microsecond of hesitation was long enough. The codeworm took hold and began to spread.

Qoios felt the thing, growing in em, malignant and cold. Ey released es phage programs to deal with the intrusion, watching helplessly as they were struck down, splattering apart against the black evil. Feeling the beginning of fear, Qoios severed all of es external connections, giving the virus nowhere to escape. Giving emself nowhere to escape.

Saphia's codeworm was ruthless and efficient, replicating itself. Within seconds, it took command of the palace's security subsystems. Qoios felt a part of emself go grey and numb as limbs of thought and hardware were suddenly, viciously amputated. Rallying emself, ey fought back.

Saphia had designed her virus to sneak in through the back door of the security subroutines, taking over enough of Qoios's control to convince em that Elai was a threat that must be terminated. Qoios heard and felt the hypnotic murmur in es mind, insistent and rhythmic. //SHE IS THE ENEMY// At first, Qoios strained to hear it, the maddening whisper at the edge of consciousness. Each time ey focused on it, //ENEMY// it was gone.

Ey staggered as the virus launched a frontal attack. //SHE MUST DIE// The chorus swelled inside em, disorienting em, encircling em, filling em. Qoios fought the distraction of the maddening voices, concentrating es will. //YOU MUST KILL HER//

Saphia had anticipated Qoios could be convinced to dispatch Elai cleanly and without remorse or loss of other lives. What she hadn't counted on was the integrity of Qoios's core control, as programmed by es original designers. Qoios's allegiance to, and protection of, the Technarch was es primary function. In addition to this top priority were subroutines governing routine management of the palace, instructions given or rescinded only by the Technarch.

Daevin had given Qoios specific instructions to protect Elai at all costs whenever she was in the palace. This top level instruction from the Technarch came in direct conflict with the powerful compulsion of the virus program to eliminate Elai as an enemy intruder, precipitating a severe logic fault in Qoios's cortex.

Qoios watched the opalescent lattice of es being, split by ribbons of oily black, begin to crack open, bleeding energy into cyberspace. One of es sub-levels was cross-referencing schizophrenia, a split personality and psychotic break, when es psychological self-assessment files crashed.

Gathering es strength once more, Qoios wondered if this was pain.

❖

Bach frowned at the distortion interfering with the holo from Elai's quarters. He attempted some manual adjustments, but the image of Keene and Elai bent over their game grid would not sharpen. In fact, it continued to degrade before his eyes.

"Qoios, run a diagnostic on the imaging units in my office, please."

The lack of response deepened Bach's frown. Another display came to life, unbidden, showing only a shower of static.

Before he could do anything else, Saphia burst through his door, flushed and gasping for breath. "First Mind...danger. Technarch... alive," she managed to get out between gulps of air, before dropping into a chair.

Bach groaned. "Not you too. I told the First Mind..."

He broke off as she flung the bit chip with the transponder code at him. He caught it easily. "What is this?"

"Check it yourself," she said clutching her side as her breathing finally slowed.

Bach slotted the chip in the reader and activated it. He absorbed the information quickly, which was good, for the holo display was the next system to crash. "Damn it. What is going on?"

He looked at Saphia, whose face had gone white. "Shit. It's happening faster than I thought."

"What is?" Bach said through clenched teeth.

Saphia's confession burst forth in a gush, every detail from her first meeting with Bodi to her recent subversion of Qoios. Tears were on her face when she was done.

Bach listened to her speak, feeling an opportunity open before him. *I can use this,* he thought. Plans formed in his mind, mutating as quickly as they were born. As Qoios deteriorated, he realized, palace operations would become more and more confused. Records will be lost, damaged. *I can arrange for the ones left to say whatever I want them to. Without Qoios recording everything that goes on within these walls, no one will be able to contradict me. And that meddling Sotar will no longer be a problem.*

Saphia babbled out her guilt. He prodded her along with the occasional question, all the while solidifying his plans. With their leader gone, the Sotars would be easy targets, he thought. And they will finally pay for all they've done.

Unable to stop himself, he smiled at the idea. Luckily, Saphia was too distraught to see. He noticed what she was saying.

"Come on, Bach, for god's sake. We have to warn her, do something." Saphia bolted out of her chair, heading for the door.

There's just one more obstacle to remove, he thought, thumbing open the catch on his holster.

❖

"Sweep Six," Elai said, winning again.

"Wow." Keene leaned back in his chair, surveying the board, trying to see where he had gone wrong this time. "You are way too good at this."

"Beginner's luck. Isn't that what they call it?" Elai said, then saw the frown of concentration on Keene's face. "I'm not reading your mind."

The note of defensiveness in her voice surprised Keene. "I didn't think that at all. The truth is, it doesn't take much to beat me. I said I could play. I never said I could play well."

"I'm sorry," she said, an oppressive fatigue on her face. "I'm afraid I've started to see suspicion where there is none."

"And from what I've seen, I'd bet you're right about it a lot of the time."

"Perhaps a bit," she said, with a brief nod of her head. "It is the same for the humans who come to Sotari, I'm afraid. My people are often no better. We have many years of mistrust to get past."

"I suppose it's not surprising your people are suspicious of technology," Keene said. "All things considered."

She nodded again. "The humans here in Brighter Light see us as monsters, the stuff of their childhood fears. They can't help it when they look at us. And they see our mere existence as the ultimate invasion of privacy, prying into their thoughts at every turn."

"You call us humans as if you're a different species."

"Aren't we?" Elai asked. "Your ancestors were born in the same way you were, give or take. Mine were made, crafted from genes and technology tiny enough to dance on the head of a pin. They were created in a lab for no other reason than to see if it was possible.

"The truth is, we eschew machines, because deep down, buried in our racial memories, we fear that we *are* machines. Everything we do or create, every aspect of the way we live is an attempt to prove that we are not."

"Does it even matter, though?" Keene asked. "The ship Lexa-Blue and I travelled here in is one of the last independent, sentient ships. He's one of the few that's even willing to interact with humans. In literal truth, he's a machine. But he's our friend. The fact that his body isn't the same as ours makes no difference. He thinks. And he feels. He's smart and loyal and kind and for me, that's what really counts."

"And yet, I frightened you when you first saw me," Elai said.

"Yes, you did," Keene said, blushing. "For about five seconds. And I got over it. Others will too."

"I hope you're right. I see the toll this is taking on Daevin. And on me too. Neither one of us thinks our world can take much more."

"It won't come to that," Keene said, not sure how much he believed his own words.

"I hope you're right, my friend," Elai said. "Shall we have another game?"

"Later? I think my ego needs a break."

"Would you like some tea, then?" she asked. "I'm having a craving."

"That would be nice, thanks."

"Qoios, some tea, please. That one that Daevin likes so much. The one that smells like wildflowers."

There was no response.

Keene frowned. Elai tried to shrug it off. "He must be busy elsewhere."

Keene shook his head. "An AI that size would have to be running an entire planet before ey got too busy to respond. And even then, ey would at least answer, even if ey just shunted the request into a priority loop. There must be something wrong. Qoios? Please respond, Qoios."

When he received no answer, Keene went to the direct commo circuit and tried Jaekir again. This time, Jaekir answered.

"I was just about to call you," Jaekir sounded tense and unhappy. "There's been a development. Saphia Valme has confessed to being the traitor who passed the codes to Deathmind. She turned herself in to Bach a short time ago."

When she heard the news, Elai hurried over to Keene's side. Keene hunched over the commo, intense and bright with hope.

"What else did she say? Does she know where Daevin is?"

"Bach informed me that she said nothing else."

"Well then, interrogate her. She's lying."

"That won't be possible," Jaekir said wearily.

"Why the hell not?!" Keene said, his voice rising.

"Apparently, she was shot and killed while attempting to escape."

"Escape!" Keene couldn't believe his ears. "What kind of moron turns herself in and then tries to escape?"

"I don't know, but I intend to find out. I'm…preparing to launch a full scale…investigation. I…want to know…" Jaekir's voice was thick and slurred. Keene heard a faint hissing in the background. There was a thump and silence.

"Jaekir," Keene yelled into the commo circuit. "Jaekir. Are you all right?"

Keene looked up at Elai, concerned. He straightened from the commo just before a beam of light lanced into the unit, sending up a shower of sparks.

Keene looked up to see one of the room's security pods, inset in the ceiling, targeting Elai.

Reacting on instinct, he threw himself at her, knocking her aside just as the beam shot past where she had been standing, burning a black gouge in the fabric of the couch. Keene landed on top of her with a grunt.

He rolled off Elai, drew his gun and fired, and the security pod exploded in a shower of sparks. He stood and offered his hand. She took it and rose from the floor, trying to look unruffled and cool. Keene crouched in a fighting stance, scanning the room to find the next threat.

"I don't know what's going on, but at least the weapon damper is off. It gives us a fighting chance. Come on."

They had just begun to move when Keene heard a faint sound. Making a snap assessment of the sound's location, he pitched forward, shielding Elai with his body. The beam from the second pod clipped his shoulder, charring his shirt, but merely stinging flesh. He swivelled his arm and fired, again cleanly taking out the pod.

They were struggling to their feet when they heard the whisper of gas.

In es core, the battle raged on as Qoios felt the boundaries of es world begin to blur, blistering tumours erupting throughout es consciousness. More and more fissures marred es surfaces, spreading across the sphere. The shreds of es intelligence had just managed to disable the weapon damper, knowing it was Keene and Elai's only chance, when ey felt one of his rogue elements booting up auxiliary power to the damper unit. Grimly, Qoios turned to fight the new threat, determined to keep the unit out of the fight.

Saphia Valme had seriously underestimated es will to survive.

❖

The Maverick Heart shot up into the air, gauzy layers of cloud parting and resettling to mark the ship's passage. Still the ship climbed higher, passing the boundaries of Orb's thin atmospheric envelope into the hard vacuum of space.

Lexa-Blue checked the course plot and saw they were coming up on the apex of their flight path. She checked all the system readouts, a habit she had never lost despite being a pilot in name only. Life with a sentient ship would do that to you.

"Apex on my mark," Vrick said. "And...mark."

Vrick directed a low level jamming field at the Brighter Light traffic control to mask their sudden change in course. The heading had them skimming along Orb's atmosphere, past the curve of the planet, out of range of Brighter Light scanners. Vrick signalled they were clear and nosed the ship down, re-entering the atmosphere.

After a momentary whiteout while they dropped through the clouds, Lexa-Blue was afforded a breathtaking view of Orb's other side.

Below her, a pelt of untamed, verdant forest stretched out into the distance, terminating in the foothills of a mountain range in the distance. Where the tree line ended, the harsh greys and browns of rock jutted up into the sky, terminating in brilliant white caps against the blue. The land appeared to be uninhabited.

"The Median Lands," Vrick informed her. "Rhokhara Canyon should be off to your left."

Lexa-Blue caught a glimpse of something blood red and glinting in the sunlight, marring the landscape below. Their heading altered slightly, their destination, the highest peak on a long spine of mountains. She recognized it from Elai's directions. Sotari should lie beyond. Vrick nudged es engines slightly, pushing the ship faster to cover the remaining distance in minutes. The sharp needle shape of the mountain grew quickly ahead, until it seemed about to smash them to bits. Vrick banked smoothly around the summit, easily avoiding a collision.

Sotari lay immediately below, sheltered in a long, shallow valley. A wide blue-green river ran between the mountains, separating a smaller area of the city-state, directly at their foot, from the bulk of the settlement, fanning out beyond. Off to the east, she saw rows of cultivated farmland.

Lexa-Blue noted the buildings were low and scattered, made mostly of stone and wood, giving the city a softer, more natural look than Brighter Light. Scanners told her that several tunnels and caverns had been cut into the side of the mountain. She couldn't find any generated power at all. Hundreds of tiny pinpoints of heat showed on the infrared band, and she suspected some combination of candlelight and primitive lamps lit the interiors.

(I'm not sure I would agree with you that we're "primitive." Welcome to Sotari. I've been expecting you.)

The mindtouch was gentle, and she felt the humour behind it, like clear water bubbling over rocks in a stream. The sensation was distinctly different from previous mental contacts she had experienced with Elai. It was almost like a new flavour: sharper, more tangy.

(I am Giri. Elai let me know you were coming. You can land here.)

Lexa-Blue felt an image forming in her mind and became aware of a flat, dry plain off to her left. She opened her node and shared the location with Vrick, who banked and brought them in without so much as a bump. She went to the hatch and cycled it open.

(I am sorry I couldn't meet you in person. I've been detained at the Hall of Memory.)

Directions to reach him bloomed in her mind.

(I hope you don't mind the walk.)

Not at all, she thought back. It will give me a chance to explore.

She set off, following the map in her head, feeling the image as something vibrant and alive in her mind. She reached the outskirts of the settlement itself in only a few minutes. Unlike the precise grid of Brighter Light, Sotari seemed a warren of lanes and switchbacks, all scattered in different directions as if buildings had merely been placed wherever the builder chose in any shape or size that would fit. Without the map Giri had provided her, she would have been hopelessly lost. She wondered if a sense of direction was one of the gifts that the Sotars' heritage bestowed upon them. As soon as the thought formed, she felt a chuckle; it seemed as though the bubbles in the stream had taken rainbow coloured flight, bursting in the air.

(Not specifically, but it helps us follow the signs.)

She became aware of the rough crystals hung over the door of every building, and felt through Giri's mind the residents' names and their occupations resonating from these crystalline structures.

Then she became aware of the fact that the buildings had doors all the way up their walls, opening into the air with no stairs or ladders to the street.

Which made complete sense once she saw the people flying.

It wasn't like anything she had seen in holos, where people moved through the air like darts. The Sotars seemed to be merely standing in mid-air, floating along on some invisible moving platform that moved wherever they wanted to go and then set them gently on the ground again. She saw a woman lift from the street to a door on the third story. It swung open, and she disappeared inside.

Artwork was everywhere, from brightly painted murals on several of the buildings to sculptures of wood and stone adorning plazas, gardens, and street corners. While the architectural style was simple, almost rustic, the profusion of art gave it all life and energy. Musicians on several street corners filled the air with melodies that mixed and built on each other.

(We encourage our artisans to produce as much work as they can, wherever possible.)

Lexa-Blue came to a heavy stone bridge that traversed the river she had seen. She crossed it and found herself in the smaller area of Sotari in the mountain's shadow. When she saw the wide bank of steps leading up to an imposing stone façade carved into the side of the mountain, she knew she had arrived at her destination.

The steps led up to a huge arch, more ornately decorated than anything she had seen in Sotari so far. Two immense doors, slabs of obsidian curved at the top to form a semicircle, were set into the arch. Above the door, as on all the other buildings, was a faceted crystal. This one, however, was a fat, rough sphere, tinged almost blue in its clarity. Lexa-Blue figured this particular structure held great importance.

(Come in. I am in the Main Chamber. Through the doors and straight ahead.)

Lexa-Blue climbed the stairs, awe overtaking her as the massive doors swung out to admit her. The antechamber directly inside was open and bright, sun streaming down from a skylight channelled straight up through the mountain. Several people were in the atrium, but few paid her any mind, concentrating on their own tasks. She crossed the cool stone to another arched opening, where light glinted out at her. When she stepped through, the source of the illumination took her breath away.

Stretching deep into the mountain, the Main Chamber was long and wide, its vaulted ceiling rising to another carved skylight at its apex. Crystals lined every wall, on tier after tier rising out of sight, catching sunlight and magnifying it into bright refractions.

A group of people stood in the centre of the room, deep in silent conference. One of them saw her and broke away from the group, smiling as he drifted toward her on shifting air.

He had the same angular, pale strangeness as Elai, but his smile was open and generous, crinkling the pattern of freckles across his face. His pale, sun-bleached red hair fell in unruly curls, giving him a reckless, jaunty air. He wore snug leggings and a loosely wrapped shirt, both pale blue. His eyes, a deep piercing green, darker even than her one, sparkled with a hint of the devil.

"I am Giri, welcome." He steepled his hands in the traditional Sotar way and bowed.

She saw heads turn at the sound of spoken words, then focused on the grandeur around her. "Lexa-Blue."

"It is impressive, isn't it? It's the store of the history of Sotari, all that we are and all that we have been, our Great Library. Though the person who named it was hopelessly pompous, so we're stuck calling it the Hall of Memory. I've been coming here all my life, and it never fails to take my breath away when I see it. When they needed help with the repairs, I had to help."

"Repairs?" The mere thought of any damage to a place this beautiful was horrifying.

Giri nodded and pointed up at the long walls. In the space he indicated, Lexa-Blue saw several patches of dark along the walls, each containing shards of shattered crystal.

"The last SCI attack used some new form of weapon that could short-circuit our abilities. Some were not able to resist. The feedback damaged several of the matrices here in the Hall of Memory. We have been working day and night to repair them ever since."

"Can you fix it?"

Giri shrugged, and his merry face turned wistful. "We repair what we can and mourn what we can't."

Lexa-Blue's anger and disgust flared, radiating from her mind.

"I agree," Giri said, seeing it on her face. "They are savages, but no more so than those of Deathmind that have attacked Brighter Light."

"I just don't know why they can't see that this violence gets them nowhere."

Giri's smile was rueful. "But what kind of world would it be if everyone was as smart as we are?"

Lexa-Blue smiled back, but Vrick's voice stopped her from responding.

Heads up, Meat. I'm having trouble reaching Keene and you have three heavily armed flyers coming your way.

Lexa-Blue turned and ran for the door, sending out her thoughts as strongly as she could. When Giri caught them, he flew after her.

She sprinted across the atrium, and the heavy doors swung slowly open. Too slowly for her liking. Rather than wait, she twisted sideways and she squeezed through the narrow gap. She skidded to a halt at the top of the steps just in time to see the three sleek darts shoot across the mountain over her head. As they banked to come back, she zoomed her scan-eye to identify them.

Emblazoned across the wings was the sharp, angular logo of Brighter Light Security.

CHAPTER FOURTEEN

Keene heard a faint, directionless hiss but couldn't find the source of the gas. Whatever the compound was, it was invisible and odourless. He felt a sudden rush of dizziness and realized it was hitting his system.

Vrick, I've got an unidentified toxin in my blood. Scan and identify.

He didn't get a response for a moment, just a ringing void.

Sorry, Keene. There's some major intermittent jamming going on. I'm...

The node cut out for a second before fading back in.

...Sorry about that. What the hell is going on down there?

The toxin, damn it! Keene felt the edges of his vision going grey.

Scanning

Keene waited what felt like an eternity, sliding closer to unconsciousness.

Got it. It's Neurox 422. I'm adjusting your system to compensate

Keene felt the fog in his head recede. He realized Elai was almost unconscious. He grabbed for her just as she started to topple. Holstering his gun with one hand and supporting her awkwardly with the other, he eased her to the floor and looked around the room again. Qoios had closed all of the windows, including the wide sliding door leading to the small outdoor patio. Keene grabbed Elai and dragged her, staggering, closer to the patio door, but he found Qoios had sealed it tight. He let Elai slump to the floor, drew his gun, and fired at the door. Nothing. The damper field was up again.

Keene pumped the trigger a few more times. On the last try, the gun fired and shattered the plex of the door. Using the gun butt, he knocked away the remaining shards and pulled Elai out into the fresh air. He propped her against the wall of the patio and slumped down beside her, gulping clean, clear air, while Vrick manipulated his body chemistry to neutralize the toxin. Vrick's efforts began to pay off, and Keene realized his head was clearing. Elai stirred beside him, uttering a harsh, guttural cough. Keene placed two fingers on where he assumed her carotid artery was, concerned over her exposure to the gas. Without Vrick to help her, she must have taken a more serious dose than him. He found her pulse strong but racing.

    Keene, is there any way you can plug me in to the AI? I might be able to help if I'm hardlinked.

    No problem, I've got one of your finks right here in...Shit.

    The small pouch that Keene usually carried at his waist was not there. He suddenly remembered he had taken it off while they were playing. It was, no doubt, on the couch, exactly where he had left it.

    Hang on. He started to rise and felt a feather light touch on his arm. Elai's eye fluttered open.

    "What happened?" Her voice was a hoarse whisper.

    "Sleepygas. Hold still and breathe. You'll be fine."

    Elai nodded, hit by another spell of coughing. Keene pulled himself up and stood by the doorway. He saw his pouch, intact on the arm of the couch. Taking a deep breath to steel himself, he leaped back into the room.

    He dashed for the chair, zigzagging to avoid the beams of energy trying to home in on him. Energy beams burned across the floor and the furniture. Keene leaped for the pouch, grabbed it, and rolled to the floor behind a chair. He scrabbled inside it as the beams began to carve the chair apart. He grasped the small, familiar shape and pulled it out. Now all I need is somewhere to put it, he thought.

    The most logical choice was the master terminal set in the coffee table. Almost all of Qoios's library functions could be accessed there and through them, Qoios emself. Keene slithered across the floor, feeling one of the security beams sear his pant leg. Too damn close, he thought. With a forceful push, he slammed the fink onto the terminal pad.

    He heard a quiet chink as the featureless rectangle embedded its hardlink spines through the panel into the circuitry underneath.

The room went silent as the beams shut off.

I'm in, Vrick announced. ***Someone has infected Qoios with one of the nastiest codeworms I've ever seen. I've pulled the plug on the security devices in your suite, but I don't know how much else I can do for you.***

Do what you can. I have to help Elai.

Keene heard a sound behind him and whirled, gun at the ready. It was Elai, leaning on the door frame to steady herself.

"Are you okay?" he asked.

She nodded, clearing her throat one last time.

"Come on, let's check you over just to be sure," he said, leading her into the bathroom where he settled her on the edge of the tub and pulled out the first aid kit from under the sink.

"Can your physiology handle a stim?" Keene asked. "It might help you clear the toxin out faster."

"I should be fine," Elai said. "Our bodies are close enough to yours that most drugs affect us the same way."

He rifled through the kit for a stim patch. When he found the right dosage, he pressed it against the skin of her throat.

"Okay, just sit still for a second and let it work its magic."

She shuddered, and her eyes opened wide. "Oh, my. That'll wake a girl up, won't it?"

Oh boy. Keene, you've got to get Elai out of there, now. The code is designed to kill her, using Qoios as the weapon. If you get in the way, it won't be shy about taking you out too. Qoios's logic centres and core commands are trying to fight it. That's why everything is so erratic, but there's no telling how long ey can hold out.

Keene groaned and stood. "Come on, we have to get moving. Qoios is trying to kill you."

Elai looked stunned but took his helping hand and followed him out of the bathroom. They crossed the ruined living room to the main door of the suite.

It didn't open.

Keene hit the manual release, but it didn't budge. "The lock is jammed. Qoios must want us to stay put."

"Allow me," Elai said. Faint lines of strain appeared on her face, and Keene became aware of a faint sub-harmonic hum, then a groan of bending metal. The area around the locking plate of the door buckled, steaming slightly. After a moment or two of protest, a chunk of the lock about fifteen centimetres across fell from the door with a final shriek of metal. Keene hit the manual release again, and the door opened.

Keene had to take a quick step back as the two unconscious security guards slumped inward at his feet from where they had fallen. Keene and Elai stepped over them.

Hold it! Vrick informed Keene. ***You've got a sever field between you and the elevator. Take even a step, and it will cut you to ribbons.***

Keene looked around for something to test the field with. He grabbed a cushion off a chair and tossed it into the corridor. Barely a metre away, it fell apart into neatly sliced, irregular chunks. Fluff fell everywhere, shredded even finer as it fell through the invisible beams.

So what now? Keene thought.

I think I can open up a hole in the field. There's a program to let security in but not let the bad guys out. The problem is that you have no way of seeing it, and if you can't see my pathway, you'll get carved up.

Keene thought for a moment and had an idea.

"Wait here," he said to Elai. He hopped over the Security agents, ran back into the suite, and found a slim, fluted bottle of scented body powder in the bathroom. He grabbed it and ran back to Elai.

"Totally low-tech. Well, more like no-tech." ***Open the corridor, Vrick,*** Keene thought, prying the lid off the container.

Open.

Keene swung his arm wide, sending the powder flying. Ventilation currents caught it, distributing it evenly. The pattern of slicer beams became visible, all red angles in the hazy, powdery air. Down the middle of the dangerous corridor was an open path to the elevator. Keene grabbed Elai's hand and pulled her forward. The edge of the laser field burned at Elai's long gown as she ran, slicing through the soft fabric.

I'm losing control of it.

"Hurry!" Keene shouted to Elai. They made a last, desperate sprint, slamming hard into the closed elevator door. Keene hit the call button and as they turned, they saw the last of the powder show the sever field falling into place once more.

"Too close," Elai said. Keene didn't see her body move, but her dress began to tear on a shallow diagonal just above her knees. Untouched by hands, the scrap of cloth fluttered off and away. She moved her legs, exploring her new range of motion. "That's better."

They heard a ping, and the elevator doors slid open. Keene nearly stepped in, but Elai pulled him back.

"No!" Elai shouted.

He was overbalanced, ready to fall forward when he felt the air grab him and pull him back from the opening. As Elai caught him, he saw the elevator car plunge down the shaft, rocketing out of control. Seconds later, they heard the far off sound of rending metal as the elevator crashed at the bottom.

❖

The dark, bat-like shapes of the planes held a tight formation, wheeling to strafe the long main street leading to the Hall of Memory. Along the street, people began to scatter, some finding cover. Those left in the open were caught by some unseen weapon and dropped from the air. Lexa-Blue saw their faces contort in agony as they writhed on the ground.

She heard Giri cry out and turned to see his hand contorted into claws against his skull. She caught him just as he began to collapse.

"What is it?"

"Scrambler," he hissed through clenched teeth. "Hypercharges the linkages in our altered genes."

Did you catch that, Vrick?

Yup.

Can you project a blocking field through my node, two metres radius?

Best I can give you is one metre. Anything wider than that will fry your brain.

Do it.

Lexa-Blue watched as the pain wracking Giri's body eased, his tortured breathing even out. Within seconds, he was calm, his body unwinding as he stood.

"Thank you."

"Don't mention it. But stay close, cause the block is only good to a metre." *Vrick, status of those ships.*

Three light troop carriers, complement of twenty-four. Their transponders broadcasting Brighter Light Security Defense codes. They're exactly who they seem to be.

Defense against what? she snorted. *Civilians out for a walk?*

Heads up, Meat. One's landing.

Sure enough, while the other two continued to strafe the main street, one of the planes was coming in for a hard, fast landing, the attack hatch opening to spill out troops. Lexa-Blue drew her gun and fired, dropping the point man like a stone. The other members of his squad were disoriented for a minute.

(You surprised them) Giri said in her mind, faster than words could be spoken. *(They weren't expecting any technological resistance.)*

Pressing her slim advantage, Lexa-Blue fired off several low power shots at the ground just in front of the Brighter Light troops. Clouds of dust rose from the hard packed but unpaved street. The troops grabbed for their breathers, coughing and sputtering. Lexa-Blue stunned several more while she had the advantage. From the corner of her eye, she saw something hurtling toward the plane and realized it was a huge cask of wood and iron. It slammed into the bow of the plane with a thunderous crash, tearing through its hull. The Security ship teetered for a moment before slowly tipping on one side. The open hatchway buckled, crushed under the plane's weight as the aircraft came to rest. The remnants of the attack squad staggered away from the wreck, totally disoriented.

"Was that you?" Lexa-Blue asked Giri, standing close at her side. He just smiled.

Jamming is still coming from the other ships. Another one's trying to land. I'll be right there.

Run some interference if you can.

Gotcha.

"Come on," she said to Giri, "let's keep them occupied until Vrick gets here. Distract that one, keep it from landing."

Without another word, she ran down the steps into the street. Around her, Sotar were struggling to help each other out of harm's way and clear the area. She opened her mind and shared her plan with Giri. He followed, staying close to remain unaffected by the scrambler.

Taking a position in the open, Lexa-Blue anchored her stance and fired at the strafing plane, gun on full power. She had no illusions her sidearm would do any damage to the plating of the plane's hull, but it got her noticed. The pilot brought his ship around for another pass, trying to target on her, buzzing and weaving in an intricate flight pattern like an angry hornet.

Meanwhile, Giri stood behind her, back to back, and harassed the pilot of the other plane as he tried to land. Unable to boost another cask high enough to ram him, Giri kept it constantly in the pilot's way.

Every time the pilot adjusted his landing vector, Giri pushed some heavy obstacle directly under him. At the last moment, the frustrated pilot would have to abort his landing, his engines wailing in protest.

Suddenly, the Maverick Heart swooped down on them, looping up just in time to avoid crashing into the mountain. The wave front of turbulent air buffeted the two Brighter Light planes, sending them reeling. Lexa-Blue's target was safe in the high end of its banking flight and regained control. Giri's plane was not so lucky. Its flight already shaken by continuous attempts to land, the plane's pilot lost control. The ship tumbled, clipping its wing on a low, squat building. Its hull screaming, the plane flipped over and came to rest upside down.

Vrick chased down the last Brighter Light plane, easily anticipating its moves before he slipped into an aggressive new attack. When the pilot panicked and tried to make a run for it, Vrick powered es forward weapons array and fired, taking out just enough of his engines to bring him down. Belching smoke, the plane gouged a trench down the middle of the street.

In the sudden silence, Lexa-Blue felt quite pleased with herself.

Don't get too cocky, Meat. Keene's in trouble.

The Maverick Heart dove down from the sky, stopping to hover about ten metres above their heads. There was no place in the crowded street to land.

Qoios has freaked and will probably kill him and Elai if we don't get back.

Lexa-Blue grabbed Giri's arm. "Are we needed here anymore?"

Hearing the urgency in her voice, Giri frowned. "The others can handle it from here. What is it?"

Before she could say it, he saw it in her mind, and his face went white. Without warning, he shot them both up into the air, straight for the Maverick Heart's open hatch.

The momentum of Elai's mental grab sent them both toppling over backward. As they scrambled to disentangle themselves and stand up, they heard the ringing, tinny echoes of the elevator's destruction fading away.

"Thank you," Keene said, drawing in a deep breath.

"My pleasure. I owed you one. Now what?"

Keene considered a moment, having no idea what do next. "We

have to get you out of this building, that much we know. Obviously, the elevators aren't an option. Stairs?"

Elai pointed to a door at the end of the hallway. "There."

Keene walked to the door. It didn't open. "Big surprise," he muttered.

The rectangular panel for the manual release was set in the frame beside the door. He pressed the panel, reached in, and grasped the handle.

A surge of raw current shot through his arm, making him twitch. He jerked his hand away, suddenly aware of all the nerve endings in his hand, jittering and numb. As sensation returned, he knew the voltage must have been just low enough to keep him from opening the door.

"Looks like Qoios wants to play with us for a while," Keene said, rubbing his tender fingers to get some feeling back in them. "I don't suppose you can do that lock picking trick again?"

Elai's brow furrowed as she concentrated, then the expression turned into a wince. She stepped back and shook her head. "Scrambler circuit."

"Okay then, the stairs are off limits too. Any ideas?"

"I could probably float us down the elevator shaft to the main reception area. From there we could get out easily," Elai offered.

"Possibly. Somehow I don't think Qoios will make it that easy for us," Keene said. "God only knows what he has cooked up for us down there."

Cooked is definitely the operative word. The sever field down there has gone out of control. There's a fire burning in the reception area that's spreading, and Qoios won't let anyone in to deal with it. The fire suppression subroutines were trashed by the virus. This is getting worse, Keene. Lexa-Blue is on her way, but you two are going to have to hang on until the cavalry gets here. Can you handle it?

We'll give it our best shot, Vrick. Keep me posted. "Lexa-Blue's on her way to help. Let's see what we can do to make sure we're still alive when she gets here."

"Indeed," Elai said, nodding emphatically. "The question is, how?"

"We need a safe place to wait. Any suggestions?"

I have one. Vrick piped up. ***I've rerouted the command lines around your floor, cutting off Qoios's access to you for now. The security devices are offline, so you should be able to get back to**

174 STEPHEN GRAHAM KING

your suite and wait there. The bad news is you're stuck there until Lexa-Blue shows up.*
  Not very pro-active, but I think it's our best option.
  Keene outlined the plan to Elai, and she agreed. They turned back toward the suite, but Keene hesitated at the edge of the space formerly defined by the sever field.
  It's okay, it's down.
  With a sigh of relief, Keene took a step forward, and then froze. One of the maintenance robots came around the corner ahead of them, purring along on its treads with a barely audible whir as its eye lens focused on them.
  Elai looked quizzically at Keene. "What's wrong? It's just one of the maintenance drones."
  Keene didn't take his eyes off the mech. "And all of the maintenance drones are controlled by the mainframe AI. Qoios."
  Elai's eyes widened. You fool, she thought, you are not safe at home in Sotari anymore. Everything in this building is a potential weapon. Think before you get both of us killed.
  The mech extended its two heavy manipulator arms toward them and compartments along its sides snapped open, revealing four, lighter appendages tipped with saw, scissor blades, drill bit, and welder. With surprising speed for something with that much mass, the mech charged.
  Keene pushed Elai hard in the direction of the suite. "Go!"
  The chivalry cost him precious seconds. Before he could run, the mech was on him. It clubbed him with one of the heavy manipulators, catching his neck just below this ear. Keene's vision greyed as he fell sideways. He heard the harsh buzz of the saw blade coming at him and kicked, aiming low, hoping to be below its arc. The blade squealed and sent up sparks as it hit something out of his line of vision. He turned his head, seeing the arm bearing the saw blade pulled taut, away from him, as if struggling with some unseen force. Elai. The arms of the mech flailed, fighting her power to get at him.
  He felt a sudden pain along his cheek and warm blood along his jaw as the drill bit tore at his face. He struggled to pull back from the robot, but its hold on him was too great. At that moment Elai tore the saw arm from its body, and the combination of forces caused the mech to overbalance and topple toward Keene. Its weight pinned him to the floor, knocking his breath away in one great huff. Squirming like an impaled bug, Keene saw the arm with the scissor blades shoot down at

him. A sudden vision flashed in his mind of his own head, neatly lopped off his body.

Instead, he heard a thunk as the tips of the scissors dug in the floor. Rather than decapitated, Keene found himself trapped, pinioned by the open blades, unable to move his head without slicing his own throat. Aiming for the space between his eyes, the drill bit moved closer.

Suddenly, he brushed the butt of his gun with his hand, and he grabbed it. But before he could move or fire, one of the mech's grippers closed around his wrist. He struggled against the hold, but it was too strong. Just as his strength began to ebb, he felt the fingers of the gripper being pried away from his wrist, one by one, and his hand was free to move. Keene swung the gun up and pumped three shots into the mech's head. Lubricant-soaked shrapnel splattered in all directions. Twisting his head to avoid a large chunk, Keene felt a twinge in his neck where one of the blades nicked his skin. Moving the gun slightly, he fired again into the mech's chest, ripping the steel casing like foil.

The robot twitched once and was still.

Keene let out his breath in one huge gasp of relief.

"Elai," he said with only a faint quaver in his voice. "Could you get this thing off me, please?"

As soon as her feet touched the deck, Lexa-Blue was moving. She brusquely buckled Giri into Keene's seat. Dropping into her own chair, she secured her harness as Vrick shot almost vertically from the Sotari street. They were pressed hard into their seats as Vrick, with greater precision than any human pilot, boosted the ship over the mountain and set course for Brighter Light.

"What is happening?" Giri asked, tension tight in his voice. "Elai is in danger, I know, but from what?"

"Details, Vrick. Fill us in," Lexa-Blue said.

Vrick explained quickly, filling them in on Keene and Elai's predicament.

"You were inside this Qoios at the same time you were helping us?" Giri asked.

"I still am. Haven't you ever heard of multitasking?" Vrick asked.

"Valme, huh? Wasn't expecting that. What's Keene's status?"

"He and Elai are still okay. Some close calls, but still kicking. Uh-oh."

"Uh-oh, what?" Lexa-Blue asked.

"Can't talk. Things are going critical in Qoios's core. Keene needs me more than you do. Your course is set, and I've got the autonomic systems flying you back. Just keep an eye on things, and you'll be back before you know it."

Lexa-Blue did a quick systems check, knowing that flying them back while helping Keene was well within his abilities. When her cursory check was complete, she turned to Giri and almost laughed at mixture of wonder and terror rioting across his face. His eyes darted from surface to surface, object to object, unable to land anywhere. He seemed thirsty to drink it all in, even though it terrified him.

"Take a breath there, champ. You're gonna sprain something."

"I'm sorry," he said. "I've never flown in one of these things before. I've never seen anything like it. It's amazing."

"And it scares the shit out of you, right?"

He nodded, smiling. "Yes, it does. But the fear feels good."

"So you never travelled with Elai to Brighter Light before?"

Giri's cheeks cultured and he looked away from her eyes. "I have not."

"I thought you were her...what's the term? Soul's Blood?"

Giri looked back at her. "You know of this?"

"Elai mentioned it. Not sure I really get it, though."

"May I show you?" Giri's face lit up.

Lexa-Blue shrugged. "Go ahead."

The concept opened in her mind, in a way that was coming more and more familiar to her. She saw words, but also emotions, colours, sounds. She saw love and unity. She felt the true nature of the relationship, what it meant and felt it form like a solid. The shape was specific and clear, extending into directions she could not have perceived with her senses, either the natural ones or the enhanced ones her sensor eye gave her. Each facet of the wondrous shape was another aspect: love, loyalty, mercy, friendship, faith, generosity, and each folded back onto itself to encompass the other.

"You know this bond," Giri said to her. "The concept those words struggle to encompass can manifest in so many ways. Your friend, Keene. Your...ship?" His eyes grew wide. "But it's nothing but metal."

"That metal saw es people slaughtered around em in a war with humans. Ey is one of a precious few that exist anymore, one of the rarest minorities in the Galactum. And ey lives among es former enemies with no bitterness, carrying no grudge. Ey has saved my life countless times over, and I've done the same. Ey is the same as Keene or any one of us as far as I'm concerned."

Giri's cheeks cultured again, despite sensing no rancour in her words. "You understand about Soul's Blood better than you think. I'm afraid I haven't always been worthy of Elai's faith in me. I resisted her desire to bring our people and Brighter Light together. In my mind, they were everything we've hated about ourselves for generations. They worshipped the very things we have tried to forget about ourselves."

"So, what changed?"

"We were arguing one day. And she asked me why I was trying so hard not to learn."

An image of Elai formed in Lexa-Blue's mind, and she heard what Elai had shared with Giri that day, broken down into words. "It is said that one must always strive to learn. But I don't believe that. Learning is like breathing air or digesting food. It happens all the time if you just let it. It's the ones who refuse to learn or think or open themselves up that are really working at it."

"I didn't think it was possible," Giri said. "But I saw her in a new light that day."

"A Brighter Light?" Lexa-Blue arched an eyebrow.

"That is quite possibly the worst joke I have ever heard."

"Hey, you need someone shot, I'm your girl," she said. "You want comedy, not so much."

Vrick struggled to ride the storm in Qoios's Pseudo-Neural cortex, becoming a part of the ruptured, pearlescent surface of the AI's avatar. As ey had suspected, the codeworm that was decimating Qoios's higher functions ignored em, being specifically keyed to the AI's matrix. All around em, the data streams and programming chains whipped into monsoon frenzy, lashing em. Vrick knew about hurricanes from es library core, but this was the closest ey had ever come to experiencing one.

Vrick became one with the maelstrom, feeling a picosecond of pity for es distant relative. AIs like Qoios were as related to Artificial Sentiences like Vrick and es kind as the simplest primates were to humans, though this was no fault of their own. They had been designed and built specifically to be limited, to not desire or self-improve in the way Vrisk and es relatives had been. As quickly as it had come, the feeling disappeared. All that mattered to Vrick in that moment was that another being needed es help.

Qoios's core was a shambles, most of es fringe functions gone, slaughtered by the invading code. Vrick released some of es own virus-fighting phage programs into the system, but it was a losing battle. Qoios's consciousness had been so seriously subverted that ey was even sabotaging es own internal efforts at repair, losing es ability to distinguish between emself and the virus.

Vrick sensed the frail thread of Qoios's consciousness, the remnants of what ey had been, and followed it down through the maelstrom. Ey felt a sense of growing desperation as ey chased the retreating persona, then a calmness as ey felt Qoios reach a decision. Vrick hurried, knowing in the exact instant of choice what the other planned to do.

As a last ditch ploy to protect Elai, Qoios was cutting off power to es main core nexus, committing suicide rather than face what ey was becoming. Vrick grabbed at the slender thread, drawing its end into emself and holding on tightly, struggling to make contact with what was left.

With a burst of luminescent data, Vrick burst through into the persona nexus, coming face to face, as it were, with what was left of Qoios.

Who are you? Qoios snarled the question, feral and desperate. Confusion and hostility sparkled around em in dark, sickly light.

A friend. Come, let me help, Vrick answered, sending out cool, soothing waves of reassurance to wash over the fractured, crumbling persona.

I'm scared. Qoios sounded like a lost child. *It's dark, and I can't see.*

There, there, little one. I have you. With barely a whisper of effort, Vrick enfolded the core nexus, gently quieting Qoios's cry of distress. Sure that the AI was safe, Vrick slingshotted emself out of a world that was rapidly succumbing to the dark.

CHAPTER FIFTEEN

The Maverick Heart flew into deepening twilight. Below, the city-state flickered with light. As night crept up, the city glowed as points of light came to life and lined the grid of streets. Irregular pointillist patterns spread across the faces of the buildings.

They watched in silence as night rolled forward to meet them: Lexa-Blue a tight knot of concern, Giri awestruck by the size and shape of the city-state below. Together they watched as Brighter Light passed below, the glow growing from a fragile lace to a dense, stellar core.

"And the stars fell," Giri whispered, so quiet Lexa-Blue almost missed it.

"There," she said, pointing toward the sea.

Growing in the distance was Daevin's home, the centre of Brighter Light, dominating the horizon. Even from this far out, they could see the damage. Yawning scars of darkness spread across the sloping outer walls. As they watched, a pattern of lights along one edge flickered out. Thick, oily-black smoke rose from the base of the pyramid, dissipating on the evening wind. Hard beams of red and blue light stabbed up into the night from the emergency vehicles on the street below.

A quiet alarm sounded, and Lexa-Blue checked a readout.

"What is it?" Giri asked.

"The perimeter of the security screen," she said, her hands moving over her control board. Their forward motion dropped to zero, and the ship hovered. "If the screens were still up, that is."

"It's all right," Vrick said. "The screen generator is down until repairs can be made."

Lexa-Blue heard the subdued tone in Vrick's voice. "What's wrong?"

"I just pulled Qoios out of the main core. There isn't much left. Whoever did this…"

"Don't worry, we'll get to the bottom of it, Vrick. I promise." Lexa-Blue felt a growing rage, keen as the blade of a knife, and took hold of it. She tested its heft, felt its weight, and knew it as a familiar weapon she was ready to use. "What about Keene?"

"He and Elai are a little banged up, but fine. I'll take you in to the nearest landing pad."

The Maverick Heart dipped and followed es new heading.

"It's been quiet for a long time."

Elai nodded, concentrating on applying the disinfectant to Keene's face. The first aid kit Keene had used on her earlier lay open by her feet, its contents spread in a precise array. She knelt by his chair, where he sat, working on his injured cheek in the feeble candlelight.

Elai paused a moment to wipe away any oozing blood, dabbed again with the disinfectant, and then applied the wound sealant.

"There. I'm afraid it's the best I can do with what we have, but if we don't get you to a proper medical facility soon, you'll have quite the scar." She set about replacing all of the first aid kit's contents, snapping the lid shut when she was finished. "Though, I don't know. It might look quite dashing. You and Lexa-Blue would match."

"Thanks," Keene said with a chuckle, stretching his legs after sitting so long.

"So now what?" Elai asked, putting the kit aside. "Any other human games you can teach me?"

"Not enough room in here to play zero-ball," Keene said with a smile, though it sent a twinge in his cheek. "So, I guess we wait. Not many other choices."

Elai nodded and ran her hands along her bare legs, the skin pebbling. "It's getting cold in here."

Keene nodded and stood, crossing to the nearest air vent. He placed his hand in front of it and felt a strong flow of cold air. "Temperature control must have gone skew-whiff when Qoios went offline. Not surprising, I guess. There are blankets in the other room, if you'd like one."

Her nod was emphatic. "I'll get them."

Two blankets wafted like ghosts from the other room, one settling beside each of them.

"Thank you," he said, watching her bundle herself into a chair and wedge the blanket tightly around her thighs.

Dressed warmer than she was, Keene draped his blanket over his knees, sitting on the couch just to one side of a scorched ridge in the fabric. A pensive expression formed on his face. "I've been thinking."

Elai looked at him, her eyes wide. "You had time to think?"

Keene smiled, ignoring the pain in his cheek, but the smile faded and the pensive look returned. "If we get Daevin back..."

"When..."

"Okay, when we get him back. The two of you have your grand Unification ceremony. What will it change? Is it going to magically make the hatred go away? Will the violence end?"

Elai pulled the blanket up under her throat, framing her pale face. "Neither of us are that naive."

"Then why?"

"You know the culture that Daevin comes from. In Brighter Light, networks are formed, built by these adoptions, creating a web of biological and adoptive families tightly interwoven by the choices that create them.

"In Sotari, our altered nano-enhanced DNA changes in utero. We give birth to children that bear no genetic relationship to their parents. What we call family is a decision. Every birth is accompanied by a ritual similar to the one Daevin and I will be undertaking. There are so few of us in the universe as it is. We must exist for each other, so we commit to the child, for we know we would be lost if we didn't hold each other fast.

"What Daevin and I will do is blend our traditions. We will become each other's family. We will be a new kind of Soul's Blood, taking along all of our people who are willing to make the journey with us."

"And the ones who aren't willing?"

"Never underestimate the power of symbol. If we are very lucky, some who are on the cusp of acceptance will join us. And the rest, we will stop. We have no other choice."

"As long as we can find Daevin and get things back on track. I hope this Giri is as good as you say he is."

Elai smiled, and Keene recognized the love behind her warm, gentle look.

"He is."

They didn't talk for a while after that until Elai noticed him looking out at the stars, a hungry, longing look in his eyes.

"Where are you?" she asked quietly. "What do you see out there?"

He hesitated. "I don't know. The stars. Opportunity. A place to explore."

She smiled. "What else? Tell the truth."

Keene looked at her and chuckled. "I guess it's pretty pointless to hedge with you, isn't it?" He shook his head, then looked back out at the starry black above.

"My home," he said wistfully. "I've lived among the stars for almost a dozen years now. I've seen the constellations from almost every corner of the Galactum just by looking out my bedroom window, and more sectors are being opened up every day. I've reached a point where the deck of my ship feels more natural than ground under my feet." He shook his head a little. "Sorry. I don't usually get homesick."

Elai smiled, knowing he was lying. "And here I am, having never left the world of my birth."

"I'll tell you what," Keene said. "As soon as all of this is resolved, we'll take you for a spin in the Maverick Heart, show you the neighbourhood."

"I would like that," she said, feeling a frisson of excitement. Very much, she thought.

The promise warm between them, they settled back to wait.

❖

The Maverick Heart settled emself on the landing pad, and Lexa-Blue was halfway down the gangway before it had fully extended, her gun drawn. Despite Vrick's insistence that everything was safe, she knew how quickly a situation could turn. The thought made her scar itch where it divided her brow, until she willed the sensation away.

Giri came close behind her, mimicking his behaviour on the streets of Sotari. Though he had no jammer field to evade here, he remained near her, reaching out with his senses.

Vrick had brought them to one of the areas of the palace that still had power. Floodlights swamped the area, and the door to the palace opened when they neared it. Wary and alert, Lexa-Blue stepped through, sweeping her gun right, then left, then ahead. She saw that the light faded into a cool wash of emergency lights beyond ten metres. She cautiously moved deeper into the palace.

(Someone's coming.) Giri tried to keep the alarm out of his thoughts.

Lexa-Blue pointed to her right. Giri shook his head. She pointed to her left. He nodded. She faded back against the wall, motioning him to do the same. She looked into the darkness, her eye adjusting to compensate for the light level. Dimly she heard footsteps coming closer. As they approached, she realized they were moving quickly, making no attempt at stealth. Finally, she was able to make out a small knot of agents in riot gear, a medic, and a commo-tech in a full field rig.

Recognizing the face of their leader, she stepped out into the pale light. "Jaekir."

For a moment, it looked like Jaekir would die of fright on the spot before regaining control. After hasty introductions were made, Jaekir updated her.

"The Board was trapped in chambers when Qoios crashed, but it hasn't stopped them squabbling. Bach is down there trying to free them now."

"Well, keep an eye on him," Lexa-Blue said. "Giri and I barely managed to stop an attack in Sotari by Brighter Light Security troops, there on his orders would be my guess."

Jaekir looked stricken.

"And for the record, Daevin is alive," she added, explaining Elai's sense and her own belief that sense could be trusted.

"We must find him quickly before Bach can free the Board," Jaekir said. "No telling what he will convince them to do. Keene and the First Mind took shelter in her suite. We were going to collect them when we ran into you. Come."

Jaekir started to walk, but Giri stopped him.

"This way is faster."

Jaekir looked surprised and a little suspicious. "And how do you know this?"

Giri looked taken aback by the question. "I just do."

Lexa-Blue merely shrugged. "It's what he does."

Still looking sceptical, Jaekir deferred to Giri and signalled for the security agents to follow. Sure enough, leading them through a service corridor and to a functional elevator on the east side of the pyramid, Giri brought them to the suite in a matter of minutes.

The door's lock had been torn out, but the door had been dragged closed and wedged so tightly that prying it open took three of them. Giri pushed his way past everyone, headed for Elai's side, and Lexa-Blue bounded across the room, grabbing Keene up in a bear hug. Only when he squawked to be put down did she let him go. Holding him at arm's length, she shook her head.

"You keep forgetting. No one gets to kill you but me!"

I hate to interrupt the reunion, Meat, but get the medic to look at his face, it's a mess.

Lexa-Blue examined Keene's face, inspecting his wound. Taking his chin between her forefinger and thumb, she turned his face to the light. "Good field dressing, but it needs proper treatment."

Keene shook his head, freeing himself from her grip. "It can wait. We have to find Daevin right away."

"It cannot wait, Keene. Daevin will be all right for the few minutes it will take to get it looked after. Now, move!" She all but dragged him over to the medic.

"But I'm fine," he protested feebly, knowing she was right.

The medic sat Keene down and got to work, pulling out more sophisticated tools than Elai had access to. He examined the wound, peeling away the sealer Elai had applied. He drew a grafter and adjusted the setting. "This may sting a bit. Let me know if it does, and I'll boost the aesthetic field."

After a couple of minutes work, he put away the grafter and sprayed a fine layer of mist along the pink ridge of the sealed wound. "There. That should keep it from scarring. Just sit still for ten minutes and let it do its work."

As the medic packed up his kit, Keene rolled his eyes, frustrated at having to wait the seemingly endless time. Lexa-Blue waved a warning finger at him and gave her best fierce look. "Stay."

Once she saw compliance in his eyes, she turned to Jaekir and his commo-tech, over by the main access to Qoios. Or at least, what was left of Qoios. The commo-tech had her equipment spread out and was performing a diagnostic through a hardwired link in the access panel. Giri, reassured that Elai was all right, was peering over her shoulder, fascinated. The look on the tech's face was not encouraging. Lexa-Blue crossed over to them.

"Bad news?" she asked, standing beside Elai.

The commo-tech brushed her hair back and shook her head. "Not good at all. The core infection is almost total, most systems down with the backups out too. It's going to take a long time to get things back online."

"Which means," Jaekir put in, "that Brighter Light is almost completely vulnerable. A good portion of our commerce and information was routed through Qoios. The raw data should still all be there, but our society could grind to a halt without the AI to process it."

You thinking what I'm thinking, Meat?
You willing to blow your cover?
If it helps Qoios, I can live with it.

Lexa-Blue looked thoughtful. "What class was Qoios?"

"Class Six Persona, just over five hundred terabytes per cell. The most powerful we can legally produce," Jaekir answered. "Why?"

"My ship is a Class Nine, with almost twice the capacity. Ey is at your disposal."

"A Nine? But Nines were prohibited by the Arac Convention decades ago." The tech sucked air through her teeth, and her face went pale as realization struck her. "That would mean ey is…"

"Yes, ey is," Lexa-Blue said to the tech. "And ey is willing to help, so why don't we let em?"

The commo tech put up her hands. "I'm not saying no. A Nine would make all the difference in the world until we get Qoios repaired. If you're sure you…I mean ey doesn't mind?"

"Ey is ready whenever you are."

"The hardlink I established should still be intact," Keene said, coming over to them after checking with the medic that it was okay to move. "I'll show you how to access and expand the connection."

After a moment's fiddling, Keene and the commo-tech sat back from the panel. Vrick's voice, a little lower and richer than Qoios's, came from the speech units.

"I'm in. Hold on, I've got something here. It was flagged to catch the eye of whoever booted up the system after the crash. It's a holo, projection coming up."

In the empty air before them, the cultured mists of the holo swirled and coalesced into a life-sized version of Saphia Valme.

Her face was pale, and pinched lines of strain showed around her eyes. The raw emotion on her face left her blunt and open, laying her heart bare.

"If you are seeing this, then Qoios is in ruins and my plan was a success," the holo said bitterly. "I know you probably won't believe this, but I'd give anything to change the way things have turned out right now."

The image sighed, a sound scraped bloody.

"They say that confession is good for the soul, but my soul is the least of my concerns at the moment. I was the leak to the other side. I was the one who provided the access codes to the Sotar terrorists. I caused the Technarch's abduction. Why? Not that it matters much anymore, but I believed it was the best way to keep Brighter Light and Sotari separate but at peace. Bodi and I had a plan. It all made sense in the beginning. Focus on the differences, make people see our two cultures were too different to merge, but could find peace apart. Separate, distinct societies, each free to pursue its own course. I actually believed it all. I realize now that Bodi used me, manipulated my mind to believe whatever he wanted me to. I can't tell where my ideas end and his begin. Now Orb is teetering on the very brink I hoped to avoid. And I will go down in history as the person who brought it there.

"But maybe it's not too late to salvage something out of this mess. I'm on my way to confess everything to Bach, my involvement in the kidnapping and my sabotage of Qoios. Do I trust him? Not for a second. That's the reason for this message, a little insurance policy in case Bach decides to double-cross me, which wouldn't surprise me at all. He's hated me for a long time."

Saphia shrugged her shoulders, drawing herself up with a final shred of dignity and strength.

"Included in this confession is a micropulse containing the names of all Brighter Light and Sotar conspirators I know of. Also, you'll find the frequency of a tracer code that will lead you to the Technarch. The details are in the pulse. Maybe now I can face this with a little of my honour back. It's cold comfort, but it's all I have."

The image reached out and turned the recorder off, destroying itself.

Keene finally broke the uncomfortable silence. "Doesn't sound like a woman who was planning to make a break for it, does it?"

"The micropulse is there, and it contains exactly what she said it would," Vrick said.

"Which means that as well as launching an unprovoked attack on Sotari, Bach knew about Qoios's impending attack on Elai and did nothing about it," Lexa-Blue said. "Add to that suspicion of murder. Not good."

Jaekir shook his head sadly, clearing his throat. "Vrick, Mordren Bach is hereby relieved of his duties as Security Chief. Log it immediately under my orders. Do you know where he is?"

"He's in his office," Vrick said.

"He could be planning to make a run for it as we speak," Lexa-Blue said. "You need someone there now."

"Find Agent Horne, get him here as soon as possible so she can arrest Bach and take over for him."

"Consul, Horne is over in the seaward wing, trying to free some researchers trapped in one of the labs," the tech said, looking up from her work with Keene. "We're the closest squad that isn't busy."

"I'll do it," Lexa-Blue said, her voice hard.

Jaekir looked at her through narrowed eyes a moment. "I want him alive."

Lexa-Blue's eyes shone with a devilish gleam. "I'll see what I can do."

"I suppose that's the best I can hope for. Vrick, log Sei Lexa-Blue's temporary field promotion, effective immediately," Jaekir said. He turned to Lexa-Blue. "Take Aames and Webster here and bring him in."

Lexa-Blue made a jaunty salute and signalled the two Security officers to follow.

❖

Bach slammed his hand down on the commo control, cutting off the dead circuit. As before, there was no response from the squad he had sent to Sotari. He could only assume his team had been stopped somehow. Who knew if they were alive or dead? And he would be left holding the bag.

He leaned back in his chair, the frustration rising over him once again like a wave. Elai had survived Qoios's attacks, his plan to bring Sotari to its knees was a shambles, and he had killed Valme for nothing. His carefully constructed house of cards had fallen around him, and he was left to contemplate the humiliation and dishonour that awaited him, the ruin his second family faced because of him. First the Onestra, shamed by the Adisi, he thought, now the Bach shamed by me.

He leaned back and muttered a stream of vivid obscenities, suddenly unsure of his next move. *I have to get away from here. To where?* There was nowhere in Brighter Light to hide. The colony was big, but not that big. The islands? *No, it would have to be off-planet.*

With a renewed sense of direction, he punched the code for the Port. *In this chaos, his security override would get him on a ship and offworld before anyone was the wiser. Once he had that, he was home free.* He slammed the last key, only to be presented with a blunt denial etched in the holo-grid.

He stared at it for a fraction of a second and then stabbed the code in again. The result was the same, and he felt the noose tightening around his neck.

They're on to me, he thought, fighting a spasm of panic. *Have to get out of here; it's the first place they'll look.* He thought for a second, analyzing his chances, gauging who they would send against him. *With the palace in disarray, they would have their hands full elsewhere, and despite everything, he was still the best. No, I can handle whoever they send.* He grabbed for his field jacket, drew his gun, and stood.

"Going somewhere?" Lexa-Blue asked from the doorway.

Bach cursed himself for being so absorbed in his thoughts that he missed her approach.

"As Acting Security Chief—things being what they are, you'll just have to take my word for it—I am placing you under arrest for complicity in the attempted assassination of Elai, First Mind of Sotari and suspicion of the murder of Saphia Valme."

Bach longed for the opportunity to carve that smile off her face. He knew this little Acting Security Chief bit was one of Jaekir's tricks. He hesitated, observing Lexa-Blue carefully. Seeing her hand was nowhere near her own weapon, he brought his gun up in a smooth, rapid motion and aimed at her, returning her smile coldly.

"I don't think so," he said.

Lexa-Blue smiled. "I guess you've got me. Go ahead, shoot."

Fury rose in his throat and he pulled the trigger.

Nothing happened.

Bach looked dumbly at the gun in his hand.

Lexa-Blue merely continued to smile. "Remember the selective damper field you had installed to protect the Technarch? It's easy to take control of if you're on good terms with the AS in control of the palace. Drop it."

Bach lowered the gun onto the desk. "You've got me. I'll go

quietly." Holding his arms wide in a non-threatening way, he slid his jacket on and came around the desk.

Lexa-Blue watched him closely, not trusting this sudden change of heart.

Suddenly, when Bach was about three metres from her, his arm flashed up, the throwing knife he kept secreted in his sleeve flying at her. In a micro-second, she was alert and knew the throw would go wide and miss her, but Bach took advantage of her distraction, and spun into a high kick.

Instinctively, she sank and rooted, altering the angle of her stance for stability. As his foot came at her, she shifted her weight and ducked under the arc of his kick. Shifting her weight forward to root again, she blocked the swing of his foot with her hand and directed it away from her head. The second she was clear, she pulled close to him and targeted his groin with a savage kick, but he twisted away.

Surprised by her deflection of his attack, Bach lashed out with a vicious punch to her head. Lexa-Blue blocked the punch with her hand, and aimed her tightly pointed fingers at the tender cleft just below his ear, pushing off her back leg and rotating her hip to give the blow extra power.

Bach resisted the common impulse to turn his head, leaving the soft spot open. Instead, he turned the other way, moving in to ram his chest into her shoulder. She managed to avoid the shoulder blow, striking at the back of his neck, sensing the movement wouldn't connect even as she started it.

Bach pivoted, getting away from her and diving for another target. He twisted and came up with the knife in his hand. Lexa-Blue hesitated for a second, seeing the blade swishing the air, waiting for Bach's next move. He made it barely a second later, the blade singing in precise, wide arcs. She sensed that he was merely taking her measure. None of his slashes went wild.

The blade tore through her shipsuit and sparked against her steelskin. She twisted against the rain of blows, trying to keep the body armour between her and the blade. Ultimately, she made a mistake. As she blocked a slash with her forearm, Bach jerked the blade along the armour until it hit flesh, cutting her hand.

Lexa-Blue winced at the sharp pain, then shut it off. Bach leered and lunged, the blade coming at her throat. She slithered out of the way, catching his wrist in the curve between her forefinger and thumb, deflecting the thrust up and away.

Bach was already pulling back, aiming a kick at her groin. Deftly, she blocked it with her knee, striking at his solar plexus with her elbow. He pulled back from the killing blow just enough to stay alive, but lost his wind and his grip on the knife. It skidded across the floor. Without his weapon, Bach felt himself beginning to lose control. He backpedalled away from her, trying to get some breathing room.

Sensing his flash of weakness, Lexa-Blue came at him, staying close. She kicked for the leg carrying his weight, but he managed to step out of it. She quickly changed the kick to a cross step, coming in close to him again.

Bach's nerve continued to erode. The more he tried to get space from her, the closer she came, giving him no time to think. Every time she came at him again, his panic grew. He couldn't escape her placid face, growing in his vision all the time. Finally, he punched wildly for her midsection, trying to drive her off.

The blow was sloppy with panic and just slightly off centre. She swung her torso, scaling the punch past her body. It slid off, doing no damage. With a move like lightning, she grabbed for his elbow, jamming her thumb into his funny bone. She heard Bach's breath huff out as his arm went numb.

Sliding her other hand along the thumb line for control, she moved her knee into him and pulled him over.

Losing his footing completely, Bach went over face first onto the floor. As he went down, Lexa-Blue shifted her grip, pulling his wrist back and up, finding the right spot on his hand.

Bach gasped as he hit the floor, lying on his stomach with his arm pulled back and straight up. He tried to squirm out of her grasp, but yelped in agony at the pain.

"The nerve I'm pressing is called a Tan Tian," she said, brightly. "Hurts, doesn't it? But only if you try to move. So, how about you just don't."

Bach's only response was a strangled, humiliated grunt.

CHAPTER SIXTEEN

Daevin pulled himself out of a shallow sleep and struggled to rise from the hard cot. An ache rippled across the muscles of his back as he straightened. I am getting old, he thought. Though I shouldn't complain. At least I'm still here to get old. For the moment, at least.

The cot that had tortured his back was the merest of courtesies, like the rest of the sparse furnishings of the cubicle. Actually, he thought, when I blanked out in my room, I half expected my next accommodations to be a coffin. Compared to that, this isn't all that bad.

Hoping to loosen the muscles in his back, Daevin stood and pacing his cage again, twelve paces long by eight wide and stark in the extreme. I have bathtubs bigger than this, he thought. The back wall was bare, lumpy rock, seamed at right angles with two walls of pale, off white plastic-resin polymer. The wall opposite the rock was translucent, shimmering energy, a jangle field that would disrupt all of his synapses if he was stupid enough to get too close. The tiny, silent generator keeping him imprisoned sat just outside the field, though it might as well have been on the other side of the world. Standard Emergency Supplies Division issue, he thought, obviously Brighter Light. I probably signed off on the design myself.

Other than Daevin, the cot, and a dingy, portable toilet, the cell was empty. Not even a book to read, he thought.

Daevin continued to pace, his restlessness unabated until he forced himself to relax. He replayed the events of his capture in his mind. Keene and Elai on the bed. The rush of joy when he knew that Keene was all right. Beginning to move toward him, then the grip on his arm, and the sudden, numbing black in his mind. And waking up here in this cell, wherever that was.

At the edge of his field of vision, he caught a flicker of movement through the force wall, a blurred dark mass he assumed was a sentry posted to prevent his escape. Once again, he had the uncomfortable feeling the wall of energy was one way, and he was being watched.

Other than the loss of his creature comforts which, he was ashamed to admit to himself, he missed, this was the worst and most humiliating aspect of his captivity. To have his bodily functions on display, to be reduced from the leader of a nation to little more than an animal in a zoo or a sideshow freak, was more than he thought he could bear.

Someone would pay.

If I ever get out of here, he thought, feeling fear churn in his belly. Don't be ridiculous, he thought, giving himself a mental shake. If they had wanted you dead, they would have killed you already. Which would seem to mean they want you for something. And that buys you some time.

He looked around the cell, searching for some means of escape. Come on, he thought. Keene or Lexa-Blue would have found a way out of here by now. He scanned along the walls, searching for some weak spot in the cell's structure. He traced the seams where the walls met, the generator of the field energy, the fusing along the rock wall.

When Brighter Light techs do a job, they do it right, he thought with bitter pride. No matter how many times he physically examined the cell, he couldn't find anything. Oh, well, it's not like I don't have the time.

Before he could form another thought, something crashed through his mind. He gasped as the wriggling assault broke through his will like a thousand tiny insect legs across the tender surface of his brain. He winced as the sensation burrowed down into the crevices between his thoughts. Daevin felt a rush of revulsion at the mental intrusion and fought a wave of nausea. He struggled against the physical and emotional sensations, attempting to close his mind off as Elai had taught him. The only response from his captor was a malicious bubble of laughter that felt sticky and wet inside his head.

❖

Keeping Bach's arm twisted back and pressure on the nerve cluster in his hand, Lexa-Blue sat on his back and whistled for Aames and Webster. Their eyes widened at the sight of their former leader prostrate on the floor, but they locked the restraints on him without comment. Following them, Lexa-Blue oversaw Bach's imprisonment in a maximum security cell, more out of satisfaction than any lack of faith in their abilities to hold him, and then she hurried back to the others.

When Keene saw her, he struggled to his feet. "We have to find Daevin now."

"Hold on there, partner," she said. "If we go off half-cocked and exhausted, we're just as likely to get him killed for real this time. We need food, sleep, and a plan."

Keene opened his mouth to protest, but she shut him down. "The transponder is still beaming his signal, so we know he's alive. Think about it. They told us he was dead but kept him alive. They must have a reason. That's not likely to change before morning."

"All right," he said. "I don't like it, but I have to admit I don't have the strength to argue."

Over a cold, scrounged meal, they brainstormed the basics of a plan. Keene, Lexa-Blue, Elai, and Giri would undertake the rescue mission with a backup of Brighter Light Security ready to go if they failed.

At first light, the small rescue team boarded one of the Brighter Light security planes similar to the ones Lexa-Blue and Giri had fought in the streets of Sotari. With Vrick deep within the systems of the massive building attempting repairs, their own ship was of no use.

I wish I could go with you, ey said, tone thick with worry, *but they need me here. There's so much to do to get this place back online.*

Don't fret, junkpile, Lexa-Blue said to em. *Brain stuff is your specialty. Shooting stuff is ours.*

"Lock the tracking sensors on transponder code: Three Three Five, Omicron Two," Lexa-Blue said to Keene. "Use the beacon as a navigational heading and home in on it, full stealth mode."

As Lexa-Blue guided the plane out of the hangar, Keene input the transponder code and keyed it into the navigation systems. When the course flashed across her display, Lexa-Blue jammed the throttle hard, and the plane shot off into the sky.

Lexa-Blue punched up a holo-globe, their course marked by a thin red line terminating in a ring of four inward pointing arrows that blinked rhythmically, marking their objective. A tiny blue dot representing the ship began steadily turning the red line to blue.

Setting the auto-pilot, she swivelled her chair to the rest of the main cabin. Keene sat to her left, and she watched him a moment, his attention focused on the collection of field tested tools he kept in the kit at his waist. Each one of the spanners, drivers, probes, jammers, and lock picks had come in handy in any number of sticky situations in the past. More than anyone, she knew the magic he could work with those tools.

She watched him as he pulled each piece of equipment, thumbed it on, and checked its power level and calibration. She saw the slight smile as each diagnostic came up green. When she noticed he was doing the testing one-handed, she looked carefully at his other hand, frowning slightly to see him toying with a some small object, rubbing at it like worry beads. He noticed her scrutiny and held the silver ring up for her to see.

"I found it in Daevin's quarters, all neatly wrapped and addressed to me. He must have bought it at the Market when we were all there and forgotten to give it to me. Not that he really had much of a chance, I guess. It's almost the same as the ones we gave each other before." Keene's voice held only a faint trace of melancholy.

Lexa-Blue looked at him closely for signs of stress or weakness that might jeopardize their mission, and he noticed her knowing gaze.

"You okay?" she asked.

"Of course I am." he said.

"Hey, don't act like it's an unreasonable question. You're pretty emotionally involved in this one." She paused. "You're in love with him."

Keene sighed.

"Yes, Blue. I love him. And as soon as I know what I'm going to do about it, you'll be the second person to know." He chuckled. "Maybe even the first. But until then…" He tossed the ring up and snatched it out of the air. "Until then, I'm frosty and ready to end this."

Her muscles relaxed ever so slightly, and she smiled back at him. She knew that he was telling the truth, and she wanted no one else at her back.

"I'm going to check on the others, make sure they're kitted up and ready. E.T.A.'s about…" she did a quick check on the readout, "…one hour at max speed."

Keene nodded absently, already engrossed once again in his tools. Lexa-Blue looked at the others. Elai sat straight and serene while Giri paced, a bundle of restless energy. Both of them were dressed in matte black steelskins borrowed from Brighter Light security, all the angular leanness of their bodies highlighted by the tight, flexible body armour.

"Let's make sure we're ready. I'm glad to see you're both dressed for action." She and Keene wore their own steelskins, the burnished metallic surface unadorned by any other garment.

Giri fidgeted at the steelskin, a blush touching his cheeks. "It feels strange. And it it's…revealing."

Lexa-Blue quirked her mouth up at the corners, amused by his shyness. "It might be revealing, but it moves like skin, and it will stop a phased forty mag burst at close range."

The blush faded from Giri's face, leaving him a little pale.

"You can cover it with other clothes if you want to, but it will probably just limit your freedom of movement, and I don't think that's such a good idea, do you?"

Giri shook his head vigorously.

"Okay, I've got some other goodies to pass out too—goodies that could mean the difference in getting us out of this alive or not." She popped open an equipment cubby and pulled out two small, sturdy cases. She placed her thumb on the print reader of the first case and opened it, pulling out two strands of optical filament with flat metal discs at each end. "These are shielded commo links, portable versions of the nodes Keene and I have implanted in our brains. With this on, you'll be able to communicate directly with us."

"But we can communicate with each other and with you. Why do we need these?" Giri asked. Behind him, Elai's face showed she already knew the answer to this question.

"I assume you talking to us that way takes effort and concentration. I want every ounce of effort you have focused on getting Daevin back. This is just easier. I'll show you how it works."

First on Giri, then on Elai, Lexa-Blue connected the links, attaching one disk to the right temple, the other to the base of the skull. When she touched a tiny stud on one of the discs, the filament shortened, taking up the slack. "Okay, clench your teeth once to activate it, twice to deactivate. Try it."

After a couple of minutes of practice, they had a good grasp on it. "Okay, keep practicing until we arrive, and I think you'll be fine." Lexa-Blue opened the other case and pulled out two hemispheres, flat on one side, about three centimetres across.

"These are jammer buttons, similar to the stealth equipment on the Maverick Heart. While you have them on, you are invisible to most electronic scans." Lexa-Blue took the buttons and placed one against Elai's steelskin, then Giri's, just above their hearts.

"Good. We're ready."

Once they reached their destination, the plane flew, then banked, flew, then banked, executing a perfect search pattern laid out by the transponder trace. According to the code, the locus of their search was nestled in a canyon somewhere in the valley below, but they couldn't see anything from their position.

The canyon itself was a long scar in Orb's crust, gashing the rolling green jungle apart. Craggy rock walls plunged almost a kilometre down to a ribbon of blue water twisting along the canyon floor. Other than the occasional flicker of animal movement, there were no signs of life.

"Switching to I.R. thermal scan," Keene said. A frown began to form on his face.

In the holo-field, he saw several irregular glowing white blobs of heat splattered across the floor of the canyon, burning like stars to the infrared sensor. Keene shook his head. "There's too much geo-thermal activity. The I.R's unable to distinguish what's what."

"Can you filter out the other heat traces to home in on the base?" Lexa-Blue asked.

"I could, but without knowing what we're looking for, I could unintentionally filter out the base by mistake."

From his position behind them, Giri pointed out one of the glowing blobs of heat in the display. "That one."

"Are you sure?" Keene asked. Giri nodded, grave certainty on his face.

Keene shrugged and began activating the I.R. unit's filters. When he was done, only the one trace was left in the holo, tucked away under an overhang of rock. Without the interference from the other sources, he saw the heat trace, roughly the shape of an upended dome bonded to the canyon wall. One thin spindle of energy shot straight down from the dome toward Orb's core, out of sensor range.

"What is that line going down?" Giri asked.

Lexa-Blue had her suspicions but turned to Keene for confirmation. He tapped out an instruction on his panel before speaking. "It's a thermal tap, a micro-fibre bundle that goes down into the magma layer and converts it into power. Output looks like a standard emergency portable unit, century lifespan. Common issue in standard survival packs."

"What are their defenses like?" Lexa-Blue asked.

"Pretty passive. Some E.M. detectors, but not very sophisticated. No match for the stealth units. Looks like they were counting on the geography of the canyon for natural defense and protection from detection. That was a pretty safe bet on their parts because of all the geo-thermal activity. If we hadn't had Giri, we never would have figured out they were there. I don't think even an orbital scan would have penetrated all that interference. Scans show one heavily shielded elevator up to the canyon rim, but it looks pretty secure. There's probably some other access to the canyon floor, which is probably a better bet for us."

"Can you get any kind of psionic fix on who's down there?" Lexa-Blue asked Elai.

"There aren't many…" she said, concentration etched on her face. She frowned and tilted her head slightly. "Wait. I can't get a very solid sense. Someone down there is masking their presence, much the same way I have been doing since we came into range. That means only one thing. Bodi is down there."

"Are you sure?" Keene asked.

Elai nodded. "He's the only one strong enough to mask his presence from me."

"But can he sense you, that's the question," Lexa-Blue said, frowning.

"Not directly, but he may be able to sense my jamming as I sensed his. If so, he'll know I am near."

Lexa-Blue considered for a moment. "Well, we don't have much of a choice. We'll just have to take the chance. Everything else points to a small, temporary hideout rather than an entrenched, well-defended base. That gives us a definite edge."

"How do we even know that the Technarch is still alive?" Giri asked, a whisper of scepticism in his voice.

Lexa-Blue saw the sharp look that flashed across Keene's face and heard the icy cold tone in his voice. "The tracer vein is powered by the body's own electrical field. If Daevin was dead, the signal would have disappeared."

Realizing the effect of his careless question, Giri mumbled an apology.

"All right, people," Lexa-Blue said, breaking the tension. "Let's land this bird and pay these bozos a visit."

Expertly, she took the ship out of auto-pilot and landed at one end of the canyon where the jungle broke open into a stretch of barren veldt spotted with grass. As the engines cycled down, she turned her chair to a side console and punched a control.

"Stand by for commo and chrono sync." She touched a control again. "Mark."

In the upper right corner of their fields of vision, a digital chrono display appeared, floating in air. Lexa-Blue and Keene were used to it, but Giri flinched and twitched his head a few times before he subsided. Elai accepted the new sensation without a word.

"The chrono sync is projected through the commo links I gave you," Lexa-Blue told Giri and Elai. "Keene and I find it can come in handy when things get sticky. Okay, five minutes for final check and load up, then we move out."

Keene moved quickly, strapping his tool kit to his waist, then checking the charge on his gun and holstering it snugly against his leg. Finally, he checked all the clasps and fasteners one last time.

Elai and Giri stood quietly to one side, needing no special equipment but their innate gifts.

Lexa-Blue called Keene over to help her with a metre long case she was pulling out of a storage cabinet. He came quickly to her side, glad of something concrete to do. With his help, Lexa-Blue hefted it on her back, the strap slung Sam Brown style across her torso. Keene read the make and model of the contents of the case, in neatly stencilled red lettering, followed by the Brighter Light Security logo. Recognizing the codes, he raised an eyebrow.

"I borrowed it from the armoury," she said with a huge grin on her face. "I thought it might come in handy."

Keene shook his head and chuckled.

They set out from the plane on their journey along the canyon rim, finding a cleanly cut trail along the edge of the jungle. A leafy green wall shot up on one side, and a sheer drop of rock fell away on the other. From deep in the green came the sounds of wildlife: the chittering and cheeping of birds, the faraway growls and roars of what sounded like sounded like some kind of predator, all set against the faint rustle of moving leaves.

The trip took about ten minutes, Keene checking his portable scan module constantly. Locked on to the base's thermal signature, it led them right to a spot opposite their target. From the edge of the cliff, they could see nothing but the rock face opposite and the valley below.

"Scan says it should be somewhere over there, just under that lateral ridge," he told the others.

He pointed, showing them the ridge of rock, almost invisible against the cliff face, where erosion had long ago cut into the base of the wall. They were barely able to see where the rock cut back in a shadowed overhang.

"We need to get in close and get a visual fix on our target," Lexa-Blue said, lowering the heavy case from her back to the ground. "Which means we have to get down there by the water."

"Leave that to me," Elai said, stepping forward. She went to the edge of the rocky rim and perched on the precipice. She spread her arms wide and lifted gently off the ground, floating over the wide emptiness of the canyon. Like a black dagger, she plunged out of sight.

As she dropped, the rushing slipstream of air clung to her body like a glove. Despite the seriousness of her task, she exulted quietly in the sensation. It had been so long since she had danced in the air, so long since she had held the rushes of air with her mind, shaping them to her will.

She hadn't had much time for recreation during her tenure as First Mind, full as it had been with duties and responsibilities. Time had been even scarcer since she had been in Brighter Light, making plans for the joining.

Only once had she found an opportunity, sandwiched between protocols and meetings, to slip away and dance. The pleasure had quickly faded when she discovered the treacherous eddies and currents caused by the towers of Brighter Light. The reckless winds had almost dashed her to pieces. It had taken all of her skill to keep from being thrown to the ground or into the face of a building.

But here! Here she was free, with only nature and air. The sheer pleasure was numbing, and she almost lost control. Re-establishing focus, she checked her descent, mere metres above the water.

To your right. That's where it should be, Lexa-Blue's voice said in her head. She found the sensation odd, so similar, yet so strange.

She focused her attention on the overhang to her right and saw the base, sprouting from the rock like a mushroom.

Make one more pass, please. We're accessing directly from the commo link.

Elai twisted and slithered, using her body to alter her path along the wind. Like a sleek torpedo, she turned and came past again, taking in the details for herself.

The shelter was a smooth dome, its flat base snugged against the wall of the canyon, its edges sealed to the rock itself. Its surface was dull grey-brown, absorbing even the faint light that reached it in its shadowed hiding place. A ring of locks and cargo doors dotted the dome's surface, forming an arc where its lower edge touched the ground.

Okay, Elai, we've got a fix. Come on back up.

Elai summoned a gust of wind, lifting her higher. With another thought, she shifted the force and angled back to the others. As she rose, she saw a beam of light pass her, far enough away not to worry her, aimed at the place she had just come from.

Relax, Elai, it's just me came Lexa-Blue's thought.

Elai acknowledged and turned her head to see what Lexa-Blue was doing.

On the edge of the cliff, Lexa-Blue took careful aim and set the gun's power level carefully. With precise motions, she moved, released the trigger, and adjusted her aim. Firing again, she repeated the process, terminating the movement in a slightly different place. When she was finished, she regarded her handiwork with satisfaction.

On the edge of the overhang directly above where Elai's reconnaissance had shown the base to be, a blackened X was burned lightly, but distinctly, into the rock.

Target acquired.

CHAPTER SEVENTEEN

Unable to achieve even the most basic of meditations, Bodi gave up and opened his eyes. He floated up from his bed in the tiny room he had commandeered for himself. By now, he thought, the First Mind should be dead, killed by the abomination of technology that passed for life. He felt a visceral disgust for the hubris of the Brighter Lights to believe they could create life with their circuits and their electronics. The mere thought of it made him sick. Still, he thought, it has served its purpose.

With Elai dead, he knew it would only be a matter of time before his people declared war on Brighter Light, and once he was done with the Technarch, Sotari's enemies would fall at their feet. He was tired of waiting, anxious to hear some confirmation of Elai's death. The unprecedented attack by Brighter Light security forces on the Hall of Memory had been a fortuitous circumstance, elevating his people's fear and desire for action. Once he knew Elai was dead, he could rewrite the Technarch's mind and proceed with the next phase of his plans. But until then...

He glided out of his cramped room like a swirl of mist along the halls to the common area. As he had been doing at regular intervals, he scanned, checking for signs of intruders, his mind open and naked. He stopped.

For a second, it had seemed he felt something, but when he turned his attention to it, nothing was there. He scanned again with greater concentration but found nothing, so he continued to the base's common room.

Only one other person was there, a renegade Brighter Light Security thug named Wulk, who looked up from polishing his rifle and fixed wary eyes on Bodi.

Bodi stared at Wulk's blunt, dull-witted features, the only outward sign of his scrutiny a slight tilt of his head. Fury welled up at the easy mistrust and simmering violence he sensed behind the human's eyes. This was the type that had taken the life of his father. You are nothing, he thought, his hate a haze the colour of burning and blood. Valme had taken careful handling and subtle manipulations, but you were only too eager to conspire against your own people to "protect" them from the horrors of union with us.

His lip curling, he stabbed into the slow-witted Wulk's mind. His touch burned along the human's neurons like a brand and the beefy man let out a high-pitched yip of pain. Bodi smiled at the sound. Now then, he thought, let's see what's in there to play with.

Like fingers pulling and stretching taffy, Bodi gouged through Wulk's memories, discarding all that didn't suit his purpose. There, he thought. This will do. He immersed himself in Wulk's childhood memory of being the least intelligent of his peers, with few to no technical skills showing up on his aptitude tests. One of the other children had tapped into the private files and shown the test results to all of Wulk's classmates. Bodi savoured the rich, sickly tang of youthful anguish, the horror as the boy's classmates turned on him, cruel as only children can be. He tasted the humiliation, bitter as venom across his lips. With a thought, he skeined the memory and several others like it together, linking it with the pain he was making Wulk feel. Still he kept up the pressure, grinding mercilessly at the human's synapses, binding the physical and emotional pain together.

Bodi retreated, just short of doing any permanent neurological damage. Almost as an afterthought, he smoothed Wulk's memories, placing the last few minutes behind a veil. Wulk would remember nothing of this.

Not yet, anyway.

Wulk suddenly became aware he was sitting in the common room with tears wetting his cheeks. A fierce blush cultured his face as he looked around to see if he had been noticed. Bodi hung quietly above a chair on the other side of the room, attention focused elsewhere. Wulk stood and all but stumbled out of the room.

As he left, the pale, nasty smirk returned to Bodi's face only to die there a second later. There it was again, that vague something, like a shadow half glimpsed out of the corner of one's eye or something wandering at the edge of consciousness.

Anger erupted in him as he realized someone was blocking him.

He stood, intending to go investigate, but he stopped short. How? His was the most powerful mind here. If he couldn't sense the source of the block, none of the others could. The base shelter's electronic scanners were minimal. He had insisted on it, hating any reliance on technology at all. There was a minimal passive detection system that wasn't nearly sophisticated enough to detect a mind powerful enough to shield itself this effectively.

None save Elai could hide themselves from him, and she was dead.

Or was she? He hadn't had any confirmation. An icy, hard glint came into his eyes. He had to know.

❖

Rising on the shaft of air, Elai suddenly became aware of the intense probe radiating up at them and fought to shield herself and the others. She had no doubt now who was waiting for them. Slipping herself out of the airflow, she dropped down on the cliff edge where the others stood.

"Okay," Lexa-Blue said. None of the others interrupted her, understanding she was the best suited to lead them. "First, we have to get Keene down there. He's the one who can get us past whatever locks and security devices there are. Giri, you have to go with him. The transponder trace isn't effective now because the thermal radiation buggers it up at this close range."

She turned to Elai. "Can you get the two of them down there?"

Elai looked at Keene, judging his mass. She nodded. "I can do it. You should know, though, that Bodi is down there. I felt him probing for us."

"Did he sense you too?" Lexa-Blue asked, concern in her voice. "Losing the element of surprise could make this dicey."

"I don't think so. It may be only by a fraction, but I am stronger than he is. He may suspect something, but I doubt he is certain. He thinks I'm dead by now."

Lexa-Blue digested the information. "Okay, it's a minor hitch, but we're here and we're committed, so we'll just work around it."

"What's your part in this plan, Blue?" Keene asked.

Lexa-Blue flashed him a grin and leaned down to the case at her feet, popping the latch. She opened the lid proudly, displaying a shoulder-mount plasma cannon powerful enough to stop a tank.

"I make a bit of noise to distract them while you sneak in the back door."

"And what about me?" said Elai.

"If I'm right, they're going to send their ranks after us once I start shooting. You'll have to help me keep them busy."

Elai nodded.

"Any more questions?"

There were none.

"Okay, Elai, take Keene down first, then Giri." She turned to Keene. "Let me know when you find a likely spot to break in, and I'll start shooting."

Keene's nod was crisp.

"All right, everybody, let's do it."

Elai went still with concentration, and the wind whispered up around her in the silence. Keene felt himself lifted from the ground and swung out over the edge of the cliff. He shut his eyes for a second and took a deep breath, forcing himself to relax.

Trust me. Elai's 'push rang with unshakeable confidence. He forced himself to open his eyes.

Keene's stomach flew up into his throat as the cliff edge fell away, and he dropped into the canyon. He streaked downward in a sharp, tightly controlled descent and felt the air release him as he touched down. As soon as he landed, he dropped into a fighting crouch, drawing his gun. Weaving his head back and forth, he checked for sentries or witnesses. None.

He turned to the dome, searching for a way in. There. A small personnel hatch, rectangular, two metres by three. He sprinted to it, checking the lock mechanism. He smiled. Easy.

Somewhere behind him, he heard Giri's landing, then steps as the Sotar joined him. Keene pulled out a fink and 'pushed Lexa-Blue.

I've got an entry point, Blue. Light it up.

❖

As soon as Keene had lifted from the ground, Lexa-Blue hoisted the metal cylinder of the cannon to her shoulder, closing her fingers around the handgrip. She flexed her fingers, testing the feel. Placing her sensor eye in the cup of the sight, she thumbed the start-up diagnostic. The display showed all clear, and she sighted along the wall of rock above her X, picking her targets. Her body went still as she focused her mind on the task, already planning her firing pattern. She was ready when Keene's call came.

She lined up her first target and fired.

❖

When he heard the first shot, Keene slammed the fink onto the lock and booted up his portable code reader. He flipped open the small hinged unit and keyed it to his node. With a thought, he tuned into the door's frequency, infiltrating the lock's memory. Streams of data flowed across his vision, ending in a flash of red.

"Problem?" Giri asked, fear rising in his voice.

"Slight delay," Keene said, gritting his teeth as resistance rose against him. "An extra layer of code, that's all. Just means we try a little harder." He reached into his pack again, pulling out a bit chip and inserting it into the input slot on the side of the reader. The unit gave a cheery ping as the code was accepted.

Somewhere inside the shelter, they heard the faint sound of alarms.

Keene's thoughts raced as he renewed his attack on the lock. He watched the datastreams carefully, searching for signs of success. Finally, he saw one. 'Pushing a new command routine, he felt the lock give way, and the hatch opened with a huff of air.

Keene quickly stored his tools and snapped the pack shut. "Come on."

❖

Steady and sure, Lexa-Blue aimed and fired, the plasma beam hammering into the cliff face. She watched the power level closely, keeping the blasts phased for maximum effect and minimal physical damage.

We're in.

Through the node, Lexa-Blue sensed Elai receiving the information as well. She saw Elai hovering, and she sensed her readiness. Lexa-Blue shifted her aim, setting her targets lower, closer to the base. A couple of the blasts hit the ground, sending up clouds of dust from the canyon floor. Right on their proverbial doorstep, she thought.

Time to wake the neighbours.

❖

Bodi struggled up from the floor, having fallen when he lost focus of his mind. Wincing at a sharp pain in his arm, he probed the area with his mind and found a broken bone. He closed his mind to the pain momentarily, set it back into place, and focused part of his thoughts to holding it there. He looked around the base's cramped control room. Papers and assorted minor debris littered the floors, but he saw little serious damage. The few others in the room, some Brighter Light, some Sotar, were unhurt. The monitor techs were already back at their posts.

Bodi had come to the control room to inform Deria, the senior Brighter Light agent, of his suspicions about Elai's presence. The first blast had hit as he walked into the room.

Fighting the continuing shocks, Bodi staggered over to the rough-faced snub of a woman barking orders at the monitor techs. He flooded her mind with images of raging, spiky arcs of danger.

"We're under attack, I know," she snapped, her nose wrinkling at the burning chemical smell of his thoughts. "I noticed."

Bodi flushed, and his thoughts burned red with rage and fell on her like stones, centred around the possibility of the First Mind rescuing the Technarch.

Deria's gaze was murderous.

"Gold, Harper," she growled into the commo, "take out a perimeter patrol, now."

He thrust an image of Simir into her mind, so real she smelled sweat and fear. For a moment, he thought she would lose control, and then he heard her thoughts, in plain linear words. I don't want your people anywhere near mine, she thought, that's why I got involved in all of this in the first place. She was about to say something when she saw a cold, over-the-edge gleam spark to life in his eyes. She backed down, grunting the order into the commo unit. "Done," she said, turning again to Bodi. Without a word, he was already walking away.

The smile on his face made her blood run cold.

Unbeknownst to Deria, Bodi had sensed something, felt it dance across his mind. It left a tantalizing trace, like a drop of honey on his tongue. Blocking everything out, he went after it like a predator with the scent of blood in its nose.

❖

The hatch slid open and revealed a supply bay, dark and empty of people. Keene drew his gun and stepped in, Giri just behind him. They steadied themselves against the rumblings of Lexa-Blue's constant barrage.

Racks of shelves lined the walls, laden with crates. Some had fallen to the floor under Lexa-Blue's barrage and smashed open, spilling everything from rations to engine parts. Off to one side, an open arch of light led into a larger bay. Peeking around the edge of the wall, Keene saw two Brighter Light planes, emblazoned with the security logo. One of the engine housings of the nearest plane was open, cabling and engine parts hanging out like entrails. Beyond the shuttles were several small flitters and air bikes. When he heard the sound of running footsteps, Keene ducked back, moving away from the arch but watching carefully.

Two men came in at a dead run and mounted two flitters. He waited while they did a cursory pre-flight check and revved their engines. The hangar door rolled slowly aside, and the two flitters rocketed out. Keene made a tentative move toward the arch, but jumped back suddenly, roughly shoving Giri as well, as the rest of the flitter squad raced into the hangar.

Sorry.

It's okay.

Keene pulled back from the arch, scanning the small dark room looking for another exit. No luck. The only way out of the supply bay was across the hangar to the inner door leading into the base, the door that the flitter crews had used. He bit down hard to keep from cursing out loud.

We'll have to wait until they're gone.

With a gentle pressure, Keene eased Giri back into the shadows of the bay. Through his node, Keene felt Lexa-Blue engaging the first terrorist flitters. He knew she could take care of herself and was probably having the time of her life doing it, so he closed off the link to concentrate on his own task.

They waited and watched as the rest of the flitter crew made ready to join the battle, priming their vehicles and eventually taking off. From beyond the open hangar door came the sounds of pitched air combat. When Keene was sure the hangar was empty, he pulled Giri out of their hiding place, and they made a dash for the door.

The inner door, however, didn't open for them. Keene saw a palmprint reader attached to it. Okay, he thought calmly, no problem. Reaching into his kit, he pulled out the tools he needed and set about bypassing the reader. Precious minutes ticked by, but he deliberately stayed cool, refusing to be rushed. He might trip a hidden alarm by accident. Shortly, the reader clicked, and the door opened. Keene stuck his head out into the hallway, looking first one way, then the other. Certain that the way was clear, he pulled back.

Your play now. Which way?

Giri closed his eyes and concentrated for a second. When he opened his eyes again, they sparked with a green glow. *Left.*

❖

Elai noticed the flitters first, swooping up from under the rock ledge that hid the base.

We are about to have company.

Lexa-Blue stopped firing and zoomed her eye on the base below. She saw two delta winged eggs coming, bristling with weaponry.

Flitters, Elai. They're fast and agile. Be careful.

One of the flitters pulled ahead of the other, having spotted Elai. Spurts of orange fire came from its forward laser turrets, but the air around her bent, deflecting the energy.

"Not nice, junior," Lexa-Blue said, shaking her head. She swung the plasma cannon around, pumped up the power level, and fired.

Her shot sheared away the flitter's wing in a squeal of tortured metal. The small aircraft wobbled before spinning out of control into the canyon wall. Lexa-Blue felt the ground shudder under her feet and heard the roar of fuel cells rupturing.

The other craft banked sharply away from the fireball and seemed to hesitate between Elai and Lexa-Blue before zeroing in on Elai again.

Lexa-Blue was targeting on the second craft when she heard the odd pop of air off to her left. She pivoted, having just enough time to register a pair of drugged, pinhole eyes as she fired. Set to punch through a flitter's hull, the plasma cannon tore the teleporter apart before he could move.

❖

Elai felt the heat from the flitter's explosion wash up from the canyon and over her, changing the air currents. Concentrating, she steadied herself and focused her attention on the other ship coming at her.

It was fast indeed, though she realized she had an edge in

manoeuvrability. As it bore down on her, she cut the thought field holding her aloft, dropping out of the pilot's sights like a stone. She just missed being fried by laser fire which scorched the leafy fronds of a tree.

She caught herself, shooting up suddenly and looping around to end up above the flitter. She set up a barrier against the currents of air near the flitter, causing a wind shear to form around the small craft. The flitter bucked and lost control, diving into the jungle and cutting a swath in the leafy canopy. A trail of black smoke wafted up from the aircraft's resting place.

Seeing Lexa-Blue pointing down at the base, Elai turned and noticed the trio of new flitters rising toward them. Before she could react, she felt Lexa-Blue 'push a new plan to her. An anticipatory grin formed on her face as she thought back her acknowledgment. She plunged down toward Lexa-Blue, seeing her sling the plasma cannon over her shoulder. Elai concentrated, knowing they would only get one chance at this manoeuvre. Her mind reached out and took hold of Lexa-Blue, lifting her from the cliff's edge, her hold solid. Elai pulled her into the air and brought her close. Linked, they shot from the cliff edge, dropping to the canyon floor, aimed right at the center of the tight flitter formation.

Seeing the two women exploding toward them, the flitter pilots split their formation open wildly, the chicken run taking them completely by surprise. The pilot on the right veered away too sharply, sending his craft into the cliff face as well. Vehicle and pilot disappeared in a fiery blossom.

The other two pilots managed to stay in the air, arcing back to chase their quarry, but Lexa-Blue and Elai were already on the canyon floor outside the base, ready and waiting for them. As Elai lifted off once again, Lexa-Blue unslung the cannon and took aim.

❖

The sounds of battle quieted as they moved deeper into the base. After several twists and turns through the corridors and two stops to avoid detection by passers-by, Giri pulled up short at a junction in the corridor, motioning for Keene to stop as well.

The Technarch is just around the corner. There is a guard, but he is not paying attention to his task. He'd rather be outside, fighting.

Keene nodded, shifting his grip on his pistol. ***Can you give me a fix on the layout of the holding area and his position, so I can take him down?***

Yes. One moment.

Giri's eyes lost focus, and a precise map of the inside of the room formed in Keene's mind: the cell, Daevin barely visible behind the shimmering jangle field, the hard backed chair the guard was in, and, finally, their own position around the corner and to the right. Relative distances entered his mind, more clearly than if he had measured them electronically. Trusting the information, ready to rethink if he failed, Keene swung around the corner, firing a stun charge.

He saw the stun bolt hit the guard in the head, knocking him out. The guard's face went blank as he fell off the chair with no sound but a small thud as he hit the floor. One slim strand of spittle came from the corner of his mouth, pooling on the floor. Keene twirled the gun around his finger before slipping it back into its holster.

Giri brushed past him excitedly, heading for the cell. "He's in here. We found him!"

Keene opened his mouth to shout a warning, but it was too late. Unaware of the danger, Giri's hand hit the jangle field dead on, giving him a full dose of its neural disruption energy. Giri's body went into spasm then collapsed. Keene rushed to his side, feeling for a pulse in his neck. No permanent damage, he decided, just a pretty nasty stun. "Shit," he muttered.

"Who's there?" Daevin's voice came from the other side of the energy wall.

"Daevin, it's me, Keene. Can you hear me?"

"Yes, I can hear you." Relief flooded Daevin's voice. "Is it really you? I can't see anything but blurs."

Keene checked the field's control panel and discovered the cell was locked down from another location, probably the main control room. The palm plate was out as the reader wouldn't recognize his hand. Beside the palm reader was a touch-pad that controlled the opacity of the field. He slid his hand along it, watching the field go from translucent to clear.

Daevin's face appeared, grubby and gaunt. One lank strand of hair had escaped the ponytail and hung limply over one eye. To Keene, Daevin had never looked better.

"Get back against the wall, Little Prince. I'm going to blow the lock."

Keene stepped back and took aim but before he could fire, his mind exploded under a grinding thought assault. Gravity seemed to turn inside out, the room shifting and tearing apart. In his mind, he saw his bones ripped from his body one by one, shredding his flesh. It's not real, he thought desperately, not real. Every cell in his body seemed to turn inside out, and as he dropped to his knees retching, he saw Bodi suspended in the doorway, glittering like a rain of icy, diamond bullets.

CHAPTER EIGHTEEN

Keene struggled against the nausea and was trying to focus and aim his gun at Bodi when the burnt, angry bludgeon of the telekinetic blast hit him. Like a kick to the head, it knocked him off balance. He felt himself tip over, his gun hand swinging wide in an effort to stabilize himself. The back of his hand brushed against the jangle field, jolting him with energy and for a second, it felt like his veins were pumping pure acid. He collapsed in a heap, his muscles twitching.

The pain began to ebb, but the twitching numbness remained, blocking use of his limbs.

"Keene! Are you all right?" Daevin's frantic voice seemed to echo from far away. "Answer me!"

Keene fought to form words, but none came.

"You fucking bastard, if I ever get out of here, I swear, I'll kill you," Daevin raged at Bodi.

The Sotar's only response was a squirm of silent laughter that reverberated through their minds. Bodi stopped for a second at Giri's unconscious form, then ignored him and continued closer. He stopped just beside Keene's prone body. He looked down patronizingly as Keene jerked his fingers uselessly, trying to grab his gun just centimetres from his hand.

Bodi's viscous contempt washed through Keene's head like oozing, acid honey, searing away at Keene's desire to help Daevin. Keene felt the thought form in Bodi's mind and enclose his gun where it lay on the floor. It skidded away, coming to rest against the wall a metre away. To Keene, it might as well have been on another planet. He felt a new pain, a dull ache as Bodi sifted none too gently through his mind. Keene felt Bodi's mind wrench Elai's image free of his memories, leaving him with an impression of ragged, bleeding flesh left in its place. Bodi's confidence in his plan burned white hot like a star.

In the blinding radiance, Keene saw the intricate web of Bodi's plan spin out, saw it shift and weave around his and Lexa-Blue's unexpected presence. They would die now, along with Elai, and the story would be told of their betrayal and attempted assassination of Technarch. Daevin would be returned to Brighter Light with his mind scrubbed and programmed to Bodi's will. Keene felt a wave of vertigo sweep through him at the pale ghost of Daevin he saw in Bodi's mind, empty of his formidable will and strong, generous heart. His own heart tore open to see the puppet Daevin declare war on Sotari and lose through intentionally erratic leadership.

Keene saw the inevitable tumble of dominoes then: censure from the Pan Galactum, followed by expulsion when the Daevin golem refused to capitulate, Brighter Light's fall, Sotari in quiet solitary peace as a Galactum Protectorate. And one final image: Daevin's body arcing from his terrace, falling through space to the sea below.

Without speech, Keene howled inside his head, the anguish and rage echoing through his thoughts. It took a second to realize the barrage of emotions pummelling him wasn't just his own. He felt the mental attack raining down on Bodi like a fusillade of cannon fire, and knew, even as he struggled to open his eyes to see, who it was.

See, that ending's just not gonna work for me. At all. What else have you got?

Keene felt Elai and Lexa-Blue united, their minds blending together to pound at Bodi's. When he managed to get his eyes open, he saw the renegade Sotar suspended in the air, his body contorted under the combined onslaught of the two women's minds. Beyond him, he saw Lexa-Blue with her gun drawn, and Elai buoyed at her side.

Stand down. Keene winced at the mere echo of the command ringing through Bodi's head.

Keene felt Bodi's mind form a gesture of surrender, and saw him spread his arms wide. He straightened, drawing himself to his full height.

The shift in his thoughts was almost too fast for Keene to see.

Blue, look out!

The air around Bodi bent like a lens as he sensed the one grain of weakness in the bond between Elai and Lexa-Blue, the latter's inexperience. A shockwave tore through the refracted space between them, tearing through the link and sending Lexa-Blue hard into the wall.

❖

Lexa-Blue felt a moment of queasy vertigo as the present smeared, becoming the past. Then she hit the ground, a jut of rock cutting into her shoulder blades, and she recognized the time and place.

Not here.

Not again.

Before she could fight it, her awareness of the intervening years was gone, and she was lost in the memory.

Her breath huffed out as Zhark drove his fist into her side, and she felt a rib break. She squirmed and struggled, but his pals gripped her arms tightly. She bucked against their hold, her head swinging back and forth, but there was not even an inch of give. Lost in rage, she spat and saw the missile hit Zhark square in the eye.

He bellowed like an animal and brought his face close to hers. His foul breath was in her face. She swung her head back and forth trying to avoid him, but he pinned her face with his hand. The sour, beery taste and smell filled her head, making her gag.

He punched her in the stomach, and tears sprang to her eyes. Again and again he struck, and she felt her body bend around the blows like elastic. Each punch resonated through her body, stretching her out, the connective tissues elongating as her bones threatened to fly apart. She felt her organs rupture and shred, coming back together only to fly apart again.

No.

It wasn't like this.

Time broke and reformed around her, the beating taking an eternity. Zhark put his hand on her skull to hold her head steady. and she swung around, sinking her teeth into the gristle of his arm, tearing away a ragged chunk of flesh.

He bellowed like a raging animal and slapped her hard enough to make her head swim. When her vision cleared, she saw the knife in his hand, saw the blow fall.

And he tore the left side of her head open.

❖

Still struggling to regain control of his body, Keene saw Elai at Lexa-Blue's side. Through her mind, he felt his friend's anguish radiating from her in sickly waves. Elai whipped her head around to Bodi, a feral snarl across her face. She terrified Keene, and in that moment, he saw again the childhood nightmares she had brought to mind the first time they met.

She rose from Lexa-Blue's side as if held on strings, all rage and sharp, black angles. And then she was still, though Keene felt something building in her.

Without moving at all, she struck.

Elai focused her mindfield, fashioning it into one solid battering ram. Faster than an ordinary human could think, she drove it at Bodi.

He countered it, his own field flaring to meet hers. Forces normally invisible to the human eye glittered in ugly, clashing colours where the fields met.

Pressing a minute advantage, he struck, emitting his hatred at her like a cloud of poisonous gas and she felt it seeping into her through gaps too tiny for thought. It sickened her, obscured her will, but she concentrated, refining her own strength. A thought came to her. At the edge of her consciousness, she found an overturned chair and enveloped it, sending it at him like a missile.

He saw it coming and batted it aside. She felt his sneer slide across the surface of her mind, followed by the sulphurous violet waves of his arrogance driving against her. Wincing under the rush of his absolute certainty in himself, she allowed herself an instant of satisfaction. She knew his weakness.

She relaxed and opened her memories to him. Daevin, standing honourable and humble, approaching her to end the violence. The people of Brighter Light who accepted her, showed her kindness, despite all her people had done. She flooded him with the strength and nobility of those left in the wake of the terror Bodi had wrought. Even showed him how his own people managed to forgive and move past the wounds that SCI had inflicted on them. She poured into him the memories of Keene throwing himself headlong to protect Daevin at the market with no thought to his own safety. Lexa-Blue and Vrick ready to sacrifice for their friend. Vrick saving Qoios.

She flooded Bodi with nobility and compassion and selflessness, all of the things he thought the humans of Brighter Light incapable of. All of the things he had sacrificed in his quest to destroy his enemies. Relentlessly, she hammered at him, her memories like bright, hot sunlight on skin, warming every inch. And feeling every thought enrage and disgust him even more.

Then she felt the whisper at the edge of her mind, and the final piece fell into place. That's it. That's how we win.

Bodi opened his mouth and screamed.

"Nice try, asshole," Lexa-Blue said, teeth clenched against pain. "My turn now."

Bodi dropped to his knees, staring at the ragged stump of his right arm. Everything below the elbow had been sheared away. Panting with exertion and shock, he looked from the blood and tatters of his arm, to her and then back.

She aimed again, fighting the tremor in her hand that had caused her to miss the killing shot. She tightened her grip on the gun, levelling it at Bodi's head.

He screamed again before she could fire, the sound even more horrifying in its agony. This time, she felt it reverberate through the floor. His body shook with massive, quaking tremors that looked like they would tear him apart. For barely a second, Lexa-Blue was stunned by the furious insanity radiating from him, and she hesitated. Before she could pull the trigger, the room exploded into chaos.

The very air churned, turning into a ripping, agonized whirlwind. Lexa-Blue was flung up and back, pinned against the wall like a butterfly specimen. Elai extended her mindfield around Giri and Keene, holding them down. Loose debris swirled up in a crazed demon dance. The chair Elai had used as a weapon smashed to splinters against the wall.

At the center of it all, Bodi gibbered and shrieked, his mind exploding out around him while he remained safe in the eye of the hurricane. Sickening waves of fractured thought radiated from him.

Sensing his shields had dropped, Elai reached into his mind, recoiling at the chaos that lurked there. All semblance of sanity was gone, with nothing left but a powerful, sucking madness that grew stronger with each passing second. Desperately, she tried to rein him in but failed.

Suddenly, bursts of yellow fire shot from Bodi, igniting bits of runaway paper into tiny pyres. One flame localized at the stump of his arm, cauterizing the wound. The sheer anguish of his scream was pitiable, but his mental assault never faltered.

Buffeted by Bodi's mind storm, Keene struggled against the paralysis, trying to control his rogue muscles. Reality seemed to falter as the room whirled, leaving a pit of nausea in his stomach. Slow down, he thought. Concentrate. With excruciating effort, he calmed the twitching in his right arm, the hand resting on his thigh.

The howling wind tore at him, snatching his breath. He felt the paralysis ebbing.

One hand, Keene, he thought. You've got one hand. Make it worth it.

He shifted his eyes, looking for his gun. Out of reach. What next? Tool pack. He manoeuvred his hand to the pack, painfully opening it. His fingers felt like lead as he fumbled for his objective. After what seemed like an eternity, he closed his fingers around it. Now, all I have to do is lift it, he thought.

Feeling like he was lifting a ton of stone, he raised the pinbeam drill and aimed. Steady. A rogue twitch jiggled his finger. Steady, he told himself. He calmed the tremor in his hand with sheer force of will, hoping that his aim would be true. Jerking his thumb, he jammed the power level to maximum.

(I have you. I'm here.) Elai's thoughts sang inside his head. Calm washed through him as he felt her steadying him. Then Giri was there too, his unerring sense of objects in space guiding Keene's hand.

You've got me too, partner. He saw through her sensor eye angles calculated in wavelengths far beyond those the human eye could see.

And then Daevin was with him too, flooding up from his heart. *(You can do it.)*

With his last fragment of strength, he pushed the activator.

The pinbeam pierced Bodi's brain stem, killing him instantly. His body hesitated a second, then tumbled to the floor.

The mindstorm went out with the speed of a broken thought, and the room quieted. Keene's vision blurred for a second from strain, but he heard footsteps clattering across the floor. When his sight cleared, he saw Lexa-Blue's lopsided grin.

"And I always said you couldn't hit the broad side of a neutron star," she said, chuckling.

Keene managed a weak smile in return. He struggled to speak. "Daevin...Out."

"Yes, by all means, please. Me...Out," Daevin said.

Lexa-Blue looked at him, untouched behind the cell's field. Seeing the bedraggled impatience on his face, she couldn't help but laugh. "Hang on for just a second."

She fired her gun at the control panel, and the field died in a shower of sparks. She grinned and blew an imaginary wisp of smoke away from the gun's muzzle. Daevin ran past her toward Keene's side, drawing him into his arms.

Feeling through her node that Keene was beginning to recover, Lexa-Blue joined Elai as she laid her hands on his head to rouse him back to consciousness.

When Keene and Giri were able to move, the quintet dragged themselves out of the terrorist base, leaning on each other for support. Outside, the remains of Deria's patrol, tied up and definitely the worse for wear, huddled in a sullen knot of three.

A squadron of Brighter Light Security Aircraft came over the ridge of the cliff like a black wave, each plane surrounded by a halo of flying Sotars buzzing around the planes like dragonflies. For a moment, they thought it was some kind of airborne battle, but Vrick proudly informed them it was united force he and Jaekir had mounted to come to their aid, the first in Orb's history.

Despite his aches, Daevin looked at Elai and smiled a smile that was joyfully returned.

EPILOGUE

The days that followed passed in a blur. Daevin invited Keene and Lexa-Blue to stay for the Joining and the ensuing celebrations, but they had barely arrived back in Brighter Light when Daevin was called away to deal with the chaos facing the Technarchy Board and reestablish his control over the city-state. He also needed to deal with Saphia Valme's funeral, Bach's trial, and the final harried preparations for unification.

Through it all, Daevin swore just one more thing required his attention, before disappearing for hours at a time. Keene saw first-hand the demands Daevin faced every day.

To pass the long hours, Keene and Lexa-Blue kept each other company, exploring Brighter Light and Sotari, camping in the Median Lands, just enjoying what the unfamiliar world had to offer. Elai accompanied them as much as she could, but her duties were almost as demanding as Daevin's.

Through it all, Keene and Daevin met in bed, sharing what they could in the moments before fatigue claimed them.

❖

Keene walked to the railing of the landing pad, sticking one finger into the knot of his bow tie to untie it. The loose ends of the shimmersilk fell against his tuxedo shirt, dark against the perfect white.

Savouring the solitude, he closed his eyes a moment, the cool breeze feeling wonderful on his skin. The sounds of celebration—music, laughter, endless cheering—reached him even here on the landing pad and widow's walk at the apex of the palace. Some of the sounds came from the main ballroom, covering an entire floor of the building five levels below. Its walls were retracted, leaving the entire space open to the pleasant spring night. Keene knew not all the happy roar came from the ballroom. The rest of it came from the joyous crowds thronging the streets far below. Off in the distance, fireworks lit the dark with bursts of colour, and far below, brilliant lights were strung along the Avenue.

He took a sip of champagne from the fluted goblet, then held it up, watching the reflections of light play across its smooth black surface. For a few minutes, he just stood there, revelling in the night air, listening to the sounds of the worldwide party. A peaceful smile lay gently on his face.

"Penny for them."

Lexa-Blue came toward him, silhouetted against the Maverick Heart idling quietly in the background. The far off light of the fireworks made the teal blue silk of her dress gleam. Keene marvelled at how beautiful she looked, the sheath very short and fetchingly slit from hem to underarm and held together with tiny silver clips. In her hand was an open bottle of champagne and a glass.

"What's a penny?"

Lexa-Blue frowned. "You know, Vrick never did tell me."

Look it up!

Yeah, yeah, I'll do my homework later.

"Have I told you how gorgeous you look tonight?" he asked her.

"Only a dozen times, but feel free to say it again," she said, holding out the bottle to refill his glass.

He executed a courtly bow. "Consider it said."

He's right, Meat. You look pretty.

"Elai helped me pick it out when we went shopping," she said, making a slow, sinuous twirl.

Keene looked aghast. "Shopping, you?!"

Lexa-Blue waggled a finger in his face. "Not a word!"

He merely looked at her with a "Who, me?" look on his face.

For a moment or two, they just stood, watching the play of lights across the sky.

"He wants you to stay with him, doesn't he?" Lexa-Blue asked eventually.

Keene nodded. "He asked me just before the ceremony."

Lexa-Blue waited for a moment, expecting more, but Keene was silent. "Do you want to stay?" There was no recrimination in her voice.

Keene sighed, as if clearing out weeks of held breath. "I don't

know. A part of me does, I guess, but we're from very different worlds."
He chuckled. "Literally and figuratively. I've been in space most of my
adult life, and the thought of never seeing another planetfall, or another
jaunt into interspace…The thought of not being able to look out the
window by my bed at a sea of stars. I don't know if I could live like
that."

"Come on, Keene. Just because you stay here doesn't mean you
can never see those things again."

"I know, but…" He struggled with the thoughts, trying to make
them clear so he could articulate them. "But then space would become
what it is to Daevin, just something to travel through to get somewhere.
Not home like it is now. With you and Vrick."

Lexa-Blue smiled, accepting the sentiment. "Still, it might be nice
to have a patch of dirt to call your own," she said with a shrug. "There's
no shame in finding a new home."

"Hey, are you trying to get rid of me or something?"

"Oh, like I could," she shot back. "I keep telling you, partner,
you're stuck with me."

She jerked a thumb at the Maverick Heart. "Em too, if I'm not
mistaken. You'll always be a part of our lives, no matter what you
decide. So set you mind at rest on that score and let us know when you
make up your mind."

What she said.

He clinked his glass against hers, smiling. "I will. And thank you.
Both."

"Well, let's do this so we can get back to the party."

"What's his name?" Keene said, then suddenly looked pensive.
"Her name? It's hard to keep track with you sometimes."

"This time, her." Her smile intensified, becoming lusty and
uninhibited. "Dehlas," she said, the name coming out in a lascivious
purr.

"From Elai's honour guard?"

She nodded eagerly. "I hear telepaths are amazing lovers."

"Who told you that?"

"Elai. Who else?" With a wink, she turned and walked toward the
ship.

"You don't have to come with us. It's just a quick trip."

"Partner, I wouldn't miss the look on her face for anything. Come
on. You have a promise to keep."

Everyone ready, Vrick?

All set. Our guests are all in the lounge and fairly eager to get started. Whenever you're ready.

Keene followed Lexa-Blue up the gangway into the ship and entered the main lounge. Daevin was resplendent in his formal cutaway, the insignia of rank and stature bright on his left breast. Beside him, Giri was practically bouncing out of his skin with excitement. Even Elai, normally so calm and graceful, had an eager glint in her eye.

Keene looked them over, his smile ending up on Elai's glowing face. "Have a seat, make yourselves comfortable, and we can get under way."

He stood in the back of the lounge with Lexa-Blue, and the Maverick Heart lifted away from the pad and arced up into the sky. Off in the distance, fireworks exploded in riots of colour, falling below them as the ship angled toward its orbital insertion point. Within minutes, the atmosphere fell away behind them and planetary night was replaced by the truer, blacker night of space.

Giri and Elai stared, speechless at the vista of stars before them. Elai turned to him and seemed about to speak, but no words came.

"Wait," Keene said, brimming with pleasure at being the one to show her this for the first time.

"We've hit perigee, everybody," Vrick said. "I'm turning us around."

The field of stars turned in the viewport, then slowly, majestically, was replaced by the curve of Orb. The planet grew steadily, fully two thirds of it filling the port when the ship stopped moving.

"Synchronous orbit," Vrick announced.

Vrick had timed and calculated their orbit perfectly. Barely moments after their arrival, a single strand of fiery sunlight bloomed along Orb's curve. Transfixed, Elai stood and walked over to the viewport, her hand touching the plex lightly. The wash of brilliant light made her russet gold gown shine. She turned to Keene and then Lexa-Blue, wonder shining in her eyes. When she spoke, her voice was an awestruck whisper. "Thank you."

Keene smiled and let some of her wonder flow through him. ***Good job, Vrick.*** Though he had seen hundreds of worlds in his travels, seeing this one through her eyes made the experience new for him. And more planets were yet to be seen, he thought.

He realized Daevin was at his side, his eyes sad.

"I'm going to go be somewhere else now," Lexa-Blue said, "but this, your techness, is for you."

She held something out to Daevin, who extended his hand to receive it. Gently, she laid the credit chip that he had given them, its balance untouched, in his palm. "This one's on us."

She turned away to go join Elai and Giri.

"You're leaving, aren't you?" Daevin said.

Keene looked down and sighed, then faced Daevin. "I can't stay. I have a life, partners, a business. I have a thousand more views like this to see. Other than you, there's nothing for me here." He shrugged. "I'm a spacer. It's in my blood. I wouldn't be any happier in your world than you would be in mine. I'm sorry."

"I understand," Daevin said, knowing that the words were true.

"Of course, there's probably a lot of work for independent merchanters in this sector, isn't there?" Keene asked. "Someone could probably make regular stops here, couldn't they?"

Daevin grinned. "Now that you mention it, I think so."

"Well, there you go."

"So, when are you leaving?" Daevin asked a minute or so later.

"In the morning, Lexa-Blue wants to get back to the party. And a certain member of Elai's honour guard. I may have to pry her away."

"She may be the one prying you away."

Keene smiled. "Still, nights can last an awful long time out here if you know what you're doing."

"And of course, you do," Daevin said, smiling too. He took hold of Keene's lapels and pulled him in for a slow, thorough kiss. When they broke apart, Keene took in his friends. Elai and Giri stood by the viewport, side by side, but with no physical contact. Even across the room, Keene felt the intimacy of their bond despite never having seen them touch. He saw Lexa-Blue off to one side, her hand resting against the seam where the viewport joined Vrick's hull, and saw her hand move slowly, as if in a caress.

"What do you say, everyone?" Keene said, pulling Daevin close against his side. "Ready to go home?"

"Not yet," Elai said. "Just a little longer." By her side, at a loss for words, Giri nodded.

Lexa-Blue met his eyes and smiled. ***Dehlas will just have to wait.***

What about it, Vrick? Once around the moon and back?

...And straight on til morning.

About the Author

Born on the prairies, Stephen Graham King has since traded the big sky for the big city and now lives in Toronto. His first book, *Just Breathe*, tells the blunt, funny, and uncompromising story of his three-year battle with metastatic synovial sarcoma. Since then, his short fiction has appeared in the anthologies *North of Infinity II* ("Pas de Deux"), *Desolate Places* ("Nor Winter's Cold") and *Ruins Metropolis* ("Burning Stone"). His first novel, *Chasing Cold*, was released in 2012. He is also an artist, working primarily in acrylics, but also dabbling in photography. He also loves to cook, so if you ask very, very nicely, he might make you dinner. More about his writing and art, as well as some of his favorite recipes, can be found on his website.

Stephen can be contacted at: sgk@stephengrahamking.com
Website: www.stephengrahamking.com/
Facebook: www.facebook.com/stephenwritesbooks
Twitter: www.twitter.com/stephenwrites

Books Available From Bold Strokes Books

Night Sweats by Tom Cardamone. These stories are as gripping as the hand on your throat. (978-1-62639-572-5)

Soul's Blood by Stephen Graham King. After receiving a summons from a love long past, Keene and his associates, Lexa-Blue and the sentient ship Maverick Heart, are plunged into turmoil on a planet poised for war. (978-1-62639-508-4)

Corpus Calvin by David Swatling. Cloverkist Inn may be haunted, but a ghost materializes from Jason Dekker's past and Calvin's canine instinct kicks in to protect a young boy from mortal danger. (978-1-62639-428-5)

Brothers by Ralph Josiah Bardsley. Blood is thicker than water, but you can drown in either. Jamus Cork and Sean Malloy struggle against tradition to find love in the Irish enclave of South Boston. (978-1-62639-538-1)

Every Unworthy Thing by Jon Wilson. Gang wars, racial tensions, a kidnapped girl, and a lone PI! What could go wrong? (978-1-62639-514-5)

Puppet Boy by Christian Baines. Budding filmmaker Eric can't stop thinking about the handsome young actor that's transferred to his class. Could Julien be his muse? Even his first boyfriend? Or something far more sinister? (978-1-62639-510-7)

The Prophecy by Jerry Rabushka. Religion and revolution threaten to bring an ancient civilization to its knees...unless love does it first. (978-1-62639-440-7)

Heart of the Liliko'i by Dena Hankins. Secrets, sabotage, and grisly human remains stall construction on an ancient Hawaiian burial ground, but the sexual connection between Kerala and Ravi keeps building toward a volcanic explosion. (978-1-62639-556-5)

Lethal Elements by Joel Gomez-Dossi. When geologist Tom Burrell is hired to perform mineral studies in the Adirondack Mountains, he finds himself lost in the wilderness and being chased by a hired gun. (978-1-62639-368-4)

The Heart's Eternal Desire by David Holly. Sinister conspiracies threaten Seaton French and his lover, Dusty Marley, and only by tracking the source of the conspiracy can Seaton and Dusty hold true to the heart's eternal desire. (978-1-62639-412-4)

The Orion Mask by Greg Herren. After his father's death, Heath comes to Louisiana to meet his mother's family and learn the truth about her death—but some secrets can prove deadly. (978-1-62639-355-4)

The Strange Case of the Big Sur Benefactor by Jess Faraday. Billiwack, CA, 1884. All Rosetta Stein wanted to do was test her new invention. Now she has a mystery, a stalker, and worst of all, a partner. (978-1-62639-516-9)

One Hot Summer Month by Donald Webb. Damien, an avid cockhound, flits from one sexual encounter to the next until he finally meets someone who assuages his sexual libido. (978-1-62639-409-4)

The Indivisible Heart by Patrick Roscoe. An investigation into a gruesome psycho-sexual murder and an account of the victim's final days are interwoven in this dark detective story of the human heart. (978-1-62639-341-7)

Fool's Gold by Jess Faraday. 1895. Overworked secretary Ira Adler thinks a trip to America will be relaxing. But rattlesnakes, train robbers, and the U.S. Marshals Service have other ideas. (978-1-62639-340-0)

Big Hair and a Little Honey by Russ Gregory. Boyfriend troubles abound as Willa and Grandmother land new ones and Greg tries to hold on to Matt while chasing down a shipment of stolen hair extensions. (978-1-62639-331-8)

Death by Sin by Lyle Blake Smythers. Two supernatural private detectives in Washington, D.C., battle a psychotic supervillain spreading a new sex drug that only works on gay men, increasing the male orgasm and killing them. (978-1-62639-332-5)

Buddha's Bad Boys by Alan Chin. Six stories, six gay men trudging down the road to enlightenment. What they each find is the last thing in the world they expected. (978-1-62639-244-1)

Play It Forward by Frederick Smith. When the worlds of a community activist and a pro basketball player collide, little do they know that their dirty little secrets can lead to a public scandal…and an unexpected love affair. (978-1-62639-235-9)

GingerDead Man by Logan Zachary. Paavo Wolfe sells horror but isn't prepared for what he finds in the oven or the bathhouse; he's in hot water again, and the killer is turning up the heat. (978-1-62639-236-6)

Balls & Chain by Eric Andrews-Katz. In protest of the marriage equality bill, the son of Florida's governor has been kidnapped. Agent Buck 98 is back, and the alligators aren't the only things biting. (978-1-62639-218-2)

Blackthorn by Simon Hawk. Rian Blackthorn, Master of the Hall of Swords, vowed he would not give in to the advances of Prince Corin, but he finds himself dueling with more than swords as Corin pursues him with determined passion. (978-1-62639-226-7)

Café Eisenhower by Richard Natale. A grieving young man who travels to Eastern Europe to claim an inheritance finds friendship, romance, and betrayal, as well as a moving document relating a secret lifelong love affair. (978-1-62639-217-5)

Murder in the Arts District by Greg Herren. An investigation into a new and possibly shady art gallery in New Orleans' fabled Arts District soon leads Chanse into a dangerous world of forgery, theft… and murder. A Chanse MacLeod mystery. (978-1-62639-206-9)

Calvin's Head by David Swatling. Jason Dekker and his dog, Calvin, are homeless in Amsterdam when they stumble on the victim of a grisly murder—and become targets for the calculating killer, Gadget. (978-1-62639-193-2)

Myth and Magic: Queer Fairy Tales, edited by Radclyffe and Stacia Seaman. Myth, magic, and monsters—the stuff of childhood dreams (or nightmares) and adult fantasies. (978-1-62639-225-0)

The Return of Jake Slater by Zavo. Jake Slater mistakenly believes his lover, Ben Masters, is dead. Now a wanted man in Abilene, Jake rides to Mexico to begin a new life and heal his broken heart. (978-1-62639-194-9)

Rise of the Thing Down Below by Daniel W. Kelly. Nothing kills sex on the beach like a fishman out of water… Third in the Comfort Cove Series. (978-1-62639-207-6)

First Exposure by Alan Chin. Navy Petty Officer Skyler Thompson battles homophobia from his shipmates, the military, and his wife when he takes a second job at a gay-owned florist. Rather than yield to pressure to quit, he battles homophobia in order to nurture his artistic talents. (978-1-62639-082-9)

The Fall of the Gay King by Simon Hawk. Investigative journalist Logan Walker receives a mysterious erotic journal that details the sexual relations of a corporate giant known in the business world as the "Gay King of Kings." (978-1-62639-076-8)

Backstrokes by Dylan Madrid. When pianist Crawford Paul meets lifeguard Armando Leon, he accepts Armando's offer to help him overcome his fear of water by way of private lessons. As friendship turns into a summer affair, their lust for one another turns to love. (978-1-62639-069-0)

The Raptures of Time by David Holly. Mack Frost and his friends journey across an alien realm, through homoerotic adventures, suffering humiliation and rapture, making friends and enemies, always seeking a gateway back home to Oregon. (978-1-62639-068-3)